.44 SHOWDOWN

The two riders eyeballed Smoke Jensen suspiciously as they neared where he sat his horse, his right hand resting near the butt of his .44.

"You boys look like you been riding hard," Smoke said.

"You figure that's any of your business?" one asked.

"Just trying to be friendly. Heading down to the settlement, boys?"

The pair reined up. "You got a nose problem, you know that, mister?" the second one said.

"I don't have the problems you boys are about to have," Smoke said, turning his horse to give him a better field of fire.

The outlaws grabbed for their guns and Smoke emptied two saddles. The bigger of the two hit the ground and tried to lift his pistol. Smoke shot him between the eyes, shifted the muzzle of his .44 and put another slug in the second man's chest.

"Enjoy all the comforts of hell, boys," he said softly.

CODE OF THE
MOUNTAIN MAN

William W. Johnstone

PINNACLE BOOKS
Kensington Publishing Corp.
www.pinnaclebooks.com

PINNACLE BOOKS are published by

Kensington Publishing Corp.
119 West 40th Street
New York, NY 10018

All Kensington titles, imprints, and distributed lines are available at special quantity discounts for bulk purchases for sales promotions, premiums, fund-raising, educational, or institutional use. Special book excerpts or customized printings can also be created to fit specific needs. For details, write or phone the office of the Kensington special sales manager: Kensington Publishing Corp., 119 West 40th Street, New York, NY 10018, attn: Special Sales Department; phone 1-800-221-2647.

PINNACLE BOOKS and the Pinnacle logo are Reg. U.S. Pat. & TM Off.
The WWJ steer head logo is a trademark of Kensington Publishing Corp.

ISBN-13: 978-0-7860-2844-3
ISBN-10: 0-7860-2844-0

First printing: March 1991
Seventeenth printing: June 2012

25   24   23   22   21   20   19   18   17

Printed in the United States of America

I acknowledge the Furies, I believe in them, I have heard the disastrous beating of their wings.

Theodore Dreiser

Chapter One

No one knew why the outlaws chose to attack the town of Big Rock. It was a very stupid thing for outlaws to attack any western town. For those who inhabited the towns of the West were veterans of the War Between the States, veterans of Indian wars, buffalo hunters—men who had lived with guns all their lives. But Big Rock, located in the high-up country of northern Colorado, was known to be off-limits to anyone who sought trouble.

And most trouble-hunters were as careful to avoid Big Rock as they were to keep from sticking their hands into a nest of rattlers.

Perhaps the outlaws who struck Big Rock that day hit it because the West was taming somewhat. The bad old days were not gone entirely, but they were calming down. Maybe the outlaws felt they could pull it off. They would have fared much better had they pulled off their boots and stuck their bare feet into a bucket filled with scorpions.

"Good morning, Abigal," Sally Jensen spoke to the woman behind the counter.

"Good morning, Sally," the shopkeeper's wife said. "And how are things out at the Sugarloaf?"

The Sugarloaf was the name of their ranch. 'They' being Smoke and Sally Jensen.

Both women turned at the sounds of hooves pounding the earth. A lot of horses. Sounded like fifty or more.

"What on earth? . . ." Sally said.

A bullet busted a window of the store and tore through cans of peaches. A second bullet hit Sally on the arm and knocked her down. A child and her dog were trampled under the steel-shod hooves of the galloping horses.

It didn't take the rampaging outlaws long to discover they'd struck the wrong town as men reached for their pistols and rifles and emptied a few saddles. They raced out of town, whooping and hollering and shooting. But the damage had been done.

"Four people dead," Judge Proctor said grimly. "Including a little girl. Half a dozen more wounded. Couple of them seriously. Somebody ride for the Sugarloaf and fetch Smoke. Sally's been hit."

"Lord God Amighty!" a citizen breathed. "Them outlaws don't know it, but they just opened the gates to Hell!"

He waited until he was absolutely certain that Sally was not seriously injured. A neighbor lady would stay with her, tending to her. The hands who worked the Sugarloaf range would make damn sure no one tried to attack the ranch.

"Now you be careful," Sally told her husband. "And don't you worry about me. I'm just fine."

He bent down and kissed her lips. "I'll see you when I get back." He walked out of the house and stepped into the saddle.

Sally made no attempt to dissuade her husband. This was the West, and a man had to do what a man had to do. They were bound by unwritten yet strictly obeyed codes. Especially a man like Smoke Jensen.

He rode a big buckskin that he'd caught wild in the mountains and gentled. Because of the way he'd worked with the horse, and the bond that had been established between horse and rider, Smoke was the only human the buckskin would allow on its back.

Smoke was tall, with wide shoulders, heavily muscled arms, and lean hipped. His wrists were huge, and his big hands were as powerful as they could be gentle. His hair was ash-blond, cut short, and his eyes were a cold, unforgiving brown that rarely showed any emotion except when with his wife and children.

He wore two guns, the left-hand gun worn butt-forward, the right-hand gun low and tied down. He was just as fast with one gun as he was with the other. Some said he was the fastest man with a gun who ever lived, but he never sought out or bragged that he was a gunfighter. He was just a man one did not push. He carried a long-bladed knife that he usually shaved with on the trail. Or fought with, whichever was the most important at the time. He'd been raised among old mountain men and some called him the last mountain man. His clothing was earth-tones, his hat brown and flat-brimmed. A Winchester rifle was in the saddle boot.

Leadville was behind him and the Gunnison River just a few hours ahead. He would make the small town just about dark. There was a hotel there, and there he would bed down for the night.

He was in no hurry. He knew he would find the outlaws that had ridden into Big Rock and shot it up, killing and wounding innocent people. If their intentions had been to rob the bank, they had failed miserably. But they had left behind them a bloody main street and sorrow in the hearts of those who had to bury their dead and watch the suffering of those wounded by the indiscriminate bullets.

The sheriff of Big Rock, Monte Carson, had been wounded during the bloody battle, and could not lead the posse that went after the outlaws. Went after them, but finally had to return empty-handed.

9

The man on the mean-eyed buckskin didn't need a posse. Didn't want to be hampered by one. He knew the difference between right and wrong, and he sure as hell didn't need some fancy-talking lawyer to explain it. As far as he was concerned, lawyers should stick to writing wills and drawing up deeds and such. Keep their noses out of a man's private business. That was part of the problems facing the world today: too damn many lawyers.

He had kissed his wife goodbye, provisioned up, and ridden out from their ranch in the high lonesome of northern Colorado. Alone.

Nobody attacked Big Rock. Nobody. Not and got away with it. Smoke didn't believe in cowboys hoorahing a town. People got hurt doing that. A gun was not a toy, and when a man grew up, he put boyhood behind him and accepted the responsibilities of being a man.

Smoke had helped found Big Rock; his blood and sweat and time and effort were ingrained in the streets and buildings. And those outlaws had shot his wife. Nobody shot his wife. Ever. Not and lived to brag about it.

One lawyer, straight from the East and new to Big Rock, had said the outlaws probably had a poor childhood, and that was what caused them to behave in such a barbarous manner. They really shouldn't be blamed for their actions.

Smoke had slapped him down in the street, jerked him up by the seat of his britches and his shirt collar and dumped him in a horse trough.

Preacher Morrow had tried to talk him out of tracking the outlaws. So had Dr. Colton Spalding and some of the others in the town.

"It's the 1880s, Smoke," Judge Proctor said. "You just can't take the law into your own hands anymore."

The big man who stood by the big buckskin looked at the judge. Judge Proctor backed up, away from those terribly hard eyes.

"I'll be back," Smoke said, then swung into the saddle.

He swung down from the saddle in front of the livery stable in the small town by the Gunnison River and led the buckskin inside, stripping the saddle and bridle from him and stabling the animal.

"Feed him good," he told the boy who had appeared out of the gloom of the cavernous building. "Rub him down. Give him a bag of grain." He looked at the boy. "You sleep in this place?"

"Yes, sir. I got me a room back yonder." He pointed. The man looked familiar, but the boy just couldn't place him. He took the coin the man offered him. It was a silver dollar.

"Don't you have a home, boy?"

"Yes, sir. But my ma lets me stay here during the night so's I can earn extra money to help out."

"I'll leave my saddle here. You look after my gear."

"Yes, sir!"

"Any strangers in town?"

"Three men rode in late this afternoon. They was too cheap to use the livery. They picketed their horses down by the river. They looked like hardcases. Guns tied down low. They just looked mean to me."

"How'd they smell?"

"Sir?"

"Did you get close enough to them to smell them?"

"Yes, sir. I did, come to think of it. They sure did smell bad."

"That's not the only thing that's really bad about them. Did they bathe?"

The boy looked at the tall man with the wide shoulders and the massive arms that bulged his shirt with muscles. "Bathe? Ah . . . no, sir."

"So they still stink?"

11

"Ah . . . yes, sir. I reckon so, sir."

"I feel sorry for the undertaker."

The tall man with the two guns walked out of the livery stable, moving like a great hunting cat, his spurs jingling as he moved. He carried his rifle with him as he crossed the wide street and walked toward the hotel.

The boy hung a nose-bag on the buckskin and began currying the horse as he ate a bait of grain. The boy suddenly stopped his brushing as a coldness washed over him. "Oh, my God!" he whispered, finally placing the big man with the cold eyes. "Oh, my God!"

"Good evening, sir!" the desk clerk called. "It certainly is a quiet evening in our town."

It won't be for long, Smoke thought, as he signed the register.

The desk clerk looked at the name on the register and gripped the edge of the counter. His mouth dropped open and worked up and down like a fish. "Ah, bah, bah, bah . . ." He cleared his throat. "The dining room just closed, sir. But I can get you a plate of food sent up to your room if you wish."

"I wish. Thank you."

"We're a very modern hostelry, sir. We have the finest in up to date water closets."

"Good. Give me the key to my room, have the tub in the facilities filled with hot water, and put a fresh bar of soap in there. Lots of towels. I like lots of clean towels."

"Yes, sir. Right away, sir. And I'm sure that room I assigned you has fresh sheets. As a matter of fact, I know it does. It's such a pleasure having you here with . . ."

Those cold eyes stopped his chatter. It was like looking into a frozen Hell.

The tall man turned and walked up the stairs.

The desk clerk beat on the bell until a man appeared. "Get the marshal—right now! Tell him to deputize the boys. We got big trouble." Or somebody has, he thought, recalling those three hardcases who rode into town that day.

When the tall man walked down the stairs, four of the men the marshal had deputized took one look at him and exited the lobby, fading into the night. They wanted no part of this hombre. They weren't cowards; they were all good, solid men who had used a gun on more than one occasion against outlaws or Indians. But they were intelligent men.

"You got business in this town, mister?" the marshal asked.

"Oh, yes," Smoke replied. "But it's my business."

"Maybe I'll make it mine," the marshal stood his ground.

"That's your job. But I have a better suggestion."

"I'm listening."

"Go home. Make yourself a fresh pot of coffee. Talk to your wife and family. Tell your men to go home and gather their families around them. Get the citizens off the street."

"I don't take orders from you."

"I didn't give you any orders."

The marshal nodded his head. That was a fact. What Jensen was doing was giving him an out, to save face. The desk clerk was all ears, hanging on every word. Whatever happened here would be all over town in ten minutes. "I'm not afraid of you, Jensen."

The desk clerk gasped.

"I can see that. You're a good man, Marshal. The town should be proud to have you behind that star, and the city council should give you a raise."

The marshal cut his eyes. He was alone. His newly deputized men had gone. "Come to think of it, my wife just baked a fresh apple pie. It'd still be warm."

"Man shouldn't pass that up," Smoke said. "Might insult his wife. My wife was insulted the other day

13

when the gang those punks in the saloon was ridin' with shot her."

The marshal's eyes narrowed. No man harmed a woman in the West. Just to jostle one on the street was grounds for a good butt-whipping. "She bad hurt?"

"Caught her in the arm. They killed a little girl."

"You have a good evening, Mr. Jensen."

"Thank you, Marshal. I plan to."

The marshal left the hotel lobby. The palms of his hands were sweaty. He wiped them on his britches. He was a good, tough lawman, having gunned down Bad Jack Summers on the main street of this very town only a few months back. But Bad Jack couldn't shine Smoke Jensen's boots. The marshal sighed. Come to think of it, a wedge of pie would taste mighty good.

Smoke stepped out of the lobby and moved to the shadows, standing for a moment. He worked his guns in and out of leather a few times. The grips of the .44s seemed to leap into his big hands. He stepped off the boardwalk and into the street, walking to the saloon. He stood for a moment at the batwings, looking in, allowing his eyes to adjust to the lantern light of the interior. He pushed open the batwings, stepped inside, and walked to the end of the bar.

"Whiskey," he told the pale-faced barkeep. "Out of the good bottle. I don't like snake heads."

"Yes, sir."

Some people who made their own whiskey would drop snake heads into the barrel for added flavor.

Smoke was not much for strong drink, but he did enjoy a sip every now and then. The saloon was empty except for Smoke, the barkeep, and three unshaven and dirty men seated around a table next to a wall.

The barkeep poured a shot glass full. "That's the best in the house, sir."

"Thank you." Smoke did not touch his liquor. "Where's all your business this evening?"

14

"Everybody left sort of sudden-like a few minutes ago."

"Is that right. Well, I can sure understand why."

"Oh?" The barkeep was getting jumpy.

"Stinks in here. Smells like a bunch of damn sorry punks whose mothers didn't teach them to bathe regularly. Like that stinking bunch of crap over there at the table."

That made the barkeep real nervous. He moved farther away from the tall, well-built man with the cold eyes and the big hands with flat knuckles. Fighter's hands.

"What's that?" one of the men at the table said.

"You heard me, punk. I said you stink."

The man pushed back his chair and walked toward the bar, the big California spurs jangling. "You're pushin', mister. You ain't got no call to say somethin' like that."

"I've been around skunks that smell better than you three," Smoke told him. He lifted the shot glass with his left hand and took a small sip. It was good whiskey.

One of the men at the table laughed. "Take him, Bob."

Smoke chuckled, but the sound was void of humor. "Yeah, Bob. Why don't you take me?"

Bob looked back at his buddies. This wasn't going like it usually did. He'd been a bully all his life, and folks usually backed up and took water when he prodded them. This tall man just laughed at him. Funny kind of laugh. Guy looked familiar, too. He'd seen that face somewheres before.

The tall man turned to face Bob. Dirty, unshaven, and smelly. Smoke grimaced at the body odor. "It wouldn't be right for you to meet your Maker smelling like an over-used outhouse. Why don't you boys find a horse trough and take a bath?"

"Huh! What are you talkin' about, mister. I ain't a-goin' to meet my Maker."

"Oh, yes, you are." Smoke set the shot glass on the bar. "All three of you."

"You seem right sure of that," one of the men seated at the table said.

"I'm positive of it."

The men at the table smiled. "Three of us and one of you. You're either drunk or crazy."

"I'm neither. But I'll tell you boys that you made a bad mistake getting tied up with Lee Slater and that pack of rabid hyenas that run with him. You made the next to the worst mistake of your lives when you attacked Big Rock the other day and shot those women and kids."

The third man cleared his throat and asked, "You the law, mister?"

"I don't need the law to take care of scummy punks like you three."

The man flushed deeply. But he kept his mouth shut. There was something about this tall man that worried at him. He and most of Slater's men were west coast outlaws, working from the Canadian border down to Mexico. He didn't know a whole lot about Colorado and the men who lived there. This tall man with muscles bunching his shirt was just too damn confident. Too calm. He was cleanshaven and smelling like bath soap. Neatly dressed and his hair trimmed. But he was no dandy. The outlaw could sense that. Those guns of his'n had seen a lot of use.

"We ain't with Lee Slater now," the second man said.

"You were."

"You said 'next' to the worst mistake," the punk standing in front of him said. "So that means we made a worser one."

"You certainly did."

The three waited. The tall man stood by the bar, half turned, smiling coldly at them. The barkeep was poised, ready to hit the floor.

"Well, damnit!" the second man threw a greasy deck of cards to the table. "Are you going to tell us, or not?"

"One of the women you shot was my wife," Smoke said.

The third man sighed.

"And who might you be, mister?" the punk facing Smoke asked, a nasty grin on his face.

"Smoke Jensen." Smoke followed that with a hard left fist that smashed into the punk's face. It sounded like someone swinging a nine-pound sledge against a side of freshly butchered beef. The punk's nose exploded in a gush of blood, and the blow knocked him to the floor.

Smoke straightened up with his right hand full of .44 just as the pair at the table jumped to their feet, dragging iron. He shot the two, cocking and firing so fast the twin shots sounded like one report. One was hit in the center of the chest, dead before he hit the sawdusted floor. The second was struck in the throat, the .44 slug making a terrible mess.

The punk he'd punched on the beak was moaning and crawling to his knees when Smoke jerked him up and threw him against a wall, next to the batwings. The punk screamed as ribs popped from the impact. His eyes were filled with fear as they watched the big man walk toward him, those brown eyes filled with revenge.

The punk staggered out the batwings and fell off the boardwalk, landing in the street. "Help!" he squalled. "Somebody come help me!"

The dark street remained as quiet as the grave he would soon be in.

Smoke had holstered his .44. He stood on the boardwalk and stared at the gunslick. "You think you're bad, boy." The words were chipped ice flying from his mouth. "Then draw, you sorry piece of crap!"

"You ain't no badge-toter!" the punk slobbered the words. "I got a right to a trial and all that. You can't

17

take the law into your own hands."

Smoke stared at him, his eyes burning with a glow that the young man on the street had never seen coming from any man. It was eerie and unnatural. A dark stain appeared on the front of the young man's dirty jeans.

"You gonna let me git up, Jensen?" he yelled.

"Get up."

The punk tried to fake Smoke out, drawing as he was getting to his boots. Smoke drew and shot him in the belly. His second shot shattered the punk's sixgun. Smoke turned and walked back into the saloon, leaving the outlaw in the dirt, hollerin' and bellerin' for his mother.

"You got an undertaker in this town?" he asked the barkeep.

"Ye . . . ye . . . yes, sir!" the barkeep stammered. "Got us a right good one."

"Get him."

"Right now, Mr. Smoke. You bet. I'm gone."

Smoke reloaded and finished his drink.

"Ain't much to this bunch of trash," the undertaker griped. "I'm gonna have to sell their gear to make any money."

"You do that."

"You know their names?"

"Nope."

"Well, I got to have something to put on the markers."

"You can carve on it, 'they should have bathed more often.' "

Chapter Two

The marshal walked into the hotel's dining room early the next morning and over to Smoke's table. He pointed to a chair, and Smoke pushed it out with the toe of his boot.

The marshal ordered breakfast—the same thing Smoke and everybody else in the dining room was having: beef, fried potatoes, and fried eggs—and laid several sheets of paper on the table. "These may help you."

They were flyers, wanted posters sent out by various law enforcement agencies west of the Mississippi River, and by the federal government. One was of Lee Slater.

Lee had to be the ugliest man Smoke had ever seen in his life. Ugly and mean-looking. "He sure isn't much for looks, is he?"

The marshal chuckled. "He probably didn't win any pretty-baby contests, for sure. But he's a bad one, Smoke. Vicious. He likes to hurt people. Kills for no reason. These others ride with him. Deke Carey and Curt Holt. They're both wanted for rape and murder. Everyone in his gang is facing either long prison sentences or a rope."

"So I heard. His gang was cut down by half a dozen when they hit Big Rock. But it's still a big gang."

"The biggest still operating in the West, Smoke.

Fifty at least and some place it at closer to seventy-five. He's always run big bunches. I'll tell you what I know about him, and then I wish to God you'd leave our town before some punk huntin' a reputation learns you're here."

Smoke did not take umbrage. "I'll do my best, Marshal."

"Mind if I ask you a question?"

"Not at all."

"If you'd never seen him before, how'd you know it was Lee Slater who hit your town?"

"The sheriff recognized him. Monte Carson."

The marshal smiled. "Ol' Monte was a rounder in his day. But he was never a crook. Just a bad man to fool with."

"Marriage settled him right down."

"It usually does. Ask you a few more questions?"

"Sure."

"How old are you? Early thirties?"

"That's close enough."

"I heard what happened to your first wife and baby boy. I'm sorry. I won't dwell on that. Now you've married again—and a fine lady she is, too, so I'm told—but you're still apt to go on the prod ever' now and then. Why?"

Smoke shook his head. "Louis Longmont asked me that a couple of years ago and then answered his own question. Maybe I am the last mountain man, Marshal. There's something in me that screams out for the high lonesome. Something in me that can't tolerate punks and thugs and bullies and the like. Back in the hard scrabble hills of Missouri, while my daddy was off in the war, I kept body and soul together by eating turnips—when the garden came up, that is—and berries and what game I could kill. Many's the time I went to sleep with my belly growling. But I never stole. I never took what wasn't mine. And I won't tolerate them that do. Louis said that some people think

I have a Robin Hood complex. But that's not true. I just don't like the way laws are changing, Marshal. They're not getting better, they're getting worse. I honest to God read in a Chicago newspaper a couple of months ago, that a man shot a burglar breaking into his home and the police put the homeowner in jail! Can you believe that? What in the hell is this world coming to?"

"I know. I read about it myself. But it's the 1880s now, Smoke. You got to change with the times."

Smoke shook his head. "Not me, Marshal. Somebody does me a hurt, I'll hunt him down and settle it. Eyeball to eyeball. Man kills for no reason, or kills trying to take what isn't his, hang him. 'Cause he's no good. Now I read where the country is spending money building prisons." He shook his head. "It's a mistake, Marshal. A hundred years from now, people will see that it's a mistake. But it'll be too late then. A man who'll lie and cheat and steal and hurt people and kill at fifteen will do the same damn thing when he's fifty. I don't care if this nation builds ten thousand prisons . . . it won't matter. It won't stop them. But a bullet will."

Everybody in the restaurant had stopped eating and was listening to the most famous gunfighter in the world.

"I sass my daddy when I was a kid, he'd a-knocked me slap to the floor. Now we got so-called smart folks back East saying that you shouldn't whip your children. If that silliness continues and catches hold, can you imagine what it'll be like in the 1980s? There'll be no discipline, no respect for law and order. I whip my children, then I hug them to show them I love them and I tell them why I just put a belt to their rears.

"I respect the laws of God, Marshal. I'm an Old Testament man. Eye for an eye and a tooth for a tooth. Hurt me or mine and I'm comin' after you. And man's laws be damned!"

The marshal sighed and ate his breakfast. "I hope to God I'm not the lawman who ever has to come after you, Smoke."

"That day's coming, Marshal," Smoke admitted. " 'Cause I'll never change. Someday, a posse will come after me, hunting me down like an old lobo wolf. And when they do, the land's going to run red with blood. Because I won't go down easy.

"Marshal, if a man is hungry, can't feed his family, just come to me and I'll give them food. If they're down on their luck and really want to work, I'll give them a job, find one for them, or give them money to keep on hunting for work and eat while they're doing it. But if I catch someone stealing from me, or hurting my family, or threatening me, he's dead on the spot.

"It's a funny thing about laws and lawyers, Marshal. You take a small town that just has one lawyer, he can make a living and that's just about it. Let a second lawyer move in, and damned if they don't both get rich."

Smoke pulled out and rode past the graveyard, located on a barren hilltop just out of town. Three mounds of earth were waiting to be shoveled in the holes.

The marshal had told him some names of men who rode with Lee Slater: Curly Rogers, Dirty Jackson, Ed Malone, Boots Pierson . . . to name just a few. They were all trash and scum. Back shooters and torturers. He had asked if Smoke planned to take on the whole gang by himself?

"Just one gang, isn't it?"

Smoke headed south, staying between the Cebolla and Cochetopa Rivers. Although the outlaws' trail was days old, it was not that difficult to follow. Their campsites were trashy reminders of just how sorry a bunch of people he was tracking. Tin cans and bottles and bloody bandages and torn, wore-out clothing clearly marked each night's site.

With San Luis Peak still to the south of him, Smoke came up on a woman sitting in front of a burned-out cabin. Only the chimney remained. He noticed several fresh-dug graves by the side of the charred ruins. The graves had not been filled in.

The woman's face bore the results of a savage beating. She looked up at him through eyes that were swollen slits. "You be the law, mister?"

"No. As far as I know there is no law within a hundred miles of here." He swung down from the saddle and walked to her. She had fixed her torn dress as best she could; but it was little more than rags. "You had anything to eat?"

"A biscuit I had in my pocket. The outlaws tooken everything else. Before they put the house to the torch. I ain't able to move."

Smoke took a packet of food from his saddlebags and gave it to her. "I'll get you a dipper of water from the well."

"I wouldn't," she told him. "They killed my kids' dogs and dumped them in the well."

"Then I'll get you some water from the creek."

"I'd appreciate it. I tried to get around, but I can't. They kicked my ribs in. Left me for dead. I don't think I got long 'fore I join my husband and girls. Ribs busted off and tore up a lung. Hurts."

He found a jug and rinsed it out, filling it up with water from the creek. Looking at the woman, he could see that she was standing in death's door. Sheer determination had kept her hanging on, waiting for help, or more probably, he guessed, someone to come along that would avenge this terrible act.

"Who dug the graves, ma'am?"

"I did. The outlaws made me. Then they used my husband for target practice. Made me and my girls watch. He suffered a long time. My girls was ten and twelve years old. They raped me and made them watch. Then they raped the girls and made me watch. Then they thought they had kicked me to death. I lay real still and fooled them. They done horrible things to me and the girls. Things I won't talk about. Unnatural things. I been sittin' here for three days, prayin' and passin' out from the pain, prayin' and passin' out. Wishin' to God somebody would come along and hear my story."

"I'm here, ma'am."

She drifted off, not unconscious, but babbling. Some of her words made sense, most didn't. Smoke bathed her face and waited. The woman's face was hot to the touch, burning with fever. While she babbled, smoke unsaddled Buck and let him roll and water.

"Who you be?" she asked suddenly, snapping out of her delirium.

"Smoke Jensen."

"Praise God!" she said. "Thank you, God. You sent me a warrior. I thank you."

"Lee Slater's gang did this?"

"That's him. I heard names. Harry Jennings, Blackjack Simpson, Thumbs Morton, Bell Harrison, Al Martine. They was a Pedro and a Lopez and a Tom Post." She coughed up blood and slipped back into delirium.

Smoke took that time to walk to the graves and look at the shallow pits. His stomach did a slow roll-over. The man had been shot to ribbons. His wife had been right: he died hard over a long period of time. The naked bodies of the children would sicken a buzzard. The kids had been used badly and savagely. People who would do this deserved no pity, no mercy . . . and the only justice they were going to get from Smoke Jensen was a bullet.

He filled in the holes and took a small Bible from his saddlebags. He read from the Old Testament and then set about making some crosses. He made four,

24

for he knew the woman wasn't going to last much longer.

"Them names was burned in my head," the woman said. "I made myself memorize them. They was Crown and Zack. Reed and Dumas and Mac. They was a Ray and a Sandy and some young punks called themselves Pecos, Carson, and Hudson. Three more pimply faced punks hung with them three. They was all savages. Just as mean and vicious as any man amongst 'em. They was called Concho, Bull, and Jeff."

Smoke rolled one of his rare cigarettes and waited, squatting down beside the dying woman.

"I recollect hearin' a man they called Lake and another man they called Taylor. Dear God in Heaven it was a long two days they stayed here." She looked at him. Her eyes were unusually bright and clear. "Did I dream it, or did you put dirt over my family?"

"I buried them and read words from the Bible."

"Thank you. I'm sorry, but I don't remember no more names of them outlaws."

"I'll find out who the rest of them were. Did they all . . . ah? . . ." He didn't know quite how to say it. But the woman did.

"Yes. Several times. One of my girls died while they was abusin' her. You got kids of your own, Mr. Smoke?"

"Yes."

"Then you know how I must feel."

"I believe so."

"I heard them say they was goin' to take over part of Colorado."

"The only thing they're going to take over is a grave, ma'am."

"That's good. You got a hole dug for me?"

"Yes."

"I reckon it's about time then." She closed her eyes, smiled, and said, "Thank you, God, for sending me a warrior." Then the woman leaned her head back

25

and died.

Smoke buried the woman and moved on, making camp a few miles from the scene of cruelty and savageness. He would try that little town on the Rio Grande, on the southern edges of the La Garita Mountains; see if any of the scum had ridden in there. What was the name of that place? Yeah, it came to him. Somebody had named it Gap.

Wasn't much to Gap, Smoke thought, as he approached the town from the north. A saloon, a little hotel, a general store, a cafe and barber shop. Maybe two dozen houses. He swung down in front of the small livery and looked at the man sitting in a cane-bottomed chair in front of the place.

"That horse has got a mean eye on him," the man said.

"Feed him, curry him, and take care of him," Smoke said, dropping the reins. "Give him all the grain he wants. And don't get behind him. He'll kick the crap out of you."

"Gonna cost you extra for me to take care of that wall-eyed bastard."

Buck lifted his head and showed the man his big teeth.

"Don't call him names. He's sensitive about that."

"I'll make a deal with you," the man said. "You stable and feed him, and I'll just charge you for what he eats."

"That's fair enough. Livery looks full."

"Bunch of lawmen in here, U-nited States marshals; stayin' over to the ho-tel. Chasin' some gang, they is." He squinted his eyes. "Don't I know you?"

"Never been here before in my life."

"You shore look familiar. I seen your pitcher somewhere. Maybe on a wanted poster?"

Smoke laughed. "Not likely. I ranch up north of

here, outside of Big Rock."

"That's Smoke Jensen's country. He's kilt a thousand men."

"Not quite that many."

"You know him?"

"I know him. You got a marshal in this town?"

"Yep. Right over there's his office." The man pointed. "Name is Bradley."

Smoke took his gear and checked in at the hotel. He got the last room available. He registered as Jen Sen.

"Funny name," the desk clerk said. Then he looked into the coldest eyes he'd ever seen. "No offense meant, mister."

"You been in this country long?" Smoke asked.

"Just got in from Maryland a few months back."

"Then learn this: you belittle a man's name out here, and you'd best be ready to back it up with guns or fists."

"Here, now!" a man said. "There'll be none of that around me."

Smoke turned. A man stood before him with a big badge on his chest that read: "Deputy U. S. Marshal."

Smoke took in his hightop lace-up boots and eastern clothes. He wore a pistol in a flap holster. He looked at the other men. They were all dressed much the same.

"Who in the hell do you think you are?" Smoke said, taking an immediate dislike for the man.

"United States Marshal Mills Walsdorf."

"Come to bring peace to the wilderness?" Smoke said with a smile.

"I do not find law enforcement a humorous matter, sir. It's very serious business."

"I'd say so. That's what that woman told me, in so many words, just before I buried her a couple of days ago."

"What? What? Where did this take place?"

"North of here. Gang of scum rode through and

27

shot her husband to ribbons. Then raped the woman and her two children. Same gang of trash that shot up Big Rock."

"Did the woman identify the gang?"

"She did."

Mills waited. Tapped his foot impatiently. "Well, speak up, man! Who were they?"

"Lee Slater's pack of filth."

"Scoundrels!" one of Walsdorf's men muttered darkly.

"Which direction did they head, man?" Walsdorf demanded in a tone that told Smoke the man was accustomed to getting his way, when he wanted it.

"South."

"Oh, say, now!" another Fed said. "I find that hard to believe. We've been here several days and have seen no sign of them."

He didn't exactly call him a liar, so Smoke let the remark slide and leaned against the front desk. "Where are you boys from?"

"From the Washington, D.C. and Chicago offices," Walsdorf replied.

Smoke sized up Mills Walsdorf. About his own age, and about his size, although not as heavily muscled in the arms and shoulders. His hands were big and flat knuckled and looked like he'd used them in fights more than once.

"You look familiar," Mills said. "I've seen you somewhere."

"I do get around."

Mills spun the register book and snorted at Smoke's name. "Jen Sen. That's obviously a phony name. Are you running from the authorities?"

"If you represent the authority, I wouldn't see any need in it."

"I think, sir, that I do not care for your attitude."

"I think, sir, that I do not give a damn what you care for."

Mills drew himself up and stared Smoke in the eyes. "You need to be taught a lesson in manners, sir."

"And you think you're just the man to do that, huh?"

"I've thrashed better men than you more than once."

"Cut your bulldog loose, Walsdorf," Smoke said easily. "Just anytime you feel lucky."

Jen Sen, the desk clerk was musing. Jen Sen. Jensen. Smoke Jensen! "That's Smoke Jensen, Marshal," he said softly.

The color drained out of Walsdorf's face. A sigh passed his lips.

"Hear me well, Mr. U.S. Marshal," Smoke said. "Lee Slater and his gang attacked Big Rock about ten days ago. They killed several people, including a little girl. And they wounded my wife, Sally. The former Sally Reynolds. You've probably heard the name, since her family owns most of New England. Nobody shoots my wife, Walsdorf, and gets away with it. Nobody. Not Lee Slater's bunch, not a marshal, not a sheriff, not the President of the United States. There's a little town up on the Gunnison, where the Taylor River feeds into it. I found three of Slater's men there. I hope somebody buried them shortly after I rode out 'cause they damn sure smelled bad alive.

"Now, I'm going to find the rest of that gang, Walsdorf. And I'm going to kill them. All of them. And I don't need some fancypants U.S. Marshal from back East stumbling around screwing up what trail there is left. You understand me?"

Mills drew back in astonishment. Nobody, nobody had ever spoken to him in such a manner. He shook his finger in Smoke's face. "Now, you listen to me, Mr. Smoke Jensen. I realize that you have some reputation, but the West is changing. Your kind is on the way out, and it's past due in coming. Now I . . ."

"Jensen!" the shout came from the street. "Smoke Jensen! Step out here and die!"

"Albert," Mills said, "step out there and see what that man is bellowing about."

A man filled the doorway, paused, then stepped inside. He wore a badge pinned to his shirt. He looked at Smoke. "That's Chris Mathers. He's a local troublemaker. Pretty good with a gun. Better than I am. You killed his big brother several years ago. He used to ride for a scum named Davidson."

"I remember Davidson. Ran an outlaw town. I killed him and his personal bodyguard, man by the name of Dagget. I don't remember any Mathers."

"Smoke Jensen!" the shout came. "You're a coward, Jensen. A dirty little boot-lickin' coward."

Smoke slipped the hammer thong from his guns.

"There'll be none of this!" Mills said.

"There's no law against it," the local marshal shut him up. Momentarily. "This ain't back East where you kiss every punk's butt that comes along. So why don't you just close your mouth and see how we do it in the West."

Smoke stepped out onto the boardwalk. "I don't have any quarrel with you, boy," he told the young man in the street. "So why don't you just go on home, and we'll forget you calling me out."

"Big tough man!" Mathers sneered. "I always knowed you was yellow."

"He's givin' you a chance to live, boy," the local marshal told him, standing well to one side. "Take it. You'll never get another one after this day."

"You shut up," Mathers told him, without taking his eyes from Smoke. "Make your play, gunfighter."

Smoke just stood and looked at him.

"I said draw, damn you!" Mathers screamed.

"I got nothing against you, boy. Far as I know, the marshal has no charges against you. So you're not wanted. Go get your horse and ride on out of here."

"He's giving him every chance," Albert said, watching from the hotel lobby's right front window.

"Yes, he is," Mills agreed. "He's a tough man, but seems to be a fair one."

"I'll kill you where you stand, Jensen!" Mathers shouted. His hands hovered over his guns. "Draw."

"I'll not sign your death certificate, boy," Smoke told him. "You'll have to draw on me."

"Are you ready to die, Jensen?" Mathers shouted.

"No man is ever ready to die, boy."

Mills grunted, arching an eyebrow at the philosophical uttering from the mouth of the West's most famous gunhandler. He just didn't understand these Western men. They could be incredibly crude, then turn about and quote Shakespeare. They could brand cattle and endure the squalls of pain from the cow, then turn right around and shoot somebody who tried to hurt their pet dog.

Mills reluctantly concluded that he just might have a lot to learn about the West and the people who lived here.

"Now!" Mathers yelled, and grabbed for iron.

Smoke's right hand Colt seemed to leap into his hand. Mathers felt the slug strike him. His own gun was still in leather. The bullet shattered his breast bone and sent bone splinters into his heart. The young man looked up at the clear blue of the sky. He was on his back and could not understand how he got in that position.

"Holy Mother of God!" Albert muttered. "He's fast as a snake."

Townspeople began gathering around the fallen young man.

"I'll pray for you, young man," the local minister said, clutching his Bible and leaning over Chris Mathers.

But he was talking to a corpse.

Smoke punched out the empty and let it drop to the boardwalk. It bounced and rolled off into the dirt.

"I didn't come into your town to cause trouble,

31

Marshal."

"I know that. What you probably done was save me a lot of trouble. Mathers was born to it and had a killing coming."

Smoke's smile was a grim one. "A hundred years from now, that very statement will come back into the minds of a lot of good, decent, law-abiding people, Marshal." He walked back into the hotel.

Mills Walsdorf had stepped out onto the boardwalk. He cocked his head to one side and had a puzzled expression on his face upon hearing Smoke's words. "Now . . . what in the world did he mean by that?"

"I could try to explain it to you, Mills," the local marshal said. "But people like you never seem to understand until it's just too damn late."

Chapter Three

Smoke lingered over his coffee after breakfast, pondering his next move. He didn't want to pull out and have Mills Walsdorf and his Eastern U.S. Marshals tagging along behind him. For the life of him he couldn't understand why the government would send men from the big cities out West to catch Western born and reared outlaws. It just didn't make any sense.

Of course, there were a lot of things the federal government did that didn't make any sense to Smoke.

Like sending seven U.S. Marshals out to round up a gang of fifty or sixty outlaws. That wasn't a dumb move; that was just plain ignorant. Especially when the marshals didn't know the country, weren't familiar with Western ways, and rode their horses like a bunch of English lords and dukes out on a fox hunt.

"May I join you?" Mills broke into his musings.

Smoke pointed to a chair.

"I can't get used to having no menu," Mills said.

"It's on the chalkboard over there," Smoke replied, cutting his eyes.

"I know where it is! I'm not blind." He paused, then said, "I'm afraid we got off on the wrong foot yesterday afternoon, Mr. Jensen. I should like to make amends and offer you some employment."

"The first part is fine with me. Forget the job offer."

"You would be doing your country a great service by joining us and helping to bring an end to this reign of terror put upon the land by Lee Slater and his men."

"I intend to put an end to it, Mills. Permanently."

"The men deserve a fair trial."

"They deserve a bullet, and that is what they're going to get."

"You're going to force me to stop you, Mr. Jensen."

Smoke's eyes were amused as he gazed at the man. "I'd be right interested in knowing how you plan on doing that, Mills."

"By arresting you for obstruction of justice, that's how."

Smoke chuckled. "First you better get yourself a federal warrant for my arrest. Nearest telegraph station is south of here, across the San Juan Mountains. The federal judge is in Denver. I know him. You'll play hell getting him to sign a warrant against me. And if you get another to sign it, I'll get the judge in Denver to cancel it. But that's only part of your problem. The biggest problem facing you would be trying to arrest me."

"You're very sure of yourself, aren't you, Mr. Jensen?"

"The name is Smoke. And yes, I am. You ever heard of the Silver Camp Shootout?"

"Yes. That was the setting in one of those Penny Dreadfuls written about you. Pure fiction, of course."

"Wrong, Mills. Pure fact. There were fifteen salty outlaws in that town when I went in. There were fifteen dead men when I rode out. I wasn't much more than a boy—in age. You ever seen a cornered puma, Mills?"

"No."

34

"You ever try to brace me, Mills, and you'll see one."

"Are you threatening me?"

"Nope. Just telling you the way it'll be."

"I can have a hundred U.S. Marshals in here in a week, Smoke."

"You'll need them. I was raised by mountain men, Mills. I know areas in this country that still haven't been viewed by white men. I'll get you so damn lost you'll have a beard a foot long before you find your way out. I know where to ride, and where not to ride. And that last part is far more important than the first. And as far as you and your boys taking me in, forget it. You'd have to pay too terrible a price. I've had as many as five slugs in me, and stayed on my feet shooting. The men who put those slugs in me are rotting in the grave. I'm sitting here drinking coffee. I'd think about that if I was you."

"I don't think you'd draw on an officer of the law, Smoke."

"I wouldn't want to do it. I surely wouldn't. Most of them just get out of my way and leave me alone. They know I'm not a criminal; they know I work hard and try to live right. Western lawmen also know that you got to put a rabid animal down. There is no cure for what they've got."

"Men are not animals, Smoke."

"You're right. Many men aren't nearly as good as animals. Animals don't kill for no reason. They kill to protect their mate or their cubs. They fight for territory and food. Only man kills for the fun of it. And there are lots of species of animals who won't tolerate a rogue animal. One of their kind goes bad, the others will drive it out or kill it."

"I can't make you understand," Mills said, shaking his head.

"One of us can't," Smoke said. He stood up and

walked out of the dining room, climbing the stairs to his room.

"Keep an eye on his room," Mills said, after waving one of his men over. "Just sit right there in the lobby. It's the only way out."

Smoke had paid in advance, as was the custom, and in his room, he gathered up his gear, slung the saddlebags over his shoulder, and climbed out the window, swinging up to the roof. He jumped over to the next building, climbed down, and walked through the alley to the livery, entering the back way.

"Figured you'd be along shortly," the stableman said, walking back to meet him. "Heard them Eastern lawmen want to capture Lee and his bunch alive for a fair trial and all that."

"That's their plan." Smoke threw a saddle on Buck and secured his gear.

The man spat in the dirt. "I'll go get you a poke of food for the trail."

Smoke tried to give him money. The man shook his head. "This one's on me. I'll be right back."

By the time Mills Walsdorf discovered that Smoke was gone, Smoke was halfway between Gap and Beaver Creek.

"He's what?" Mills jumped up.

"He's gone," Winston said glumly. "Liveryman said he pulled out this morning."

"How?" Mills yelled.

"On his damn horse, I suppose!" the marshal said.

"Oh! . . ." Mills brushed the man aside and ran up the stairs to Smoke's room. It was empty. "Climbed out the window, up to the roof, and went down into the alley. Damn! Tell the men to provision up and get mounted. We're pulling out. We have got to see that justice is done. It's our sworn duty. This lawlessness has got to stop. And by God, I intend to be the one to stop it."

"Yes, sir."

Smoke cooked his supper, rested, and then wiped out all signs of his camp before moving on several miles to make his night's camp. He made a cold camp, not wanting to attract any visitors by building a fire. As he lay rolled up in his blankets, his saddle for a pillow, his thoughts were busy ones.

Was he wrong for being what many called out of step with the times? Was he too eager to kill? Had he reached that point that many men good with a gun feared: had he stepped over the line and begun to enjoy killing?

He rolled over on his back and stared at the stars.

He knew the answer to the last question. No, he did not enjoy killing. He did not enjoy seeing the light fade from a man's eyes as the soul departed.

Was he too eager to kill? He didn't think so, but that might be iffy. He had killed a lot of men since those days when he and his father had left that hardscrabble rocky farm back in Missouri and headed west. But they were men who had pushed him, tried to kill him, or had done him or a loved one harm. What was that line from Thoreau that Sally loved to quote to him? Yes. He recalled it. "If a man does not keep pace with his companions, perhaps it is because he hears a different drummer. Let him step to the music which he hears, however measured or far away."

But is my drummer beating out the right tattoo? he wondered. Am I marching toward the wrong side of the law? What would I really do if Mills Walsdorf tried to arrest me? Would I draw on a badge?

He drifted off to sleep before an answer came to him.

He slept soundly and was up before dawn, waiting until the sun broke over the horizon before building a small fire to boil his coffee and fry his bacon. He sopped out the grease with part of a loaf of bread the liveryman had put in his poke and then broke camp.

He crossed Beaver Creek and would stay to the east of Wolf Creek Pass and Park Creek. This time of the year, early spring, Wolf Creek Pass would be chancy. He was pretty sure Slater and his pack of hyenas would stay clear of Pagosa Springs—which means "Indian healing waters." The town was not a new one, and was populated by men who would not look kindly upon outlaws coming in and raising hell.

And Pagosa Springs was also where Smoke, when he was about nineteen years old and still running with the old mountain man, Preacher, had gunned down Thompson and Haywood. A few days prior to that, he had put lead in two men in a tough mining town named Rico.

The name Smoke Jensen was legend in Colorado and those states bordering it to the west, north, and south.

It was wild and beautiful country he was riding through. Still wild and beautiful despite the onslaught of settlers from the East. This was not farming country, although a few were running cattle in the area. There was a little bit of a town down near Mix Lake, just north of the Alamosa River. That would be ideal for Slater and his crud to hit.

Faint tracks indicated that Slater and his bunch had split up into small groups, but they were all heading in a southeasterly direction. More south than east. That would put the little settlement directly in their path.

And since Smoke had learned that the bunch had worked the west coast for most of their outlaw careers, and really knew little about this country, he had one up on them there. For he had traveled this country since a teenager, and knew short cuts that only mountain men and Indians knew of.

He turned south and put Del Norte peak to his right, riding right through some of the most rugged country the state had to offer . . . and that was saying a mouthful. He climbed higher and higher and nooned with a spectacular view for his dessert.

Uncasing his field glasses, he began a slow careful sweep of the area. He spotted half a dozen smokes from cook fires, all well to the north of his location. He smiled. Slater and his bunch were hopelessly tangled up, taking the rough and rugged way to the settlement.

Smoke smiled as he chewed on a biscuit filled with roast beef. Come on, Slater, he thought. I'll be waiting for you.

The settlement was still half a day's ride ahead of him when he ran into two unshaven and thoroughly mistrustful-looking men riding down the narrow road.

The riders eyeballed him suspiciously as they neared where Smoke sat his horse, his right hand resting near the butt of his .44.

"You boys look like you been riding hard," Smoke said. "Plumb tuckered out."

"You figure that's any of your business?" one asked.

"My, aren't we grouchy today. Just trying to be friendly, boys."

The other rider muttered curses under his breath.

"Heading down to the settlement, boys?"

The pair reined up. "You got a nose problem, you know that, mister," one said.

"I don't have near the problems you boys are about to have."

"Huh? What do you mean by that?"

"What I mean is, if you boys think the reception

you got up in Big Rock was hostile, you're about to learn that was a picnic compared to what's looking at you now."

The outlaws had moved their horses so that they both faced Smoke.

"I think, mister," the bigger of the two said, "that you got a big fat mouth. And I think I'll just close it — permanently."

"Before you do that, I got a message for you."

"From who?"

"From that woman and her two daughters you raped and killed up north of here."

The two men sat their horses and stared at Smoke.

"And from her husband that you trash used for target practice."

"You're about ten seconds away from dyin', mister."

Smoke turned Buck, giving him a better field of fire. "Enjoy all the comforts of hell, boys," Smoke spoke softly.

"What's your damn name, mister?" the other punk asked.

"Smoke Jensen."

The outlaws grabbed for their guns, and Smoke emptied two saddles. The bigger of the two scum hit the ground and tried to lift his pistol. Smoke shot him between the eyes, shifted the muzzle of his .44 and put another slug in the second man's chest.

The dying man said, "You'll never leave this part of the country alive, Jensen."

"Maybe," Smoke told him. "But that isn't doing you much good right now, is it?"

The outlaw cussed him.

"Tsk, tsk," Smoke said. "Such language while on the way to meet the Lord."

The outlaw died in the dirt, a curse on his lips.

Smoke stripped the saddles from the horses and turned them loose. He took the men's guns and money and shoved the dead over the side of the mountain road. Several miles down the road, he came to a cabin and halloed it.

A man, a woman, and two wide-eyed kids peeked around the corner of the cabin that was set well off the road in a thick stand of timber.

"I'm friendly," he told him. "Can I water my horse?"

"You can," the man told him. "I'll not turn no man away from this house who's in need."

"Thanks kindly. Some outlaws tried to rob me up the road a piece. They weren't very good at their work." He placed the rifles and pistols on a bench next to the house. "They're part of a much larger gang that'll be coming along this road shortly, I'm thinking." He handed the man a wad of greenbacks he'd taken from the dead outlaws. The eyes of the man and woman widened in shock. "I took this off the dead men, figuring I'd run into someone who needed it more than me. You folks look like you've hit some hard times here."

"You're a saint, mister," the woman said. "There must be several hundred dollars there."

"Probably. I didn't count it. And I'm no saint, ma'am. Was I you folks, I'd pack me some food and bedding and take off for the deep timber until the trouble is over. Get those kids out of harm's way."

"We'll do that, mister. You the law?"

"No. I've been tracking these outlaws since they rode into a town near where I live and shot it up. One of the people they shot was my wife."

"What's your name?" the woman asked.

"Jensen, ma'am. Smoke Jensen."

They were still standing with their mouths hanging open when Smoke rode away.

* * *

Smoke made the settlement by late afternoon and stabled his horse at the livery.

"They got rooms for let over the saloon," the liveryman told him. "They ain't much, but they're better than nothin'. Bonnie's Cafe serves right good food if the cook ain't drunk." He peered at Smoke. "Don't I know you?"

"I doubt it. First time I've ever been here. This town have a name?"

"It's had three or four. Right now we're 'twixt and 'tween."

"You got a marshal?"

"Nope. Had one but he left 'cause we couldn't pay him . . . among other reasons. Had a bank but it closed. Got one stage a week comes through. Heads north. You wanna go south, you're in trouble. Starts out in Monte Vista and makes a big circle. Alamosa, Conejos, through here, and back up the grade."

"You ever heard of the Lee Slater gang?"

"Nope."

"You will." Smoke gathered his gear and walked to the saloon, dumping his saddlebags on the bar.

"Got a room for few days?" he asked the barkeep.

"Take your choice. They're all empty. The best in the house will cost you a dollar a night. Dollar and a half for clean sheets."

Smoke tossed some coins on the bar. "Change the sheets. I want a room facing the street."

"You got it. Number one. Top of the stairs and turn right. You cain't miss it," he added drily.

"Tubs inside?" Smoke asked hopefully.

"You got to be kidding! Tubs behind the barber shop. Want me to have one filled up?"

"Please."

"Fifty cents."

Smoke paid him and stowed his gear in the room. He walked over to the barber shop and bathed, then

42

had the barber shave him and cut his hair.

"Lilac water?" the barber asked. "Two bits and you'll smell so good the ladies'll be knockin' on your door tonight."

Smoke handed him a quarter. "How many people in this town?"

"Sixty-five, at last count. We're a growin' little community, for sure. Got us the bes' general store within fifty miles. Freight wagons jus' run yesterday, and she's stocked to the overflowin'."

Perfect for Slater and his bunch, Smoke thought. They might not get much money out of this place, but they could take enough provisions to last them a month or better while they raided towns, then disappeared back into the mountains.

"Any strangers been riding through?"

"Yeah, they has been, come to think of it. Yesterday, as a matter of fact. Some real hard-lookin' ol' boys. Stopped over to the saloon and had them a taste, then looked the town over real careful-like. Made me kind of edgy."

"Who runs this town?"

"Mayor and town council. Why?"

" 'Cause you got a big bunch of outlaws probably planning to hit this place within the next few days. I've been on their trail for several weeks. Lee Slater's bunch out of California. They hit my town up north of here and killed several people."

"Lord have mercy! And us without no marshal."

"You want a lawman?"

"Sure. But we can't pay no decent wage."

"You go get the mayor and the town council. Tell them I'll work as marshal for a time—free."

"You got any qualifications to do the job?"

"I think so."

"You sit right there. Here's a paper from Denver. It ain't but three weeks old. I'll be right back."

The mayor was the owner of the general store, and the town council was the blacksmith, the saloon-keeper, and the liveryman.

They listened to Smoke and shook their heads, the mayor saying, "That many outlaws would destroy this town. You figure that you'd do any good stoppin' them, mister?"

"I think so."

"You ain't but one man," the saloonkeeper said. "Hell, we don't even know your name."

"Smoke Jensen."

The barber sat down in his chair, his mouth open in shock. The liveryman cackled with glee.

"Here's the badge and raise your right hand, sir," the mayor said, after he found his voice.

Chapter Four

Smoke was leaning up against an awning post in front of the saloon when Mills Walsdorf and his men rode slowly into town. Three very boring and totally uneventful days had passed with no sign of any of the Slater gang. Mills gave Smoke a very disgusted look as he noticed the star pinned to Smoke's chest. He turned his horse and stopped at the hitchrail.

He dismounted and sighed as his boots touched the ground. The horse looked as tired as he did.

"Have a good ride, Mills?" Smoke asked.

"Very funny, Jensen," the federal man said. "Did you kill those two men we found off the side of the road a few miles back?"

"Yes. I did. They accosted me on the trail, and I was forced to defend myself."

"My God, man! You could have at least given them a decent burial."

"They weren't decent people."

"You're disgusting, Jensen. The vultures had picked at them."

"They probably flew off somewhere and died."

Mills ignored that. "Did you really think you could lose us?"

"Only if I wanted to. You may be city boys, but you probably know how to use a compass."

45

"To be sure. I'm curious about that badge you're wearing."

"I think it's made of tin."

A pained look passed Mills' face. He sighed. "You are a very difficult man to speak with, Jensen. I meant . . ."

"I know what you meant. I believe the Slater gang is heading this way. The town didn't have a marshal. I volunteered and they accepted my unpaid services."

"Well, we're here now, so you can feel free to resign."

"Oh, well, hell, Mills. That makes me feel so much better. What are you going to do when the Slater gang hits town, talk them to death?"

A flash of irritation passed the federal marshal's face. He cleared his throat and said, "I intend to arrest them, Jensen. Then we'll try them and see that they get long prison sentences."

"How about a rope?"

"I don't believe in capital punishment."

"Oh, Lord!" Smoke said, looking heavenward. "What have I done for you to send this down on me?"

Mills laughed at Smoke. "Oh, come now, man! You're obviously a fellow of some intelligence. You surely know that the death penalty doesn't work . . ."

"The hell it doesn't!" Smoke said. "They'll damn sure not come back from the grave to commit more crimes."

"That's not what I mean. It isn't a deterrent for others not to commit the same acts of mayhem."

"Now, what bright fellow thought up that crap?"

"Very learned people in some of our finest Eastern universities."

Smoke said a few very ugly words, which summed up his opinion of very learned people back East. He turned and walked toward the batwings, pausing for a moment and calling over his shoulder. "There're rooms upstairs here, Mills. Take your baths across the street behind the barber shop. Don't try supper at Bonnie's Cafe this evening. The cook's drunk. That apple, turnip, and carrot stew he fixed for lunch was rough."

Mills and his marshals were sitting at one table in the saloon, Smoke sitting alone at another playing solitaire when the batwings shoved open and half a dozen men crowded into the saloon, heading for the bar. They eyeballed the U.S. Marshals and grinned at their hightop lace-up boots, their trousers tucked in.

Mills cut his eyes to Smoke. The gunfighter had merely looked up from his game, given the newcomers the briefest of glances, and apparently dismissed them.

The men lined up at the bar and ordered whiskey. "Hear you got some law in this town, now," a big cowboy shot off his mouth. "I reckon me and the boys will have to mind our P's and Q's. We sure wouldn't want to run afoul of the law."

The cowboys laughed, but it was not a good-natured laugh. More like a sarcastic, go-to-hell braying of men who looked for trouble and did not give a damn about the rights of anyone else. Smoke didn't know if they were outlaws or not. But they damn sure were hardcases. Standing very close to the outlaw line.

"Evenin', Luttie," the barkeep said.

Smoke had been briefed on the men. The one with the biggest mouth was Luttie Charles, owner of the Seven Slash Ranch. The foreman was named Jake. Neither man was very likeable, and both were bullies, as were the dozen or so hands the ranch kept on the payroll.

"Yeah," Jake said, after tossing back his whiskey. "Where is this new marshal? I want to size him up and maybe have some fun."

Smoke had also learned that the last marshal the town hired had not left because the town couldn't pay him, but because he'd been savagely beaten by men from the Seven Slash, although low pay had played a part in it.

"I hope it ain't one of these pretty boys," a hand said, turning and sneering at Mills and his men. "That wouldn't be no contest a-tall."

I wouldn't sell Mills and his men short, Smoke thought. I got a hunch those badge-toters have a hell of a lot more sand and gravel in them than appears. They've been dealing with big city punks and shoulder-strikers and foot-padders for a long time. You boys just might be in for a surprise if you crowd them. Especially Mills. He's no pansy.

Luttie turned to stare at Smoke, sitting close to the shadows in the room. "You, there!" he brayed. "What are you doing?"

"Minding my own business," Smoke said in a quiet voice. "Why don't you do the same?"

To a man, the Seven Slash riders turned, looking at the partially obscured figure at the table.

"You got a smart mouth on you, mister," Luttie Said. "Maybe you don't know who I am."

"I don't particularly care who you are."

48

The Seven Slash riders looked at one another, grinning. This might turn out to be a fun evening after all. It was always fun to beat hell out of someone.

"Git up!" Luttie gave the command to Smoke.

Smoke, in a quiet voice, told him where he could put his order—sideways.

Luttie shook his head. Nobody talked to him like that. Nobody. Ever. "Who in the hell do you think you are?" Luttie roared across the room.

"The new town marshal," Smoke told him, shuffling the deck of cards.

"Maybe he's sittin' over there in the dark 'cause he's so ugly," a hand suggested.

"Why don't we just drag him out in the light and have a look at him?" another said.

"And then we'll stomp him," another laughed.

"That's Smoke Jensen," the barkeep said.

The hands became very silent, and very still. They watched as Smoke stood up from the table. Seemed like he just kept on gettin' up. He laid the deck of cards down on the table and walked out of the shadows, his spurs softly jingling as he walked across the floor. He stopped in front of Luttie.

Luttie was no coward, but neither was he a fool. He knew Smoke Jensen's reputation, and knew it to be true. As he looked into those icy brown eyes, he felt a trickle of sweat slide down the center of his back.

"If there is any stomping to be done in this town," Smoke told the rancher, "I'll do it. And I just might decide to start with you. I don't like bullies. And you're a bully. I don't like big-mouthed fatheads. And you're a big-mouthed fathead. And you're also packin' iron. Now use it, or shut your

49

goddamn mouth!"

Luttie was good with a gun, better than most. He knew that. But he was facing the man who had killed some of the West's most notorious gunfighters. And also a man who was as good with his fists as he was with a six-shooter.

"I got no quarrel with you," Luttie said sullenly. "The boys was just funnin' some."

"No, they weren't," Smoke told him. "And you know it. They're all bullies, just like you. I've heard all about how you and your crew comes into this town, intimidating and bullying other people. I've heard how you like to pick fights and hurt people. You want to fight me, Luttie? How about it? No guns. Just fists. You want that, Luttie?"

"I shall insure it is a fair fight," Mills said quietly, opening his jacket to show his badge.

"Luttie," Jake said. "Them Eastern dudes is U.S. Marshals."

The rancher's sigh was audible. Something big was up, and he didn't know what. But he knew the odds were hard against him on his evening. "We'll be going, boys," he said.

Luttie and his crew paid up and left the saloon, walking without swagger. The crew knew the boss was mad as hornets, but none blamed him for not tangling with Smoke Jensen. That would have been a very dumb move. There was always another day.

"What the hell's he doin' here?" Jake questioned, as they stood by their horses.

"I don't know," Luttie said. "And what about them U.S. Marshals? You reckon they're on to us?"

"How could they be?" another hand asked, surprise and anger in his eyes. "Not even the sheriff suspects anything."

"I don't like it," Jake said.

"Well, hell! How do you think I feel about it? Come on. Let's ride."

"You push hard, Mr. Jensen," Mills said. "There might have been a killing."

"You figure his death would be a great crushing blow to humanity?"

Mills chuckled. "Sometimes your speech is so homey it's sickening. Other times it appears to come straight from the classics. I'm new to the West, Mr. Jensen . . ."

"Smoke. Just Smoke."

"Very well. Smoke. I have much to learn about the West and its people."

"We saddle our own horses and kill our own snakes."

"And the law?"

"We obey it for the most part. Where there is law. But when you come up on people rustling your stock, a man don't usually have the time to ride fifty miles to get a sheriff. Things tend to get hot and heavy real quick. Someone starts shooting at you, you shoot back."

"I can understand that," Mills said. He smiled at Smoke's startled expression "I'm not the legal stickler you think I am, Smoke. There are times when a person must defend oneself. I understand that. But there are other times when men knowingly take the law into their own hands, and that's what I'm opposed to."

"Like you think I'm doing?"

Mills smiled. "As you have been doing," he corrected. "Now you are sworn in as an officer of the law. That makes all the difference."

"And you really believe that?"

"In most cases, yes. In your case, no."

Smoke laughed.

"You became legal—in a manner of speaking—simply as a means to achieve an end. The end of Lee Slater and his gang. What would you do should Lee and his men attack this town, right now?"

"Empty a lot of saddles."

"And be killed doing it?"

"Not likely. I'm no Viking berserker. Anyway, I don't think he's going to attack this town."

"Oh? When did you change your mind?"

"During the course of the day."

"And what do you think he's going to do?"

"I have an idea. But it's just a thought. I'll let you know when I have it all worked out. And I will let you in on it, Mills. You have my word."

"Fair enough."

"Are some of you going to be in town tomorrow?"

"Yes. We're waiting on word from the home office. We sent word where we'd be from that little settlement on the Rio Grande. The stage runs in a couple of days."

"I appreciate you staying close. I'll pull out early in the morning to do some snooping. Be back late tomorrow night."

Smoke could tell the man had a dozen questions he would like to ask. But he held them in check. "I'll see you then."

Smoke pulled out several hours before dawn, pointing Buck's nose toward the east, staying on the south side of the Alamosa River. Luttie's Seven Slash Ranch lay about twenty miles south of the town.

Luttie was up to something besides ranching. Those hands of his were more than cowboys; Smoke had a hunch they were drawing fighting wages. If that was true, who were they fighting, and why?

At the first coloring of dawn, Smoke was on a hill overlooking Luttie's ranchhouse. He studied the men as they exited the bunkhouse heading for chow in a building next to it. He counted fifteen men. Say three or four were not in yet from nightherding; that was a hell of a lot of cowboys for a spread this size.

So what was Luttie up to?

Smoke stayed on the ridges as long as he dared, looking things over through field glasses. For a working ranch, there didn't seem to be much going on. And he found that odd.

Come to think of it, he hadn't seen any cattle on his way in. What he had seen were a lot of signs proclaiming this area to be "posted" and "no trespassing allowed." Odd. Too many odd things cropping up about the Seven Slash Ranch.

It was time to move on; his position on the ridge was just too vulnerable. He tightened the cinch and swung into the saddle. He hadn't learned much, but he had learned that something very odd was going on at the Seven Slash Ranch. And Smoke didn't think it had a damn thing to do with cattle.

"So what is going on?" Mills asked.

The men were sitting on the boardwalk in front of the saloon, enjoying the night air. Mills was contentedly puffing on his pipe, and Smoke had rolled a cigarette.

"I don't know. Luttie could say he stripped his

range during roundup, and a range detective would probably accept that. But he hasn't run any cattle in several years on the ground that I covered today. Any cattleman could see that. So why does he have the big crew, all of them fighting men?" Smoke smiled. "Maybe I know."

"Share it with me?"

"It's just a guess."

"A lot of good police work starts right there."

"It might be that he's hit a silver strike and wants it all for himself, mining it out in secret. But a better guess is that he's running a front for stolen goods."

"I like the second one. But I have some questions about that theory. Why? is one. He's a rancher who has done very well, from all indications. He is a reasonably monied man. I suppose we could chalk it up to greed; however, I think, assuming you're correct, there must be other reasons."

"Why, after all the years of outlawing on the west coast, would Lee Slater put together a gang and come to Colorado?" Smoke questioned. "The west coast is where all his contacts and hiding places would be."

"Where are you going with this, Smoke?"

"I don't know. I'm just trying to put all the pieces together. I may be completely off-base and accusing an innocent man of a crime. All I've got is gut hunches. Can you do some background work?"

"Certainly. But on whom?"

"Luttie Charles and Lee Slater."

That got Mills' attention. He took the pipe out of his mouth and stared at Smoke. "How could they be connected?"

"Maybe by blood."

The Lee Slater gang seemed to have dropped off the face of the earth. Five days went by with no word of any outlaw activity in the area.

The sheriff of the county and two of his deputies rode into town, and Sheriff Silva almost had a heart attack when he learned that Smoke Jensen was the new town marshal.

"By God, it is you!" he said, standing in the door to the town marshal's small office. He frowned. "But why here, of all places?"

Smoke laid it out for the man, but said nothing of his suspicions of Luttie Charles.

The sheriff nodded his head. "We heard he was in this area. If he is, he's found him a dandy hidey hole."

Smoke had him an idea just where that might be. But he kept that to himself. "Can you make me a deputy sheriff of this county?"

"Sure can. It'd be a honor. Stand up and raise your right hand."

After being sworn in, Smoke and Sheriff Dick Silva sat in the office and drank coffee and chatted. Mills and his men were out of town, roaming around, looking for signs of the Slater gang.

"It could be," the sheriff said, "that Slater learned about the new silver strikes to the north and east of here. The big one's up around Creede, but we've got some dandy smaller ones in this area."

"Any gold?"

"A few producing mines, yeah. The stage line is putting on more people, and they'll be running through here every other day commencin' shortly. This town'll boom for awhile. But you know how that goes."

Smoke nodded his head. The rotting ruins of

former boom towns dotted the landscape of the West. They flourished for a few months or a few years, until the gold or silver ran out, and then died or were reduced to only a few hangers-on, scratching in the earth for the precious metals.

"I've seen a few boom towns in my life."

"You rode with Ol' Preacher, didn't you, Smoke?"

"Yes. He raised me after my dad was killed. I knew all the old mountain men. Beartooth, Dupree, Greybull, Nighthawk, Tenneysee, Pugh, Audie, Matt, Deadlead. Hell of a breed of men, they were. I hated to see them vanish."

One left, the sheriff thought, taking in the awesome size of the man seated before him. Smoke's wrists were as large as some men's arms. If he hit you with everything he had, the blow would do some terrible damage to a man's face.

"Tell me everything that's on your mind, son," the sheriff urged in a quiet tone. "You've been steppin' around something for an hour."

Dick Silva was no fool, Smoke thought. He's a good lawman who can read between the lines. But what if he's a friend of Luttie's, or on his payroll? How to phrase this?

"I had a little run-in with Luttie Charles the other night," he said, figuring that was the best way to open up.

The sheriff spat and clanged the cuspidor. "I don't have much use for Luttie. When he first come into this country, years back, he was a hard-workin' man. I didn't approve of the way he built up his ranch—he was one of them homesteader burners, if they got in his way—but the sheriff back then was easy bought and in his pocket. I ain't," he said flatly. "Luttie steps cautious-like around me."

56

"I took a ride over to his place the other day. He appears to be a man who don't like visitors."

"All them posted signs?"

Smoke nodded.

"They went up about five years ago. 'Bout the same time the bottom dropped out of the beef market — for a while — and Luttie took to hirin' hardcases to ride for him. I've run off or jailed a few of his hands. But he's got some bad ones workin' for him."

"And no cattle," Smoke dropped that in.

"You noticed too," the sheriff said with a smile.

"Of course, there is no law that says a man has to run cattle on his ranch if he doesn't want to."

"Exactly. But it sure makes me awful curious about just how he's earnin' a livin'." He shook his head. "I know where you're goin' with this, Smoke. But I have no authority to go bustin' up onto his property demandin' to know how he earns his livelihood. And a judge would throw me out of his chambers if I tried to get a search warrant based on our gut hunches."

"Oh, I know."

"Say it all, Smoke." Sheriff Silva smiled. "You're one of my deputies now. You can't hold back from the boss."

"I've got a hunch there is some connection between Slater and Luttie. I've asked a U.S. Marshal to check their backgrounds. He's doing that now. Probably be a week or more before anything comes back in."

"You'd make a good lawman, Smoke."

"I've toted a badge more than once," he replied with a smile. "County, state, and federal. Mills Walsdorf doesn't know that, though."

"What do you think of the man?"

"I like him. I thought he was a pompus, stuffed-shirt windbag when I first met him. But he sort of grows on you. He sure has some funny ideas about enforcing the law. He doesn't believe in the death penalty."

The sheriff almost choked on his chew. "What?"

"Says it's barbaric and doesn't accomplish anything. Says criminals aren't really to blame for what they do."

"Say what?"

"Says it's home life and pressure from friends and so forth that cause criminals. Rejection and things like that. Says all sorts of real smart folks back in fine Eastern universities thought all this out."

Sheriff Silva shook his head. "I hope them thoughts of his don't never catch on. In a hundred years, criminals would be runnin' the country."

Chapter Five

It was a very weary and dejected-looking band of U.S. Marshals that rode back into town late in the afternoon. After a bath and a shave, Mills walked over to Smoke's office. He was almost dragging his boots in the dirt from exhaustion.

"Cover a lot of ground, did you?" Smoke asked, pouring the man a cup of coffee from the battered pot on the stove.

"More than I care to repeat anytime soon." Mills sat down with a sigh and accepted the cup of coffee. "And didn't accomplish a damned thing."

"No," Smoke corrected. "Don't look at it like that. You accomplished a great deal, in fact."

"I'd like to know what?"

"You saw the country, and if you're just half as smart as I think you are, you committed it to memory. You know where good water is now. You found some box canyons and now know to stay out of them. You found good places to bed down for the night. You found where outlaws might hole up. You know where good river and stream crossings are located. And you saw some of the most beautiful country in all the world."

Slowly, a smile crinkled the marshal's mouth. "Yes. You're right on all counts, Smoke." He peered over the rim of his coffee cup at the new gold badge on Smoke's chest. "Say, now. Where did that come from?"

Smoke told him of Sheriff Silva's visit.

"The sheriff checks out as a good, honest lawman. He's a rancher that got caught up in the market bust years back and turned to police work. His ranch rebounded, but he was hooked on police work by that time, and the people of the county like him. He earns enough money from both vocations to insure he can't be bought."

"Find out anything about Luttie Charles?"

"A few things. The people around here don't like him and don't trust him. He says he came here from Texas, but people doubt that. Oklahoma Territory seems to be the general consensus. Early on he let it slip that he's fairly knowledgeable about that part of the country."

"So why would he lie about it?"

"You know the answer to that as well as I do. He's hiding something in his past. But he could be running away from a wife. It's certainly happened to other men."

"With Luttie, it's more like a rope he's running from."

"Agreed. But proving it is another matter. I have feelers out. It'll take some time."

"You'd better get some rest. You look like you're all in."

"Yes. I'll see you in the morning."

Smoke did some paper work then locked up the office and stepped out into the gathering dusk of evening. He began his walking of the settlement's streets. That didn't take long, and he headed for Bonnie's Cafe for a cup of coffee.

Movement at the edge of town stopped him.

Smoke stepped into a weed-grown space between the empty bank building and the general store and waited.

There it was again. But at this distance, he couldn't tell if the movement was human or animal. He removed his spurs and put them in his pocket while he waited and watched, not staring directly at the mysterious shape, for some people can sense being watched. The form began to take shape as it drew nearer, staying in the shadows. It was a man, no doubt about that, and moving slowly and furtively.

The man ducked down the far side of Bonnie's Cafe, and Smoke took that time to run silently across the street and into the alley that ran between the combination saddle shop/gunsmith building and the saloon.

Staying close to the building, but not brushing against it, he pulled iron and eased the hammer back just as the man stepped into the rear of the alley.

Smoke dropped down to one knee and said, "You looking for someone, partner?"

The man fired, the muzzle blast stabbing the darkness with a lance of flame. The bullet slammed into the building, a foot above Smoke's head.

Smoke let the hammer down, and his slug brought a scream of pain and doubled the man over. A rifle barked from across the street, and that slug howled past Smoke's head. Smoke flattened on the ground and rolled under the building, hoping a rattlesnake was not under there and irritated at being disturbed.

The rifle barked again, just as lamps were turned up in the homes and businesses of the settlement.

"Goddamnit, Jesse!" the man Smoke had shot screamed. "You done killed me!" He moaned once and said no more.

Running footsteps reached Smoke, followed by the sounds of galloping hooves. He rolled out from under the building just as Mills and his men came running out of the saloon, in various stages of dress, or undress. Mills had jerked on his high-top boots, not laced up, and put on his hat. He was dressed in hat, boots, and long-handles.

"Bring a lamp over here," Smoke called. "One's down in the alley."

"Don King," the barber said, as the dead man was rolled over into his back. "Rides for Luttie Charles."

"He don't no more," Bonnie said, peering over the man's shoulder.

"I heard him yell that someone named Jesse shot him," Mills said.

"He put the second slug in him," Smoke said. He looked at the barber. "You act as the undertaker?"

"Yes, sir, Mr. Smoke. I do a right nice job, too, if I do say so myself."

"Leastwise, he ain't never had no customers complain," Bonnie said.

"Stretch him out in your place, then," Smoke told the man. "It's cool enough so he'll keep for a day. Mills, you and me will take a ride out to break the sad news to Luttie Charles first thing in the morning."

"I'll be up at five."

They left before dawn and were on Seven Slash range as the sun was chasing away the last of the shadows of night. They stopped at a wooden, hand-painted sign nailed to a tree.

TRESPASSERS WILL BE SHOT

"Certainly gives a person a warm feeling of being wanted, doesn't it?" Mills said drily.

Smoke laughed. Despite their differences of opinion concerning law and order, he liked the federal marshal. He was looking forward to seeing the man get into action. He had a hunch Mills would be hard to handle if you made him mad.

Mills shifted his badge to the front of his coat. "So they'll be sure to see it," he said.

"Makes a dandy target," Smoke told him. "Might stop a bullet if it was fired from a far enough distance."

"You're so full of good cheer early in the morning."

"Thank you."

"Just hold it right there, boys," the voice came from behind them. "And keep them hands in sight."

"I'm a United States Marshal," Mills said, without looking around. "And this is Deputy Jensen. I have six of my men fifteen minutes behind us . . ."

Pretty good liar, Smoke thought. Quick, too.

". . . Cease and desist and come forward."

"Do what?"

"Get your butt around here so's we can see you," Smoke made it plainer.

"I don't take orders from you."

"You think you can get both of us?" Smoke asked. "If you do, you're a fool."

"Just sit your saddles." The man walked around to face them.

"Now you've seen me," Smoke told him. "If you ever again put iron on me, I'll kill you. Now put

63

that rifle away."

"Just pointing that weapon at me could mean prison for you," Mills told him.

"All right, all right!" the hardcase said, lowering the muzzle. "I'm just following orders from the boss. What do you want here?"

"To see your boss," Smoke told him. "Let's go."

"He ain't up yet. He don't get up 'til eight. Likes to work at night."

Smoke smiled.

"Jesus Christ!" Luttie hollered, as Smoke grabbed him by the ankle and dragged him out of bed. "What the hell's goin' on here?" Luttie's butt bounced on the floor, and he came up in his long johns swinging both fists.

Smoke staggered him with one punch, grabbed him by the neck and the back-flap and threw him down the stairs of the two story ranch house.

"Your approach to law and order is quite novel, to say the least," Mills observed.

"It gets their attention," Smoke told him, as they walked down the stairs to stand over a dazed and befuddled Luttie.

Smoke tossed Don King's personal effects to the floor. "Those belong to one of your hands. He tried to kill me last night. Somebody named Jesse shot him after I did. Get Jesse out here and do it now."

"No one named Jesse works for me," Luttie muttered, crawling to his bare feet.

Smoke drew, cocked and fired so fast it was a blur. He put a slug between Luttie's bare feet.

"Yeeeyow!" the man hollered and danced, as the splinters dug into his feet.

"I said get Jesse here," Smoke said.

"Jesus Christ!" Luttie bellered. "Jake, go get Jesse over here." He glared at Smoke. "I hate you!"

"I'm all broken up about it. Aren't you going to be neighborly and offer us some coffee?"

"Hell with you!"

"Disgusting lack of hospitality," Mills said.

"Hell with you, too," Luttie told him.

The men stood and stared at each other for a moment.

The foreman, Jake, reentered the house. "Jesse didn't come back last night. His bunk ain't been slept in."

"We have a description of him," Mills said. "I'll get a federal warrant issued for his arrest, charging him with murder and attempted murder of a law officer."

"Now both of you get out of my house!" Luttie yelled.

Smoke looked at the man's soiled long-handles. "You need to do something about your personal hygiene, Luttie."

"Get out of here!" the man screamed.

"What do you want done with the remains of poor Don King?" Smoke asked.

"Bury him!" Luttie yelled. "In the ground."

"He didn't have but two dollars on him," Mills said. "A good box costs far more than that. I personally would suggest one lined with a subtle shade of cloth, perhaps with a soft pillow on which to lay his poor dead head. A simple service will suffice, with the minister reading from the . . ."

"Shut up!" Luttie roared. "Goddamnit! I don't care if you read from a tobacco sack. Just get out of my house and put the man in the ground. Send

65

me the bill."

"You're a true lover of your fellow man, Luttie," Smoke said, trying to keep a straight face. It was hard to do: the buttons on Luttie's back flap had torn loose, and he was trying to hold it up with one hand.

"I'm sure the service will be tomorrow," Mills said, continuing to play the game with Smoke. "Shall I tell everyone you'll be in attendance?"

Luttie started jumping up and down like a great ape in a cage. "GetoutGetoutGetoutGetout!" he screamed.

"I think we have overstayed our welcome," Smoke said. "Do you agree, Marshal?"

"Quite. Shall we take our leave?"

"Oh, let's do!"

Luttie was screaming obscenities at them as they rode away. Both breathed a little easier when they were out of rifle shot.

"Luttie, them two ain't got a lick of sense!" Jake said, when he had calmed Luttie down. "And a crazy man's dangerous!"

That set Luttie off again, jumping around and hollering.

"I think he needs a good dose of salts," a hardcase suggested. "Maybe his plumbin's all plugged up?"

"For a man that don't believe in going to the extreme with law and order," Smoke said, "you sure can jump right in there and help stick the needle to suspects."

"Oh, I think a bit of agitation is good for the soul. The man is unbalanced. You realize that?"

"Uh-huh. And now I hope you're not going to tell

me that because he's about half nuts he shouldn't be shot if he drags iron on someone."

"There is some debate on that, I will admit. But a dangerous person is dangerous whether he's normal or insane. Besides, there are degrees of insanity. Luttie Charles is not a drooling idiot confined to a rocking chair. He simply lost control back there for a moment. He's a very cunning man." He chuckled. "Wouldn't you lose control if someone grabbed you by the ankle and jerked you out of a sound sleep, then knocked you down and threw you down the stairs?"

Smoke smiled. "I might at that." He shook his head. "That was sure some sight."

Laughing, the men put their horses into an easy canter and headed back to town. Smoke noticed that Mills had stopped bobbing up and down like a cork in the water and was riding more and more like a Westerner.

The next several days were long and boring. Providing Jake had been telling the truth back at the ranch house, Jesse had left the country.

"If that's the case," Mills observed, "it's probably for fear that Luttie would shoot him because he and that other wretch failed to kill you."

Later on that day, shortly after the stage had run, Mills came to the marshal's office. "This is it," he said, smiling and waving a piece of paper. He sat down. "It seems that Lee Slater—and Slater is his Christian name—was born in Oklahoma. He left their farm when he was about fifteen, after raping and killing a neighbor girl. He had a younger brother that disappeared shortly after robbing a stagecoach and making off with a strongbox filled with thousands of dollars. The boys were named Lee and Luther." Mills smiled again. "Luther's middle name was Charles."

"It's good enough for me, but I doubt a jury would convict on it."

"Nor do I. My superiors have given me orders to stay out here until Lee Slater and his band of thugs are contained." He sighed. "At the rate I'm going, I may as well move my belongings out here and transfer my bank account."

"Oh," Smoke said, pouring them both coffee. "It's not that bad. I tell you what I'll bet you: you stay out here a few more months, Mills, and this country will grab you. Then you won't want to leave."

"I'm afraid you may be right. Do you have any sort of plan, Smoke? I seem to be fresh out."

The gunfighter shook his head. "No, I don't, Mills. It seems to me—and I'm no professional lawman—that all we can do is wait for something to break, then jump on it like a hound on a bone."

Mills had noticed that Smoke had adopted a small cur dog he'd found wandering the town, eating scraps and having mean little boys throw rocks at it. After a lecture from Smoke Jensen about being cruel to animals, Mills was of the opinion the boys might well grow up to be vegetarians. Smoke had been rather stern.

Smoke had bathed the little dog and fixed it a bed in the office. The dog now lay in Smoke's lap, contented as Smoke gently petted it.

"You're a strange man, Smoke," Mills had to say. "You don't appear to care one whit about the life of a person gone wrong, yet you love animals."

"Animals can't help being what they are, Mills,"

Smoke said with a gentle smile. "We humans can. We have the ability to think and reason. I don't believe animals do; at least not to any degree. We don't have to rob and steal and lie and cheat and murder. That's why God gave us a brain. And I don't have any use for people who refuse to use that brain and instead turn to a life of crime. You read the Bible, Mills?"

"Certainly. But what has the Bible got to do with animals?"

"A lot. I think animals go to Heaven."

"Oh, come now!" Mills gently scoffed.

"Sure. And our Bible is not the only Good Book that talks of that. Our Bible says in Ecclesiates: 'For the fate of the sons of men and the fate of beasts is the same; as one dies, so dies the other. They all have the same breath, and man has no advantage over the beasts; for all is vanity.' Paul preached about it, too. And my wife, who is a lot more religious than me, says that John Wesley came right out and outlined what he thought animals would experience in Heaven. John Calvin also admitted that he thought animals were to be renewed."

Mills shook his head. "You never cease to baffle me, Smoke. You're a . . . walking contradiction. You mentioned some other Good Book. What are you talking about?"

"The Koran. You haven't read it?"

"Good God, no! And you have?"

"Yes. Sally ordered a copy for me. I found it very interesting."

Mills studied the man for a moment. Before him was the West's most notorious gunfighter—no Jensen wasn't notorious; "famous" was a better word—and the man was calmly discussing the world's religions. And sounding as if he did indeed know what he was talking about.

"You think you'll go to Heaven, Smoke?" Mills asked gently.

"I don't know. God loved His warriors. I do know that. But I like to think that maybe there is a middle ground for men like me."

"Like Valhalla?"

"Yes."

"Another personal question, Smoke?"

"Sure."

"How many men have you killed?"

"I honestly don't know, Mills. Over a hundred, surely, and possibly two hundred. I've got a lot of blood on my hands, I won't deny that. Jesse James gave me my first pistol, way back during the war, when I was just a kid in Missouri. A Navy .36, it was. I carried that old pistol for a long time. And put some men in the ground with it."

"What happened to it?"

"I think it's in a trunk up at the ranch house."

"You have children, Smoke?"

"Oh, yes. They're in France with their grandparents, traveling and getting an education. Baby Arthur had to go for medical treatment. Their mother couldn't go because she gets deadly ill on ship."

"Outlaws killed your first wife, didn't they?"

"Yes. And smothered my baby son in the cradle while they were raping Nicole."

Mills knew the story. It was legend. At first he thought it was all a big lie. Now he knew it was all true. How a young Smoke Jensen tracked them down and killed them all. Castrated one of them and cauterized the terrible wound with a white hot running iron.

Frontier justice, Mills concluded, doesn't leave any room for gray areas. It's all black and white and very final.

"I found Sally about a year later," Smoke said. "We married and have been together and very happy since then. You married, Mills?"

The U.S. Marshal shook his head. "No. I haven't found the right woman yet, I suppose." He smiled, rather sadly, Smoke thought. "But I'm still looking."

"I hope you find you a good woman, Mills. There's one out there. Just keep looking."

One of Mills' men, Winston, stuck his head in the office door. "About half a dozen men riding in, Mills. They look like thugs to me."

Smoke smiled. Probably half the men in the West look like thugs. He put the little dog in its bed and walked to the window. Winston had been correct in his assessment of the riders.

Deke Carey and Dirty Jackson were among the six men. He'd seen pictures of Deke, and Smoke had had a run-in with Dirty some years back, when both had been much younger.

"You know them?" Mills asked.

"I know them."

Mills watched as Smoke slipped the leather thongs off the hammers of his .44s. "It's come to that?"

"It's come to that." Smoke stepped out on the boardwalk.

Chapter Six

Dirty cut his eyes as the six outlaws rode slowly past the marshal's office. His smile was savage.

"We'll arrest them," Mills said.

"On what charge? There aren't any warrants on them that I'm aware of."

"Then we have no right to interfere with their freedom of travel."

Smoke chuckled at that. "Deke there, he's a backshooter, a thief, and a child molester. Dirty has done it all: cold-blooded murder, rape, robbery, torture, kidnapping. I told him years ago that if I ever laid eyes on him again, I'd kill him. And that is exactly what I intend to do."

"But you said there are no warrants on them!"

"None in Colorado. But I've been holding one just for him for years."

"Where is it?"

Smoke patted the butt of a .44. "Right here in Mr. Colt. Now, Mills, you and I have become friends over the past week or so. But this is personal between Dirty and me. He killed a little girl in Nevada some years back. He bragged about doing it and then left town just ahead of the posse. He's fixing to come to trial over that killing.

72

Right shortly."

"But . . ."

"Mills, lead, follow, or get the hell out of my way."

Smoke stepped off the boardwalk just as the outlaws were entering the saloon. Seconds later the saloon emptied of locals.

Smoke pushed open the batwings and stepped inside, Mills right behind him. Smoke heard Dirty asking for a room for the night.

"Not in this town, Dirty," Smoke called out. "The only room you're going to get is a pine box. And if there isn't enough coins in your pocket to buy a box, we'll roll you up in your blankets and plant you that way."

Mills gasped at the sheer audacity of Smoke.

Dirty turned and faced Jensen. The man was big and dirty and mean-looking. He wore one gun tied down and had another six-shooter shoved behind his belt. "You got no call to talk to me like that, Jensen."

"You ever ridden back to Nevada to put flowers on the grave of that little girl you killed, Dirty?"

Dirty flushed under the beard and the dirt on his face. "I was drunk when that happened, Jensen. Man can't be held responsible for what he does when he's drunk."

"Yeah," Smoke said sourly. "The courts will probably hold that to be true one of these days. But 'one of these days' don't count right now."

Mills grunted softly.

"Give him a drink," Smoke told the barkeep. "On me. Enjoy it, Dirty. It's gonna be your last one."

Deke Carey moved away from the bar to get a

better angle at Smoke.

"Stand still, Deke," Smoke told him. "You move again and I'll put lead in you."

Deke froze to the floor, both hands in plain sight. "You think you can take us all, Jensen?"

"Yes."

Mills had moved to one side, one thumb hooked over his belt buckle. Smoke had noticed several days before that the federal marshal carried a hideout gun shoved behind his belt, under his jacket.

"Who's your funny-lookin' friend, Jensen?" another of the six asked.

"I am United States Marshal Walsdorf," Mills informed him.

"Well, la-tee-da," a young punk with both guns tied down said with a simper. "A U-nited States Marshal. Heavens!" He put a hand to his forehead and leaned up against the bar. "I'm so fearful I think I might swoon."

Mills was across the room before the punk could stand up straight. Mills hit the smart-mouthed punk with a hard right fist that knocked him sprawling. He jerked him up, popped him again, and threw him across the room. The punk landed against the cold pot-bellied stove. The stove fell over, the stovepipe broke loose from the flue collar, and the two-bit young gunny was covered with soot.

"Show some respect for the badge, if not for me," Mills said.

"I don't like your damn attitude!" another gunny said. "I think I'll just take that badge and shove . . ."

The only thing that got shoved was Mills' fist, smack into the gunny's mouth. Mills hit him two more times, and the man slumped to the floor, bleeding from nose and mouth and momentarily out of it.

Mills swept back his coat, put his hand on the butt of his short-barreled Peacemaker .45 and thundered, "I will have law and order, gentlemen!"

"Halp!" the soot-covered punk yelled. "I cain't see nothin'. Halp!"

"Let's take 'em, Greeny!" Dirty said.

But Smoke was already moving. He reached Dirty before the man could drag iron and loosened some of Dirty's teeth with a short, hard right.

Greeny swung at Mills and almost fell down as Mills ducked the punch. Mills planted his lace-up boots and decked the outlaw.

Smoke jabbed a left fist into Deke's face three times, the jabs jarring the man's head back and bringing a bright smear of blood to his mouth. He followed the jabs with a right cross that knocked Deke to the floor.

"By the Lord!" Mills shouted. "This is exhilarating." He just got the words out of his mouth when the punk hit him on top of the head with the stovepipe and knocked him spinning across the room.

Smoke splintered a chair across the punk's teeth, the hardwood knocking the kid up against a wall.

The barkeep climbed up on the bar and jumped onto Deke's back just as the man was getting to his boots. Deke threw the smaller man off and came in swinging at Smoke.

Bad mistake on Deke's part.

Smoke hit him with a left-right combination that glazed the man's bloodshot eyes and backed him up against the bar. Smoke hit him twice in the stomach and that did it for Deke. He kissed the floor and began puking.

Dirty hit Smoke a sneak punch that jarred Smoke and knocked him around. Smoke recovered and the men stood toe to toe and slugged it out for a full minute.

Mills was smashing Greeny's face with short, hard, brutal blows that brought a spray of blood each time his big fists impacted with the outlaw's face.

The soot-covered kid climbed to his boots and decided to take on the barkeep.

Bad mistake on the kid's part.

The barkeep had retreated to the bar and pulled out a truncheon, which he promptly and with much enthusiasm laid on top of the punk's head. The punk's eyes crossed, he sighed once, and hit the floor, out cold.

Dirty backed up and with Smoke's hands still balled into fists, grinned at him and went for his gun.

Smoke kicked the man in the groin, and Dirty doubled over, coughing and gagging. Smoke stepped forward and kicked the murderer in the face with the toe of his boot. Dirty's teeth bounced around the floor. He screamed and rolled away, blood dripping from his ruined mouth.

Deke grabbed for his guns, and Smoke shot him twice in the belly, the second hole just an inch above the first. Deke tried to lift his pistol, and Smoke fired a third time, the slug hitting the man in the center of the forehead.

Dirty rolled to his boots and faced Smoke, a gun in each hand, his face a bloody mask of hate.

Smoke had pulled both .44s and started them

thundering. He was cocking and firing so fast it seemed a never-ending deadly cadence of thunder. Puffs of dust rose from Dirty's jacket each time a .44 slug slammed into his body. Dirty clung to the edge of the bar, his guns fallen to the floor out of numbed fingers.

"Jesus!" the barkeep said. "What's the matter with him? Why don't he say something?"

"Because he's dead," Smoke said.

Dirty Jackson fell on his face.

Greeny was moaning and crawling around on the floor. The kid was beginning to show some signs of life. The other two had wisely decided to stay on the floor with their hands in plain sight.

"You others, get up!" Smoke told the two outlaws, wide-eyed and on the floor. "And haul the kid and that jerk over there to their boots."

Greeny and the punk were jerked up. "The punk goes to jail," Smoke said. "The others get chained to that tree by the side of the office."

"Hey, that ain't right!" Greeny said. "What happens if it rains?"

"We give you a bar of soap."

"Damn!" Albert said, looking at his boss. "How come we miss all the fun, Mills?"

Mills was dabbing horse liniment on yesterday's jaw bruise and ignored the question.

"You know, Smoke," Hugh said. "You really can't keep those men chained up to that tree."

"Why?" Smoke asked, scratching the little dog behind the ears.

"Because they're human beings and as such, have basic rights accorded them by the Constitution."

77

Mills smiled. He'd already gone over that with Smoke. He would have gotten better results by conversing with a mule.

"Greeny didn't think much of the rights of those people he killed up in Canada, Hugh. Lebert didn't give a damn for the rights of those women he kidnapped and raped. Augie didn't have anybody's rights in mind when he tortured a man to death." Smoke held up several wire replies. "It's all right there. Deputies will be coming for Lebert and Augie. Royal Canadian Mounted Police will be here for Greeny. And I'm going to hang the punk back yonder in the cell."

"I ain't done nothin'!" the kid squalled. "You ain't gonna hang me!"

"Oh, yes, I am, kid. I say you were the one who killed that poor man back up the trail. I say you was the one who raped and killed those poor little girls. And that's what I got you charged with. You're gonna hang, punk."

Winston started to protest. Smoke held up his hand. The cell area was behind and to the right of the main office, and the kid could not see what was going on, only hear, exactly how Smoke had planned it.

"Ever seen a hanging, kid?" Smoke called.

"No!"

"It's a sight to behold, boy. Sometimes the neck don't break, and the victim just dangles there while he chokes to death. Eyes bug out, tongue pooches out and turns black . . ."

"Shut up, damn you!"

". . . Fellow just twists there in the breeze. Sometimes it takes five minutes for him to die . . ."

"Damn you, shut up!" the kid screamed.

78

"Awful ugly sight to see. Plumb disgusting. And smelly, too. Victim usually looses all control of himself . . ."

The kid rattled the barred door. "Let me out of here!" he yelled.

". . . Terrible sight to see. Just awful. Sometimes they put a hood on the victim — I'll be sure and request one for you — and when they take that hood off — once the man's dead — his face is all swole up and black as a piece of coal."

"Jensen?" the kid called, in a voice choked with tears.

"What do you want, kid?"

"I'll make a deal with you."

Smoke winked at Mills and the others. "What kind of a deal, kid?"

"I know lots of things."

"What things?"

"We got to deal first."

"You don't have much of a position to deal from, boy. Your trial is coming up in a couple of days. The jury's already picked. And they're eager to convict. Folks around here haven't seen a good hanging in a year or more. Gonna be dinner on the grounds on the day you swing. Did you hear that hammering a while ago?"

"Yeah." The kid blew his nose on a dirty rag. "What was all that racket?"

"Fellows building a gallows, boy. That's where you're going to swing."

"I told you I'd deal!" His voice was very shaky.

"Start dealing, boy. You don't have long."

"Don't let Greeny and Lebert and Augie know nothin' about his, Marshal."

"You have my word on that."

"I'm ready when you are."

Smoke looked at Mills. "He's all yours, Mills. You wanted it legal, you got it legal." He smiled. "This time."

"Needless to say, we won't tell the kid that hammering and sawing was a man building a new outhouse."

"He might not see the humor in it."

"Get your pad and pen, Winston," Mills said. "Let's see what the kid has to say."

In exchange for escaping the hangman's noose and that short drop that culminated in an abrupt and fatal halt, the kid—his name was Walter Parsons—had quite a lot to say. He said he didn't know nothin' about Lee Slater and Luttie Charles bein' related, but they was close friends . . . or so Lee had said. But the gang was hidin' out on Seven Slash range. East of the ranch house and south of the Alamosa River. Wild country. They was plannin' to rob the miners and the stages carryin' gold and silver and Luttie was goin' to handle the gettin' rid of the boodle end of it.

How many in the gang?

The kid reckoned they was about fifty or sixty. He didn't rightly know since they wasn't camped all together. But it was a big gang.

How many people had the kid robbed and raped and murdered?

Bunches. Used to be fun, but now it was sort of borin'. All them people did was blubber and slobber and beg and cry and carry on somethin' awful. It was a relief just to shoot them in the head to shut them up.

"Disgusting!" Mills said, tossing the signed confession onto Smoke's desk. "I have never in my life heard of such depravity as that which came out of Parsons' mouth."

"You relaxing your stand on hanging now, Mills?" Smoke asked.

He received a dirty look, but Mills chose not to respond to the question.

"What are you doing to do with the kid?"

Mills shook his head. "I don't know. I can't allow the return of that vicious little thug back to a free society. That would be a grave injustice. The judge is going to have to decide that issue."

"He's never going to change."

"I know that," Mills said. "It's a dreadful time we live in, Smoke."

"It's going to get worse, Mills. Count on it. Now, then, what about Luttie?"

"We can't move against him on just the word of a common hoodlum. We've got to have some proof that he is, indeed, a part of this conspiracy. How about Greeny and Lebert and Augie? Have they agreed to talk?"

"You have to be kidding. Those are hardened criminals. They'll go to the grave with their mouths closed. They're not going to assist the hangman in their own executions."

"When will the deputies and the Royal Canadian Mounted Police come for them?"

"They said as soon as possible. Probably in a week or so."

"I've got to move the kid out of here and up to Sheriff Silva's jail. For safekeeping."

"All right. Why not do that now and as soon as the kid is gone, I'll pull those three scumbags in

81

from the tree."

"I would hate for a supervisor to ride by and see them chained out there," Winston said.

Smoke shook his head. "I'll be sure to take them some tea and cookies the first chance I get."

At Smoke's insistence Mills sent four of his men out early the next morning, taking the kid to the county seat and to a better and more secure jail. They would be gone at least three days and possibly four.

Smoke took down all the sawed off double-barreled shotguns from the rack and passed them around. "Clean them up, boys, and load them up. Don't ever be too far away from one."

"Are you expecting trouble?" Mills asked. "From whom and why?"

"Yes, I'm expecting trouble. From whom? Either Lee Slater or his brother . . ."

"His assumed brother," Mills corrected. "Yes. I see. They could not want the three we have here talking and implicating either of them. Now I see why you insisted on sending more men than I thought necessary to the county seat with Parsons. I thank you for your insistence, Smoke. Parsons would be the more likely of the four to crack—as he did."

Smoke nodded his agreement as he loaded up the sawed-off with buckshot.

Winston hefted the shotgun shells in his hands. "These are heavy, too heavy for factory loads."

"I had the gunsmith across the street load them for me. They're filled with broken nails and ball-bearings and whatever else he had on hand." He looked first at Mills, then at Winston and Moss. "Any of you ever shot a man with a Greener?"

They shook their heads.

"Close in they'll cut a man in two. Makes a real mess. Fastest man in the world won't buck the odds of a sawed-off pointed at his belly."

"You've shot men with these types of weapons?" Moss asked.

"I've shot men with muzzle-loaders, cap and ball, Sharps .52, .Navy .36 and Colt and Remington and Starr .44s and .45s. I've shot them with a Remington .41 over and under. I've used knives, tomahawks and chopping axes more than a time or two. If somebody was trying to kill me or mine, I'd drop him with a hot horseshoe if that was all I could find at the moment. Gentlemen, I just have to ask a question. You all have sidestepped it before, but level with me this time. Why in the hell did your superiors send you men out here?"

Mills cleared his throat and looked uncomfortable, and both Winston and Moss blushed.

Smoke waited.

"Truth time," Winston muttered.

"Yes," Mills said. "Quite. Smoke, we are all new to the West, and to its customs. Tenderfeet, as I've read. We've worked the cities and smaller Eastern towns, but never west of the Mississippi. The United States Marshal's office is being upgraded in manpower, and, well, while we are not amateurs in this business, we, ah . . ."

Smoke held up a hand. "Let me finish it: you were sent out here to get bloodied?"

"That, ah, is a reasonably accurate assessment, yes."

83

"Well, you might get that chance sooner than you think. Here comes Luttie with his whole damn crew!"

Chapter Seven

"Maybe they're coming in to put flowers on Don's grave?" Winston said.

Smoke turned to look at him. The man had a twinkle in his eye. Mills and Moss were both smiling. The U.S. Marshals were new to the West, and perhaps had not yet been bloodied in killing combat, but they had plenty of sand and gravel in them, and a sense of humor.

"I'm sure," Smoke said, picking up the sawed-off shotgun. "Shall we step outside and greet the gentlemen?"

Luttie and Jake rode at the head of the column, and they both gave Smoke and the federal marshals curt nods, then turned toward the hitchrails at the saloon. They dismounted, looped the reins and walked into the barroom.

"I don't think they liked the sight of these shotguns," Winston said.

"I'm sure they didn't," Smoke said. He sat down on the bench in front of the office. Mills sat down beside him, Moss and Winston stood nearby.

"I wonder what they're up to," Moss said.

"A show of force?" Mills questioned. "If so, what is the purpose? We rode right up into their lair the other day. They must know that we're not going to be intimidated."

"I don't know whether any of them is that smart," Smoke replied. "If I had to take a guess, I'd guess that this move is a diversion of some sorts."

Mills was thoughtful for a moment. "Yes. I agree. Luttie and his Seven Slash bunch keeps our attention here, while the Slater gang strikes somewhere in the county. But where?"

"No where close, you can bet on that. Around Silver Mountain, maybe." He shook his head. "And it could be that Slater's gang is going to hit the marshals escorting the kid . . . maybe to shut the kid's mouth. Or they're coming in here to try to break their friends out of jail."

"If that bunch hits my men in force, my people won't have a chance," Mills said softly.

"I just hope I've impressed upon your people to shoot first and ask questions later," Smoke said.

"You know they won't do that."

"Then if Slater and his bunch hits them, they're at best wounded and at worst dead meat, Mills. I tried to impress upon you all that this is the West. I don't seem to be a very good teacher."

He stood up and stepped off the boardwalk. Mills' voice stopped him. "Where are you going?"

"It's a warm day. A mug of cool beer would taste good right about now."

"Step right into the lion's den, huh?"

"Might as well. We did pretty well in there the last time, didn't we?"

Mills smiled. "I should be ashamed of myself for saying this, but we damn sure did!"

"We miss all the fun," Winston said glumly.

"Don't count on that continuing," Smoke told him, as they stepped up to the batwings of the saloon. "Once inside, Mills and I will stay together. Moss, take the right end of the bar. Winston, you take the left. Don't turn your back completely on these ol' boys. We'll see how smart Luttie is. If he tries to brace us, we'll put what's left of the bunch in jail and keep them there."

"What will we do with the rest of them?" Moss asked innocently.

Smoke looked at him. "Somebody will bury them."

He pushed open the doors and stepped inside, walking to the bar, the others right behind him.

Luttie and his crew had spread out all over the table area of the saloon, and that told Smoke a lot. None of it good.

"Setup," Mills mumbled.

"Yeah," Smoke returned the whisper. "Glad you picked up on it."

"What are you two love-birds a-whisperin' about?" a Seven Slash hand yelled.

"You reckon they're sweet on each other, Paul?" another said with a laugh.

"That'd be a sight to see, wouldn't it—them a-smoochin'."

"Maybe we ought to see if they'd give us an advance showin'?"

"Now that there's a right good idea," another said.

"Now, boys," Luttie said, a strange smile on his lips. "You know I can't allow nothin' like that to take place. Them fellows is lawmen. They's to be respected. Besides, that's the famous Smoke Jensen yonder. He's supposed to be the fastest gun in all the West. You boys wouldn't want to brace the likes of him, now, would you?"

His crew—and the table area filled with them—

all burst out laughing.

"I won't have no more of this, now, boys," Luttie said. "Although I'm not too sure about me givin' you orders when you're on your own time. Might be some law agin that. What do you say about it, Mr. Fancy-Pants U.S. Marshal?"

"I would say that you don't have any authority to give orders when your hirelings are off the job," he said stiffly.

"Hireling?" a cowboy said. "Ain't it a fancy title, though?"

"Not really," Mills told him, a tight smile on his lips. "It means anyone who will follow another's orders for money—such as a thug or a mercenary."

Smoke was half turned, his left side facing the crowded table area. "When he gets up, Mills," he whispered, his lips just barely moving, "kill him."

Mills shook his head minutely. "I can't do that, Smoke."

The cowboy pushed back his chair. "Are you callin' me a thug, Whistle-Britches?"

"Get ready," Smoke whispered. "Cock that Greener, Mills."

"Actually, no," Mills raised his voice. "I was merely explaining to you the dictionary definition of a hireling. If you take exception to my remark, then you must have a low opinion of yourself."

"Huh?" the cowboy said.

"Charlie," another hand said. "I think he done insulted you. But I ain't real sure."

Luttie and Jake were staying out of it. Luttie had voiced his objections about his hands' needling any further, so in a court of law, he would be clear of any wrongdoing. But courts of law didn't impress Smoke Jensen. Six-gun action was much more to his liking.

"That remark of mine would only be taken as a blot on one's escutcheon if the party to whom it was directed was in actuality, a thug or mercenary," Mills further confused the cowboy and most of his buddies, including his boss and the foreman.

"What'd he say?" Jake whispered to Luttie.

"Hell, don't ask me. Sounded dirty."

"Gawddam, boy!" another Seven Slash hand said. "Cain't you talk English?"

"I was," Mills responded.

"A blot on one's escutcheon comes from medieval times," a man spoke from a corner table. Smoke cut his eyes. The man wore a dark suit with a white shirt and string tie. He'd seen him get off the stage earlier. "An escutcheon is a shield, upon which a coat of arms was painted. In other words, it means a stain on one's honor."

"Who the hell are you?" Charlie demanded.

"No one who would associate with the likes of you," the stranger said.

"Damn, Charlie," a hand said. "I think the stranger done insulted you, too."

"Now, look here," Charlie said. "I'm gettin' tarred of being in-sulted."

"You could always leave," Smoke offered him an option.

"And you could always shut your trap," Charlie told him.

"I'm right here, Charlie," Smoke told him. "Anytime you think you have the *cojones* to brace me without all your buddies to back you up."

Nice way of making him stand alone whether he fishes or cuts bait, Moss thought. I'll keep that in mind.

89

The cowboy looked hard at Smoke and then sat down without another word.

"You just saved your own life, cowboy," the stranger said, rifling a deck of cards.

Charlie mumbled something and concentrated on his beer.

It isn't going to work, Luttie thought, staring at Smoke. The man is just too damn sure of himself and has the reputation to back it up. He's . . . Luttie couldn't think of the word, right off.

"Intimidating" was what he was searching for.

And who in the devil was that stranger sitting over there? He didn't think Jensen knew who he was either.

Smoke could sense the steam going out of the hardcases seated around the saloon. Four double-barreled Greeners at this distance would take out about half the crowd, inflicting horrible wounds on those they didn't kill outright. He'd seen men soak up five .44 caliber slugs and still stay on their boots and keep on coming. He had never seen anybody take a close-up shotgun blast and keep going.

Smoke watched as Luttie and Jake exchanged glances. Both men knew that whatever momentum they might have had was gone.

"Drink your drinks, play cards, do some tobacco buying or whatever," Smoke told them. "First one of you that makes trouble, I either put in jail or kill. Let's go, boys."

Before he could leave the bar, a young man jumped to his boots. "They call me Sandy!" he yelled. "And I say without that shotgun, you ain't nothin', Jensen."

"Don't be a fool, lad," the stranger said. "You don't have a prayer. Sit down and shut up and live."

"You don't show me nothin' either, mister!" Sandy said.

"Don't crowd me, lad," the stranger said. "I came into town to do some gambling and some relaxing on my way to California. I have no quarrel with you. So don't crowd me."

"Stand up, you funny talkin' dude!" Sandy yelled.

Smoke placed the man then. The accent had been worrying him. Earl Sutcliffe. And the Earl was not a first name. He really was an earl over in England. At least he had been until he killed a man after a game of chance (the man had been cheating); The man had been a duke, which was higher than an earl, and a man of considerable power. A murder warrant had been issued for Sutcliffe, and he had fled to America. Here he had made a name for himself as a very good and very honest gambler . . . and one hell of a gunfighter.

"That's Earl Sutcliffe, Sandy," Smoke said. "Sit down and finish your beer, and there'll be no hard feelings."

Earl Sutcliffe! Luttie thought. Now what in the hell was he doing in this jerkwater town?

"Stand up, Sutcliffe!" Sandy yelled the words that would start his dying on this day.

"Here now!" Mills said. "You men stop this immediately."

"Shut up," Smoke told him. "This is none of your affair."

Mills gave him a dirty look. But he closed his mouth.

"I said stand up!" Sandy yelled.

Earl put down the deck of cards and pushed back from the table. He slowly stood up, brushing back his coat on the right side.

"Primitive rites of manhood," Mills said in a whisper.

"Young man," Earl said. "I do not wish to kill you."

"You kill me?" Sandy snorted the words. "Dude, you the one that's gonna die."

"I don't think so. But I suppose stranger things have happened." Without taking his eyes off of Sandy, Earl spoke to Luttie. "You are his employer. You could order him to stop this madness."

"Sorry, Earl. The kid's on his own time today. What's the matter, you afraid of him?"

Earl smiled. "One more time, lad: give this up."

Sandy smiled, sure of himself, his youthfulness overriding caution. The young think of death only as something that happens to someone else, never themselves. "Anytime you're ready," he told the Englishman.

Sutcliffe shot him. The draw was as fast as a striking rattler. The kid never had a chance to clear leather. The slug took him in high in the chest, driving through a lung and slamming him back, sitting him back down in the chair he should have stayed in . . . with his mouth closed.

He opened his mouth and blood stained his lips as he struggled to speak. "You! . . ." he managed to gasp.

"Sorry, lad," Earl said, holstering his six-gun. "I tried to tell you."

"Tell me! . . ." Sandy said.

"It's too late, now," Earl's words were softly offered.

"I'm cold," Sandy said.

Mills shook his head as he watched the young man hover between life and death, with death racing to embrace him, rudely shoving life aside.

Luttie's hands sat silent, occasionally letting their eyes shift to the muzzles of those deadly sawed-off shotguns, all four of them pointed in their direction. To a man they wanted blood-revenge, but to a man they all knew that this was not the time or the place.

"I'll be damned!" Sandy suddenly blurted. "Would you just look at that!"

"What are you seein'?" Charlie asked him, his words just above a whisper.

"You hear that?" the kid said, as blood dripped from his mouth onto his shirt front.

"What are you hearin'?" Charlie asked him.

Sandy's head lolled to one side, and he closed his eyes.

"Nothing, now," Mills said. "He just died."

The Seven Slash men rode out shortly after Sandy died. They took the body with them, to be buried on Seven Slash range.

"They'll be back," Smoke said. "Tomorrow, next week, next month. But they'll be back. And when they come back, they'll do their damnest to tear this town apart."

"I concur," Mills said.

"That was pushed on me," Earl said. He had sat back down and was shuffling a deck of cards. "I really did not want to kill the lad."

"I know it," Smoke told him. "I've had a hundred pushed on me."

"What's going on in this town?" the Englishman asked. "I stopped here because it seemed so peaceful."

Smoke had the barkeep draw him a mug of beer and carried it over to Earl's table, pulling out a chair and sitting down. "How'd you like to be a deputy sheriff of this county?"

Earl looked startled. "I beg your pardon?"

Smoke smiled and Mills laughed out loud.

"If you've got some time to spare, I'm authorized to pay you fifty dollars a month as a deputy."

"Fifty dollars a month?" Earl said, a smile not only on his lips but also reaching his eyes. "My, how could I possibly refuse such a generous offer?"

"There is a bedroom in the back of the jail," Smoke said. "And you can take your meals over at Bonnie's Cafe. Providing the cook isn't drunk."

"Oh, I say, now. And bed and board is included too. I suppose I could spare a couple of weeks to lend a hand in the keeping of law and order."

"We'll be facing anywhere from fifty to seventy-five hardcases, Earl," Smoke felt obliged to tell the man. "Maybe more than that."

Earl arched one eyebrow. "This sounds intriguing. You have certainly piqued my curiosity, Mr. Jensen."

"Smoke."

"Very well . . . Smoke, it is. Let's take a stroll over to the livery and choose a mount for me. I'm very picky when it comes to horseflesh."

"Then you'll take the job?"

"But of course!"

Mills shook his head. He wondered how many warrants were out on Earl Sutcliffe. This was certainly an odd way to maintain law and order. Quite novel. He would have to do a paper on this and perhaps submit it to a New York newspaper for publication. The West certainly was a strange place, he concluded. He'd never seen anyplace quite like it.

The bartender was throwing sawdust on the pool of blood on the floor by the chair where Sandy had died as the men walked out the batwings.

Chapter Eight

Earl Sutcliffe looked at the star pinned to his shirt and chuckled.

"You find something amusing about being on the side of law and order?" Mills asked.

"Oh, I've always been on the side of law and order," the Englishman replied. "Providing it is good, fair, and just law and order."

"And in England? . . ." Mills left that open.

"In my case justice did not prevail."

"What can I say? It happens here, too."

Earl patted the butt of his six-gun. "It will never again happen to me."

"That isn't justice."

Earl smiled. "Oh, that depends entirely upon who is giving and who is receiving, doesn't it?"

"How did? . . . I mean . . ." Mills didn't know exactly how to phrase the question.

"How did an English nobleman become a gunfighter of dubious reputation in the wild American West?" Earl smiled at the U.S. Marshal.

"Thank you, yes."

"I have always been good with cards, and lucky. I soon realized that if I was going to earn my living as a gambler I had better learn to be more than proficient with a firearm. There are people who, when someone is winning, will always cry cheat."

"And you don't cheat?"

"No. That is not to say I don't know how, because I certainly do. But I don't have to cheat to win. And I don't win all the time. Just enough of the time so I earn a nice income."

"And this?" Mills waved his hand at the town.

"Why am I doing it? Why don't we just say that there is as much Robin Hood in me as there is in Smoke Jensen. Neither one of us particularly cares for the rich who use their power to remain above the law."

"I can understand your feelings on the subject. But I'm not aware of any rich person who ever wronged Smoke. Besides, Smoke is a wealthy man in his own right."

Earl laughed. "Oh, so am I, Mr. Walsdorf. My home in England has forty-five rooms. My inheritance was enormous. But what does that have to do with justice?"

Mills walked away, muttering to himself.

Smoke had been listening from a doorway and stepped out to stand by the Englishman. "He's a good man, Earl. And damn tough, too. He's just hooked on Eastern law enforcement. Or, most probably, what Eastern lawyers are teaching."

"And it's spreading, Smoke. It'll be another ten years or so before it really makes an impact out here. But it's coming."

Smoke grimaced. "First time a man gives me an order telling me I can't protect what is mine with a gun, he better get ready for a showdown."

"It's coming."

Smoke shook his head and changed the subject. "Mills is no spring chicken. He's been with the Marshal's Service since getting out of college. I can't understand why he hasn't had some of those ideas of his kicked out of his head."

"He's not been a field man for very long, I should imagine. And that is perhaps where the promotions are."

"You may be right. Well, let's get some supper and talk over some options."

"Why don't we just locate the outlaws and go in shooting?" Earl suggested.

Smoke chuckled. "A man after my own heart. I suggested that to Mills. He says that is not the proper way to go about bringing men to justice."

Earl gave Smoke a quick, bemused glance. "The man does have a lot to learn, doesn't he?"

Smoke nodded his head in agreement. "I just hope he stays alive long enough to learn it."

"I came as soon as I heard about this terrible act of violence against you, Sally," the man said.

"Thank you, Larry," Sally Jensen said. She was sitting in the parlor in a rocker, her arm in a sling.

The preacher's wife, Bountiful, was sitting in the next room, but well within earshot. It just wasn't proper for a woman, especially a married woman, to receive a man alone. Besides, Bountiful didn't trust this slick-haired New York City man, all duded up and smelling of bay rum and the like. He had something up his sleeve and she would bet on that.

Sally looked at Lawrence Tibbson and wondered what in the world he was doing out here in Colorado. She hadn't seen him in several years. And she'd been with her mother then, shopping in the city. She had allowed Larry to escort her to a few functions in college, very few, but he had never—by any stretch of the imagination—been her beau. Although he would have liked to have been.

"All your old college chums are very worried about you, Sally," Larry said.

"Worried about me?" Sally asked. "Why, for heaven's sake?"

"Well, my word, Sally! You've been shot! Living out here in this wild, lawless, God-forsaken place. And . . ." He shook his head.

"And what, Larry?"

He pursed his lips and shook his head. "Nothing, Sally."

"Larry," she said coyly, and batted her eyes at him. That used to do it in college.

It did it this time, too. He sighed and said, "Sally, the word is that . . . well, how to say this?"

"Just come right out and say it, Larry. That's the way out here."

"The day of the wild west is over, Sally. It's finished, or soon will be. Despite the play and all the articles and Penny Dreadfuls written about Smoke, the people back East are beginning to look upon him as a cold-blooded killer. And you are being dragged in the dirt as well."

It didn't come as any surprise to Sally. She'd already heard from some of her old college friends. There was a not-so-subtle movement on in some quarters back East to discredit Smoke, and mark him as a mad-dog killer without conscience. Some were even calling for a federal investigation of him, including sending some United States Marshals out West. She didn't know whether anything had come of that suggestion.

"Go on, Larry."

"I know your parents are abroad, and plan to stay for some time, but your brother Jordan is very upset about all this awful talk about you."

"Pure flapdoodle, Larry. That's all it is."

Bountiful listened for another five minutes, and then with a frown on her face she walked silently to the doorway and stepped outside. She waved at a hand coiling a rope by the corral.

"Yes, ma'am?" he said, after running over to the house.

"Ride!" she told him. "Get into town, find Monte and find out where Smoke is. Get word to him." She told him what she had overheard.

The hand threw the rope down, his face tight with anger. "I'll go in there and stomp that varmint right now!"

"No!" Bountiful told him. "Finding Smoke is more important. He might be in danger of being taken back East to stand trial in some federal court. There are in U.S. Marshals after him. They might already be with him, and he doesn't know they're to arrest him."

The hand nodded his head. "You watch that skunk in yonder, Miss Bountiful. He's just too slick for my likin'."

"I'll watch him for me and Sally. You ride."

"I'm gone!"

She stepped back into the house in time to hear Sally ask, "Larry, exactly why did you come all the way out here from the city?"

"Why . . . to take you back where you belong, Sally."

"I beg your pardon?" Sally's words were filled with astonishment.

"Sally, this is still a wild and savage land. You

don't belong out here. There is no culture, nothing that even resembles refinement . . . the nicer things in life. I have come to ask you to leave this place and return to the city. Not necessarily to be with me, although that is my highest aspiration. Sally, I believe once there, out of this horrible place, you will see things in a much different light and . . ."

Sally held up a hand. "That's enough, Larry! Actually, that is far too much. If my husband were here, he'd throw you out of the house for saying such things." Actually, what Smoke would probably do is shoot you! But she kept that thought to herself. "Larry, you must be insane to suggest such things."

"I have only your best interests at heart, Sally."

"I appreciate that, Larry. Now listen to me. I am a married woman with children. I love my husband very much, and I am quite happy here on the Sugarloaf . . ."

"The what?"

"The Sugarloaf—that is the name of our ranch, Larry. And I intend to stay here until I die, and be buried here. Is that understood?"

"Sally, haven't you understood a word I've said? What are you going to do when your husband is sentenced to prison?"

"Prison? What are you talking about, Larry?"

"A federal judge is right now contemplating issuing federal warrants for Smoke's arrest. All the wild men of the West are dead or dying, Sally. Most of the famed gunfighters and outlaws have met their just due. Very learned men in the field of crime have met and concluded that violence begets violence and also that the poor criminal has been greatly misunderstood. They have urged President

101

Arthur to abolish capital punishment and to set up programs to reeducate inmates and ban the carrying of guns nationwide . . ."

Sally started laughing. She laughed until tears momentarily blinded her. She wiped them away just about the time Bountiful stopped laughing in the next room.

"I fail to see anything amusing about this, Sally," Larry said stiffly.

"It's going to be far less amusing when somebody tells my husband he can't carry a gun, Larry. What nut came up with the idea that the poor criminal has been misunderstood?"

"I would hardly call Dr. Woodward a nut, Sally."

"Dr. Woodward?"

"Yes. He has just returned from Europe where he studied with some of the greatest doctors in the world, whose specialties include the mind . . ."

"Psychiatrists."

"Why, yes, that's right. I . . ."

"Get out of here, Larry. Leave. Now. Go on back to the city and don't come West again. This is no place for you. And don't ever again suggest I leave my husband. Now, go, Larry."

When Larry had driven off in his rented buggy, Bountiful came into the room. "You heard?" Sally asked.

"Yes. I sent a hand into town to tell Monte. He'll get word to Smoke. Do you suppose there is anything to what he said, Sally?"

"Yes. I'm afraid there is." She shook her head. "The poor misunderstood criminal. What is this world coming to?"

* * *

102

Earl Sutcliffe was doing his best not to yawn as Mills droned on. "And in conclusion," Mills said, "it is the belief of many knowledgeable people that the criminal should not be treated nearly so harshly as we have done in the past. The criminal is literally pushed into a life of crime due to peer pressure and his social and/or economic station in life."

"Incredible," Earl said.

"Yes, isn't it. You see, Dr. Woodward has found that in many cases, say, a boy from the wrong side of the tracks falls in love with the daughter of a rich man . . . of course the two worlds can never meet. That traumatizes the young man and leaves him feeling rejected and disillusioned and angry. If he then goes out and robs or kills, it isn't really his fault."

Earl sighed. "Mills, do you really believe that nonsense?"

"Nonsense, sir?"

"Yes. Nonsense. Because that is what it is. Most people who grow up in poverty don't turn into murderers. Most do their best to work their way out of a bad economic situation. Your Dr. Woodward is simply trying to cover up for a group of very sorry, worthless, no-good people who want something for nothing and will go to any lengths to get it. And the only length they deserve is the number of feet in a hangman's rope. Good day, sir." He rose from the bench and walked into Smoke's office.

Smoke smiled at him. "Did Mills make a convert out of you, Earl?"

"Not hardly. The man is well-educated but totally out of touch with reality." He looked up at the rumble of a stagecoach pulling into town.

Both men watched as Mills was handed a small

packet of mail by the driver. The man sat down on the bench and read, occasionally looking across the street at Smoke's office, a startled expression on his face.

"It concerns one of us," Earl opined.

"Any warrants out on you?"

"None that I am aware of. You?"

"I don't think so. However, anything is possible. I've been hearing rumors that are coming from back East. Somebody back there doesn't like me very much."

"So it's true, then," Earl muttered.

"You've heard them?"

"Yes. I was in St. Louis just a few months ago. I spoke with a man from Chicago who asked if I knew you. I told him only by reputation. He had heard that some federal judge back East was pushing to have some warrants reissued on you. Something about a shooting that happened years ago. Over in Idaho."

"Damn!" Smoke swore. "That was back in '73. I wasn't much more than a kid when I helped destroy the town of Bury and killed Richards, Potter, and Stratton. They were the men who helped kill my brother and my father, and who hired the men who raped and killed my first wife and killed our baby son."

Earl grunted. "Then they certainly deserved killing. Tell me, those three you mentioned—did either of them have any relative or family friend in a position of power back East?"

"Not that I know of. But it could be. But there were no warrants issued from that shooting. I'm certain of that. And I know damn well I left those men dead."

104

"Well, somebody has an axe to grind with you. And from the look on Mills' face, he isn't too happy with the letters he just received. Want a wager as to the identity of the party mentioned in those missives?"

"No bet. But he's a pretty straightforward type of fellow. If they're about me, he'll tell me."

They watched as Mills showed the documents to Winston and Moss. The men read the letters and shook their heads. Mills folded the letters and tucked them in an inside pocket of his jacket. The three of them then walked across the street and entered the office.

Mills came right to the point. "Smoke, we need to talk."

"You look like you just swallowed a green persimmon, Mills. What's the matter?"

"It isn't good news, Smoke." He poured a cup of coffee and sat down. "A federal judge in Washington is just about to put his signature to warrants. They're murder warrants, Smoke. On you. Three of them."

"The names of the men I'm supposed to have killed?"

"Potter, Richards, and Stratton."

"I killed them, for a fact. Over in Idaho, years ago. But it was a stand up and fair fight. Me against the three of them."

"Tell me about it, Smoke."

Smoke's mind went spinning back through the long years.

"All right, you bastards!" Smoke yelled to Richards, Potter, and Stratton. "Holster your guns and step out into the street, if you've got the nerve."

The sharp odor of sweat was all mingled with the

smell of blood and gunsmoke, filling the summer air as four men stepped out into the bloody, dusty street. All around the old town were the sprawled bodies of gunhands that had been on the payroll of the three men. They had taken on Smoke Jensen. They had died. Nineteen men had tried to kill Smoke in the ruin of an old ghost town out from Bury. Only three of them were still standing.

Richards, Potter, and Stratton stood at one end of the block. A tall bloody figure stood at the other. All their guns were in leather.

"You son of a bitch!" Stratton screamed, his voice as high-pitched as an hysterical woman. "You've ruined it all!" He clawed at his .44.

Smoke drew and fired before Stratton could clear leather. The man fell back on his butt, a startled expression on his face. He closed his eyes and toppled over.

Potter grabbed for his gun. Smoke shot him twice in the chest and holstered his gun before the man had stopped twitching in the dust.

Richards had not moved. He stood with a faint smile on his lips, staring at Smoke.

"You ready to die, Richards?" Smoke called.

"As ready as any man ever is," Richards replied. There was no sign of fear in his voice. His hands were steady by the butts of his guns. "Your sister, Janey, gone?"

"Yep. She took your money and hauled her ashes out."

"Trash, that's what she is."

"You'll get no argument from me on that."

"It's been a long run, hasn't it, Jensen?"

"It's just about over."

"What happens to all our holdings around here?"

106

"I don't care what happens to the mines. The miners can have them. I'm giving all your stock to the decent, honest punchers and homesteaders."

A puzzled look spread over Richards' face. "I don't understand. You did . . . all this!" He waved a hand. "For nothing?"

Someone moaned, the sound painfully inching up the street.

"I did it for my pa, my brother, my wife, and my baby son."

"It won't bring them back."

"I know."

"Good God Almighty. I wish I had never heard the name Jensen."

"You won't ever hear it again, Richards. Not after this day."

Richards smiled and drew. He was snake-quick, but hurried his shot, the slug digging up dirt at Smoke's boots.

Smoke shot the man in the shoulder, spinning him around. Richards grabbed for his left-hand gun, and Smoke fired again, the slug taking the man in the chest. Richards cursed Smoke and tried to lift his Colt. He managed to cock it before Smoke's third shot took him in the belly and knocked him down to the dirt. He pulled the trigger, blowing dust into his face and eyes. He tried to crawl to his knees but succeeded only in rolling over onto his back, staring at the blue of the sky.

Smoke walked up to the man.

Richards opened his mouth to speak. He tasted blood on his tongue. The light began to fade around him. "You'll . . . you'll meet . . ."

Smoke never found out who he was supposed to meet. Richards' head lolled to one side, and he died.

Smoke holstered his guns and walked away.

"His brother," Mills said. "Has to be. The judge's name is Richards."

"Well, then, he's just as sorry as his damn brother was," Smoke said. "And I'll tell you this, Mills: no man will ever put handcuffs on me. No man."

"Smoke . . ."

"No man, Mills. That was a fair fight, and Judge Richards can go right straight to hell and take his warrants with him."

Mills wore a crestfallen expression. "What if I'm ordered to arrest you?"

"Tell them you can't find me. Ignore it. Quit your job. But don't try to put cuffs on me. The warrants are bogus, Mills. It's a made-up charge. There were dozens of people who witnessed that fight from the hillsides around the town. Don't force my hand, Mills. It's not worth your life, or any other lawman's life."

"You'd draw on me, Smoke?" the U.S. Marshal asked in a soft tone.

"If you forced me to do it. Lord knows I don't want to drag iron against you, or any lawman, for that matter. But I won't be arrested for something I didn't do."

"Smoke, the Marshal's Service knows you're here! If Judge Richards signs those warrants, I will have no choice but to place you under arrest."

"We all have choices, Mills. We all come to crossroads sometime in our lives. Many times the legal road is not the right road."

Mills looked at Earl Sutcliffe. "And you, sir?"

"I stand by Smoke. I've talked to too many people who were at that fight in the ghost town. It was exactly as Smoke called it. I can have a dozen of the West's most famed gunslicks in here in a week . . . all to stand by Smoke Jensen. If you want a bloodbath, just try to arrest Jensen."

Mills shook his head. "I don't know what to do," he admitted. He and his men left the office.

"Goddamn a bunch of political appointees," Earl swore, which was something he did rarely. "Your government is becoming like the one I left across the waters: out of control."

"Can you imagine what it will be like a hundred years from now?" Smoke asked, sitting down and picking up the little puppy from its bed by his desk.

Earl grimaced. "That, my friend, is something that boggles the mind. But let's concentrate on the present. What are you going to do if the judge signs those warrants?"

"I damn sure won't be placed under arrest." Smoke took paper from his desk and dabbed pen into the ink well. "I'll write a friend of mine up in Denver. He's a federal judge. I'll ask him to look into the matter. I'll ask him to block those warrants until a complete investigation is done into the matter. I'll take the legal course until the road ends."

Earl did not have to ask what Smoke would do once, or if, that legal road came to a blockade. He knew only that if any man tried to arrest Smoke Jensen for something he was innocent of, the streets would run red with blood. And Earl Sutcliffe knew this, too: he would do the same thing.

There comes a time when legal proceedings came into direct conflict with a law-abiding person's basic human rights.

And this was damn sure one of those times.

Earl walked outside, leaving Smoke's pen-scratching behind him. He looked up and down the wide street of the tiny village. "Don't send good men in here to do a bad thing," he muttered. "Because if you do, you'll force another good man to turn bad. And I'll be standing by his side," he concluded.

Chapter Nine

The stagecoach ran and Smoke had mail. He tore open the letter and quickly scanned the contents. Sheriff Monte Carson of Big Rock wrote that he now had flyers from the United States government proclaiming Smoke Jensen to be an outlaw and a murderer. There was a ten thousand dollar price on his head. Events were moving very fast, and he advised Smoke to haul his ashes out of there until this matter could be resolved.

Smoke showed the letter to Earl.

"I'll go with you," the Englishman said.

Smoke nixed that. "I'd appreciate it if you'd stay on here as marshal and deputy sheriff. Mills is going to need help with the outlaws."

The man met his eyes. "The system is turning against you, yet you still have law and order in your heart. I don't know that I could feel so magnanimous toward such a system."

"Without some form of law, the country would revert to anarchy, Earl. I'll head for the high country and wait until things straighten out. I've got some good people working in my behalf."

"I'll go purchase a few things for you at the store and arrange for a pack horse. I'll have things ready to go in a hour. Did Mills receive any mail this run?"

Smoke smiled and handed Earl a letter from the U.S. Marshal's office in Washington, D.C. "I told the driver I'd see that Mills got this. Next time the stage runs, give this to him."

Earl chuckled. "I don't believe that delay will disappoint Mr. Walsdorf one bit."

Smoke grinned. "I may be on the run, but I'm going to see if I can't harass Luttie Charles and the Slater gang while I'm dodging the law."

"One-man wrecking crew?"

"I've done it before."

"You'll stay in this area?"

"Oh, yes. I'll check back with you from time to time. If the town fills with U.S. Marshals, tie a piece of black cloth on the bridge railing north of town. I'll be warned then."

"Will do."

"Take care of my little dog for me, will you, Earl?"

"I certainly shall."

"I anticipated this, so I moved my gear out of the hotel yesterday and stowed it in the shed out back."

"I'll go get you provisioned."

Smoke sat down behind the desk and cleaned his .44s and his rifle. He filled a pouch full of shotgun shells and cleaned a Greener. He put on a fresh pot of coffee to boil and then went out back to the shed. There he checked on the bag of dynamite he'd bought along the trail coming here and carefully inspected his fuses and caps, then replaced them in a waterproof pouch and rewrapped the bag in canvas.

He checked his clothing in his saddle bags and found they had not been disturbed; the same with his bedroll and ground sheet. He went back into the office and picked up the little dog, petting it.

"You behave yourself now," he said softly. "Mind Earl. You hear?"

The little dog wriggled and squirmed and licked his hand, and Smoke smiled at its antics.

Earl opened the door. "You're all set," he said. "The food should last five or six days if you're careful. I put half a dozen boxes of .44s in the pack for you."

"I'll pull out now, then. Leave the back way. Take care of yourself, Earl."

The Englishman winked at him. "You take care of yourself, friend. I told the livery man to get lost for a few minutes. You should have no trouble."

Smoke slipped out the back, picked up his gear from the shed, and made his way to the livery stable. Buck was about ready to kick in the walls of his stall. He was a horse that liked to ramble, and he'd been confined to a stall for just too damn long. He tried to step on Smoke's foot, and when that failed, tried to bite him.

"Settle down, damnit," Smoke told him, smoothing out the blanket and tossing the saddle on him, cinching it down. For once, Buck didn't try to puff up on him. Smoke stowed his gear on the pack horse, one of the strongest and best-looking pack animals he'd ever seen, and led both horses out the back. He swung into the saddle and looked back at the town.

"You better hunt you a hole, Judge Richards," he spoke softly. " 'Cause when this is over, I'm coming after you and I'm going to stomp your guts into a greasy puddle. And that's a promise, you damn shyster."

He touched his spurs to Buck's sides, and they

moved out, heading into the wild country of southern Colorado.

Smoke made his first night's camp just off the Continental Divide Trail. As was his custom, he cooked his supper over a hat-sized fire, then erased all signs of it and moved several miles before bedding down for the night. It was a cold camp, but a safe one.

Up before dawn, he walked the area several times, stopping often to listen. The horses were relaxed, and Buck was better than a watch dog. Satisfied that he was alone, Smoke built a small fire against a rock wall and cooked his breakfast of bacon and potatoes and boiled his coffee.

After eating, he washed his dishes, packed them, and sat back down for a cigarette and some ruminating.

First of all, he wanted to find the Slater gang and start his little war with them. He could not get the picture of that man and woman and the girls he'd found along the trail out of his mind. Men who would do something like that were not to be considered human beings, and it would be very unfair to call them animals. Animals didn't do things like that. Animals killed for a reason, not for sport and fun. He had promised the dying woman that her grief and pain would be avenged. And Smoke always kept his promises.

He picketed the pack animal in the deep woods, near plenty of water and graze, and saddled Buck. "You ready to go headhunting, boy?"

Buck swung his big head and looked at Smoke through mean eyes. Buck was anything but a gentle animal. Smoke could handle him, and the horse had never harmed a child. But with adults whom he disliked, and that was most of them, the animal could be vicious.

"I thought so," Smoke said, and swung into the saddle.

He climbed higher, staying in the thickest timber and brush he could find and letting Buck pick his way. Coming to a halt on a ridge that offered a spectacular view for miles around in all directions, Smoke dismounted and took field glasses from his saddlebags and began carefully scanning the area.

His sweep of the area paid off after only a few minutes. He knew where the mining camps were, and where the few homesteaders lived—this was not a country for much farming other than small gardens—and discounted them. With a smile on his lips, he put his binoculars back into the saddlebags and mounted up.

He figured it was time to be sociable and do some calling on folks.

Two hours later, he picketed Buck and hung his spurs on the saddle horn. Taking his rifle, he began making his way through the timber, carefully and silently working his way closer to what he figured was an outlaw camp. He bellied down in thick underbrush when he got within earshot of the mangy-looking bunch of hardcases.

"I'm a-gittin' tarred of this sittin' around doin' nothin'," a big, ugly-looking man said. "I say we go find us some homesteaders with kids and have our way with the girls."

"Nice young tender girlies," another man said with a nasty grin. "I like to hear 'em squall." He pulled at his crotch. "I like to whup up on 'em, too. I like it when they fight."

"Maybe we could find us a man to use as target

practice," another mused aloud. "Kill 'im slow. That's good fun."

"Slater says we got to wait," yet another outlaw said. "They gonna be shippin' out gold and silver in a few days, and we wait until then."

"Let's hit the town," a man suggested, leaning over and pouring a tin cup full of coffee from a big pot. "We're runnin' out of grub and besides, they's wimmin in that little town. I seen me a big fat one. I like fat wimmin. More to whup up on when they's fat."

Smoke shot him in the belly.

The gut-shot outlaw screamed and threw the coffee pot, the contents splashing into another man's face. The scalded punk howled in pain and rolled on the ground, both hands covering his burned face.

The gunny who liked to rape little girls jumped to his boots, his hands filled with six-shooters. He looked wildly around him. Smoke took careful aim and shot a knee out from under the man, the .44 slug breaking the knee.

The man folded up and lay screaming on the ground, his broken knee bent awkwardly. He would be out of action for a long time.

Smoke lined up a punk who'd grabbed up a rifle and put a round in the center of his chest. The man dropped like a rag doll and did not move. He had fallen into the campfire, and his clothing ignited in seconds. The stench of burning flesh began to foul the morning coolness.

Smoke shifted positions as the outlaws fell into cover and began slinging lead in his direction. He rolled for several yards and then belly-crawled a dozen more yards, coming up behind a huge old fallen log.

"Somebody pull Daily outta that far!" a man yelled. "He's a stinkin' up ever'thang."

"You pull him out," another suggested.

"You go to hell!" the first man told him. "I ramrod this outfit, and you do what I tell you to do."

The second man told the ramrodder where he could ram his orders. Bluntly.

Smoke waited, his Winchester .44 ready. He caught a glimpse of a checkered shirt and lined it up. It was a man's arm. Smoke waited, let out some breath, took up the slack on the trigger and let the rifle fire. The man screamed and rolled on the ground, the bullet-shattered arm hanging painfully and uselessly. The .44 slug had hit the man's elbow. Another out of action.

A smile of grim satisfaction on his lips, Smoke began working his way back, not wanting to risk any further shots. If he waited much longer, the hunter would soon become the hunted.

Back with Buck, he stepped into the saddle and took off in search of a hole.

"Damnit, Earl!" Mills hollered, waving the letter. "This is tampering with the mail. That's against the law."

"I didn't tamper with anything," the Englishman said. "The driver handed Smoke the mail, and Smoke told me to give this to you. I gave it to you."

"You assisted him in getting away!"

"As far as I knew, he was a free man. He could leave anytime he chose." He shrugged. "He chose to leave."

Mills stomped out of the office. The men who

117

had escorted the prisoner up to the county seat had returned. Mills started hollering for them to saddle up, they had to find and arrest Smoke Jensen.

The marshals all looked at one another. Going after outlaws was one thing. Tangling with Smoke Jensen was quite another matter.

A trio of deputy sheriffs, come to fetch one of the prisoners in jail, exchanged glances. One asked, "You boys are gonna go do what?"

"We're going to arrest Smoke Jensen," Albert said glumly.

"What the devil for?" a deputy asked.

"Federal warrants," Mills told him, walking up to the group standing on the boardwalk in front of the saloon. "The prisoners can remain in jail. By the powers vested in me by the United States government, I am hereby deputizing you men as deputy U.S. Marshals. You will accompany us in the pursuit and arrest of Smoke Jensen."

"You can go right straight to hell, too," a deputy told him. "I ain't got nothing against Smoke Jensen."

"Me, neither," another said.

The third deputy turned and started toward the alley.

"Where are you going?" Mills demanded.

"To the outhouse," the man called over his shoulder. "And as full of it as you are, you best do the same."

"You men do not seem to understand the gravity of this situation!"

"I understand this," a deputy told him. "You go after Smoke Jensen, you're gonna come back—if you come back at all—acrost your saddle."

"Yeah," the second deputy said. "If I was you, I'd

sit on that warrant for a time. Smoke is a respected rancher of some wealth. I'll wager than warrant ain't worth the paper it's written on. Besides, do you know what you'd get if you crossed a grizzly bear and a puma and a rattlesnake and a timber wolf and some monster outta Hell?"

"I have not the vaguest idea."

"You'd get Smoke Jensen. You best leave him alone. That ol' boy was born with the bark on and was raised up by mountain men and Injuns. They's tribes all over the West sing songs about how feeroocious Jensen is. 'Sides, you ever heard of gun-slingers name of Charlie Starr, Monte Carson, Louis Longmont, Johnny North, Cotton Pickens, and the like?"

"Of course, I've heard of them! What's that got to do with anything?"

"Man, how'd you like to see them ol' boys and thirty more just as randy come a-foggin' in here, reins in their teeth and hands full of Colts, all of 'em mad at you?"

"That . . . would not be a pleasant sight," Mills admitted.

"Pleasant sight! You couldn't see nothin' like it this side of Hell! Now you just pull in your horns and give that warrant time to rest, Mr. U.S. Marshal. Things will work out. You keep your nose out of Smoke Jensen's business. That way, you'll stay alive."

"I have a job to do, sir!"

"So do we," the deputy said. "But sometimes you got to let common sense take over. Smoke's killed a lot of sorry ol' boys in his time, but he ain't no back-shootin' murderer. All them he put in the ground was either stand-up fair fights—and usually

119

he's facin' two or three at a time—or punks that was after him and he waylaid 'em to shorten the odds. You think about that warrant, mister. You think a long time about it. The longer you think, the longer you got to live."

The deputies collected their prisoner and pulled out that afternoon. The RCMP were due in town within the next several days. Mills looked at Earl, looking at him.

"You'll stay to sign the papers and give the prisoner to the Canadians?"

"Uh-huh. Where are you going?"

"I have a man to arrest."

"You best use pen and paper in the office, then," Earl said solemnly.

"To do what, sir?" Mills asked.

"To leave me the name of your next of kin."

Foolishly, the outlaws in the camp Smoke attacked came after him. He led them on a goose hunt in the mountains and then tired of the game. He dismounted and took his rifle from the boot, then selected a position on a ridge where he could effectively cover his back trail.

The gang came in a rush, whipping their lathered and tired horses. Smoke emptied two saddles, and the others retreated down the slope, for the moment out of range. Smoke nibbled on a cold biscuit, took a sip of water, and waited. The old mountain man Preacher had taught him many things as a boy, one of which was patience.

After several moments, a man shouted out, "Who you be up yonder?"

"An avenging angel!" Smoke returned the shout,

then shifted positions.

He could not hear the reply, if any, but he was certain the mutterings among the scum were highly profane.

"What's your beef with us?" someone finally shouted.

Smoke shifted his eyes, sensing that conversation on the part of the outlaws would be nothing more than a cover for someone trying to slip around and flank him.

But he had not chosen his position without an eye for detail. To his left lay a sheer rock face. To his right, a clear field of fire, virtually without cover for anyone except a very skilled Indian warrior. The outlaws would have to come at him from the front.

"You deef up there?"

Smoke offered no reply. A few shots were fired at him, but they fell far short of his position. It was an impasse, but one that Smoke knew he would win simply because he had more patience than the outlaws. The men he had shot lay sprawled on the trail. One he had shot dead, the other had died only moments before, gutshot and dying hard, calling out for God to help him. The same God the girls he had helped rape and torture had called out to, no doubt.

Smoke watched as the men broke cover and ran for their horses. He waited and watched as they rode back down the trail. Smoke slipped back to Buck, booted his rifle, and took off. He would hit another outlaw camp that evening. He liked the night. He was very good in the night. The Orientals had a word for it that Smoke had read in a book Sally had bought for him. Ninja.

He liked that.

* * *

"That dude is still at the hotel, ma'am," a hand reported to Sally. "He's gonna get his ashes hauled if he don't stop with the bad mouth against Smoke."

"He'd just sue you," Sally told him.

"One of them," the hand said disgustedly.

"I'm afraid so. What's he saying about my husband?"

"That Smoke has turned cold-blooded killer. That he enjoys killin'. That he's crazy. Monte is gonna have to put him in jail for his own protection if this keeps up."

Sally nodded her head. "I wired friends back East to check into whether there is any connection between Judge Richards and Larry. They could find none—at least on the surface. I don't believe there is any connection. Larry is just meddling, hoping to discredit Smoke in my eyes."

"You want me to conk him on the head and toss him in an eastbound freight wagon, ma'am?"

Sally laughed. "No, Jim. But I'm not going to ask anyone to protect him, either. Larry is, I'm afraid, going to learn a hard lesson about the West and its people."

"He's liable to end up in a pine box, ma'am."

"Yes," she agreed. "There is always that possibility. But he's a man grown, and has to take responsibility for his words and deeds. I warned him of the consequences if he persisted in spreading vile gossip about my husband. We'll just let the chips fall, Jim."

"It won't be long, ma'am. Somebody's gonna tell that greenhorn lawyer to check, bet or fold pretty darn quick." He put his hat back on his head.

122

"And, ma'am . . . it's likely to be me that does it."

Sally watched the hand walk back to the bunk-house. She knew that the West was, in many respects, a very tolerant place. A person's past was their business. A handshake was a deal sealed. A person gave their word, it was binding. And if you bad-mouthed somebody, you had damn well better be prepared to back it up with guns or fists. It was the code, and the code was unwritten law in the West.

"Larry," she muttered, "you're heading for a stomping if you don't close that mouth."

Chapter Ten

"That's it, mister!" a cowboy said to Larry. "I've had your flappin' mouth. Now shut the damn thing and shut it now!"

Larry turned in his chair and stared at the man. The others in the cafe fell silent. For days the citizens in and around Big Rock had put up with the Easterner's bad-mouthing of Smoke Jensen. Most of them felt it was just the man's ignorance and let it slide. But it was getting wearing . . . very wearing. The cowboy from Johnny North's ranch was one of those Smoke had befriended, and he had had quite enough of Larry's mouth.

"I beg your pardon, sir?" Larry questioned, removing his napkin from his shirt-front and laying it on the table.

"I said for you to close that flappin' trap of yours," the cowboy said. "Smoke ain't here to defend himself agin your lyin' mouth. And I for one have had enough of it." He pushed back his chair and stood up, walking to Larry's table.

"Sir," Larry said, "I have a right to an opinion. That is a basic right. One only has to look at Jensen's record of brutality and callousness to see that the man has no regard for law and order and the rights of others. I . . ."

The cowboy slapped him out of the chair. Larry's butt bounced on the floor. He stared up at the man, his mouth bloody from the callused hand of the cowboy. His eyes were wide from shock.

Larry looked over at the sheriff. Monte Carson was recovering from his wounds, his left arm still in a sling where the .45 slug had busted his forearm. He stared at Larry with decidedly unfriendly eyes.

"Do something!" Larry hollered.

"What do you want me to do?" Monte questioned.

"This brute assaulted me!" Larry yelled, crawling to his knees and grabbing the back of a chair for support. "I want him placed under arrest."

"You're under arrest, Clint," Monte said, sugaring his coffee.

"The fine for disturbing the peace is two dollars," Judge Proctor said, carefully cutting the slice of beef on his lunch plate.

Twenty silver dollars hit the floor from the pockets of patrons seated around the cafe.

Willow Brook, wife of the town's only lawyer, Hunt, counted the money on the floor. "I think that means you can break the law a few more times, Clint," she said.

"What?" Larry screamed. "What kind of justice is this?"

"Western kind," Clint said, and jerked the man up by his shirt.

"Unhand me, you heathen!" Larry yelled.

Clint did just that. He tossed Larry out the front door, and the man landed in a horse trough.

"And don't come back in here!" the cafe owner yelled, once Larry had bubbled to the surface. "You are now officially barred from dinin' in my establishment."

"The cuisine was terrible anyway!" Larry yelled.

"I ain't never served nothin' like that in my life!" the cook screamed from the back.

"Ignorant oaf!" Larry said, stepping out of the horse trough with as much dignity as he could muster under the circumstances. "I'm going to sue everybody in that establishment!" He pointed at the cafe.

Monte walked to the door. "Get off the street, or I'll put you in jail for attempting to incite a riot," he told Larry.

"You'll put me in jail!" Larry shouted. He shook his finger at the sheriff. "You've not heard the last of this, sir," he warned. "I am an attorney of some reputation. I can assure you all that the consequences will be dire. I . . ."

"You got nine more chances, Clint," Monte said.

The cowboy stepped out onto the shaded boardwalk, and Larry took off running toward the Majestic Hotel. His shoes squished with every step. His ears were flame-red from the laughter he was leaving behind him.

Mills Walsdorf led his men some twelve miles out of town and halted the parade.

"What's up, Mills?" Moss asked.

"We make camp here."

"Lot of daylight left," Winston pointed out the obvious.

"We have to make plans," Mills told them, swinging down from the saddle. "And that might take several days. Perhaps even a week or more. We can't just go riding willy-nilly after Smoke Jensen."

The U.S. Marshals looked at each other and smiled. Harold said, "I wondered why you bought so many provisions."

"We must always be prepared. We're on our own now, men. No one back in town knows where we are. I told Earl we were heading east."

"But we rode north!" Sharp said.

"Precisely."

"I'll gather some firewood," Winston said, turning his head to hide his smile.

"We'll all gather wood," Mills said. "Since we're going to be here for some time."

Smoke saw to his horses' needs first, rubbing them down carefully and picketing them near graze and water. He then ate a cold and early supper. He slipped off his boots and stuck his feet into moccasins that had been made especially for him. They were Apache moccasins, with high leggings that would prevent his trousers from catching on low branches or underbrush. He blackened his face with dirt and tied a dark bandana around his forehead. He checked his guns and his knife, then picked up his rifle and slung it over his shoulder.

He knew where another of Slater's camps was, having checked the area carefully with his field glasses, spotting the smoke and mentally marking the location. This coming night was going to turn deadly for some of the outlaws.

Smoke was moving long before twilight placed its dusky hand upon the high country. He was dressed in clothing that would blend with the night and the terrain, and there was nothing on him that would rattle or clank. Moonlight, when it came up, might reflect off the brass of his .44 rounds in his ammo belt, but that was the only thing unnatural about him in the gathering gloom. He slipped through the timber and brush like a wraith.

The outlaws were a careless bunch. Smoke spotted their campfires long before he caught sight of any human movement. When he was within hailing distance of them, he squatted down and became as one with the brush. He moved only his eyes as he studied the encampment.

He concluded that Slater had split his people up into at least three bunches. Maybe four since he wasn't sure of the size of the gang. This gang of trash and thugs numbered about fifteen. They were all heavily armed, their weapons looking well-used but well-cared for.

Smoke moved closer, to better listen.

The outlaws were bitching about the inactivity and the lack of women and whiskey. They bragged about the men and women they had killed and raped and tortured. Smoke's face tightened in silent rage as the men laughed about the two little girls they'd had back up the trail.

Smoke knew which two girls they were talking about.

He'd buried them both.

He watched one man leave the bonfire-lighted area and move toward the dark timber, toward where Smoke squatted, waiting to strike. The man was removing his galluses as he walked to find a spot to relieve himself.

He was taking his last walk.

Smoke wiped his bloody blade clean on the dead man's shirt and shifted positions after rolling the body under some brush. He moved right to the edge of the encampment, very close to where an outlaw lay on his dirty blankets, his head on a knapsack probably filled with his possibles.

Smoke edged closer and looked with disgust at what was tied to the man's saddle. A human scalp. Blonde hair. Long blonde hair. He knew where that came from, too. One of the little girls he'd buried.

Smoke cut the man's throat with a movement as furtive as a ghost and as fast and as deadly as a viper. He eased the man's head down until his chin was resting on his chest. With the bloody knife in his hand, Smoke backed away, again shifting positions, working his way around to the other side of the camp. He paused along the way to wipe his blade clean on some grass.

"Hey, Frank!" one outlaw yelled. "Did you get lost out in them woods?"

Frank lay as silent as the woods.

"Frank?" the call was repeated several times by half a dozen of the thugs.

The outlaws looked at one another, suspicion and a touch of fear entering their eyes.

"Dolp ain't moved none," one outlaw observed, looking at the man with his head on his chest.

"All that hollerin' would have been shore to wake him up," another remarked.

"Well, he ain't moved. Somebody go over yonder and kick him a time or two."

A man walked over to Dolp and nudged him with the toe of his boot. Dolp's head lolled to one side and he fell over, the movement exposing the horrible wound on his neck.

Smoke eared back the hammer on his Winchester.

The outlaw screamed, "His throat's been cut."

Smoke shot him, the .44 slug severing his spine. The man slumped to the ground in a boneless heap.

The camp erupted in a mass of yelling, running men, all grabbing for their weapons and firing in every conceivable direction, hitting nothing but air.

Smoke shot one in the belly, doubling him over, and dotted another's left eye with lead. He decided it was time to haul out of there; he'd pushed his luck and skill far enough.

He left behind him a camp filled with frightened and confused outlaws. They were still shooting at shadows and hitting no more than that. However, Smoke thought, if he was lucky, two or three of them might shoot one of their own.

"They had a bad home environment," he muttered, as he silently made his way back toward his horses. "I'm going to have to remember to tell Sally about this new excuse for becoming a criminal. She probably could use a good laugh."

An hour later he rolled up in his blankets and was asleep in two minutes. He did not worry about the outlaws finding his camp. They were probably still trying to figure out what had hit them on what they considered to be home ground. And had they been more careful, it would have been safe ground. It was rugged country; no country for a tenderfoot. And a man could easily live off the land—there were bear, deer, elk, and plenty of streams in which to fish. But an outlaw wasn't going to do anything like that; they were too damn lazy and sorry. If they couldn't steal it, they didn't want it.

Smoke woke up to the sounds of a jaybird fussing

130

at him, telling him it was a pretty day and to stop all that lollygagging around in the bed. As was his custom, Smoke did not move for a moment, letting his eyes sweep the terrain around him for trouble. He spotted nothing to indicate trouble. Birds were singing, and the squirrels were jumping and dancing from limb to limb. He rolled out of his blankets and pulled on his boots, put his hat on his head, and slung his guns around his waist.

He chanced a very small fire to boil his coffee. When the coffee was ready, he put out the fire and contented himself with a cold breakfast of bread and some berries he'd picked from nearby bushes.

By now, he figured, riders would have gone out from the camps he'd attacked, and Lee Slater, if he was not a stupid man, and Smoke didn't think he was—just a no-good, sorry excuse for a human being—would be pulling in his people, massing them for some planning. That was fine. Smoke figured he'd done enough head-hunting in this area. Today he would begin his ride over to the Seven Slash range and see what mischief he could get into there.

He pondered his future as he sipped his coffee. It would be at least another day or two before his friend, the federal judge up in Denver, received his letter. Another day or two before whatever action he took—if any, and that was something Smoke had to consider—went into effect.

But a much more dangerous aspect of his situation had to be taken into consideration: bounty hunters. As soon as word hit the country that a reward was out for Smoke Jensen—and Judge Richards probably made it dead or alive—the country would be swarming with bounty hunters and those looking for a reputation as the man who killed

131

Smoke Jensen.

Well, he thought, I've done this before, so it's nothing new to me. I'll just have to ride with my guns loose and my eyes missing nothing.

He broke camp, saddled up, and headed for Seven Slash range.

"Had to be Jensen," Lee Slater spoke to some of his men. "Nobody else would be that stupid . . ."

It never occurred to Lee that stupid had nothing to do with it. "Skilled" was the word he should have used in describing Smoke's attack on his camps.

". . . He's got to be tooken out. And tooken out damn quick. He could screw up the whole plan."

"What plan?" a gunny who called himself Tap demanded. "All we been doin' for days is sittin' around on our butts. If somethin' don't happen pretty damn quick, I'm pullin' out for greener pastures."

Zack nodded his head in agreement. "I'm with Tap. We got money in our pockets and no place to spend it. They's thousands of dollars worth of gold and silver in this area, and we ain't doin' a damn thing about takin' it. I'm tarred of sittin' around. Let's get into action, Lee."

Lee knew he could not hold his men back much longer. Not and keep his gang together And he knew he had to do that because there was strength in numbers. Luttie was moving too slow to suit Lee. He couldn't understand why his brother was dragging his boots. He needed to see Luttie, but it was risky leaving the mountains just for a visit.

"Couple more days, Zack," the outlaw leader said. "I promise you . . ."

The men all looked up at the sound of a rider coming into camp. "I got news!" the rider yelled. He swung down and poured himself a cup of coffee, then walked over to Lee, waving the other men close in.

"Well?" Lee demanded. "What news?"

"Lemme drink some coffee, man!" the outlaw said. "Catch my breath. I been ridin' all night to get here." He drained his cup and tossed the dredges. "A federal judge back East done put out warrants on Smoke Jensen. Murder warrants from that shootin' over to Idaho some years back. Three warrants. The re-ward money totals over thirty thousand dollars to the man who brings him in—dead or alive."

"Well, now," Lee said, sitting down on a log. "Ain't that something? What's Jensen doin' about this sicheation?"

"He's on the run. Somewhere betwix here and the border."

Lee brought the man up to date on the attacks of the previous night.

"Thirty thousand dollars," outlaw Boots Pierson whispered. "That's a fortune. A man could live real good for a long time with that money."

"They's more news," the man who brought the word said, pouring himself more coffee. "The word is out, and bounty hunters from all over is comin' in. If we're gonna do something about Jensen, we damn well better get movin' 'fore all them other hardcases come a-lookin'."

"That there's a puredee fact," Tom Post said.

Lee looked at his men, knowing that any plans he might have had were now gone with the wind. All his men were thinking about was that thirty

133

thousand dollars reward and the reputation that went with being the man who brung in Smoke Jensen belly down acrost a saddle.

The camp of crud and no-goods broke up into small groups, all talking at once about what all that reward money could buy them. Women, whiskey, and gambling, for the most part.

"All right, all right!" Lee finally managed to shout the camp silent. "Let's plan. Now for sure we can't go after him in a bunch. He'd see and hear us coming miles away. So let's split up into groups of six. That'd be damn near ten groups workin' the mountains. Y'all talk it over and form up with men you wanna ride with. Then we'll settle down and go over what group is gonna cover what area."

The men split up into groups of six and seven, each group made up of men who had known each other for a long time, or who knew the other's reputation.

Lee had started out with a small army of crud, over seventy-five men. He was now down to nine groups of six each. Fifty-six men. He thought about that for a minute. Fifty-four men. Whatever!

Lee found him a stump of pencil and sat down, scribbling on a dirty envelope. Four were either in jail or being transported back to states that had warrants on them. Jensen had killed two on the trail coming into town. A half a dozen had left the gang after the raid against Big Rock. That meant that Jensen had killed about ten the previous night . . . give or take two or three. The man was a devil, for a fact, but he was still only one man. They would find him, and they would kill him.

Lee waved his group over to him. To his mind, he had chosen well the five men who would ride

134

with him. They were all vicious killers. Curt Holt, Ed Malone, Boots Pierson, Harry Jennings, and Blackjack Simpson.

The young punks had banded together, as Lee had figured they would, with the punk kid Pecos their leader. All the other groups were electing leaders. Curly Rogers was bossing one group, Al Martine another. Whit was fronting another group and Ray yet another. The last two were being led by Crocker and Graham.

Personally, Lee didn't give a damn which group got Smoke Jensen, just as long as somebody got him. Not that he didn't think thirty thousand was a lot of money. It was. But there was a lot more than that to be had in these mountains once Jensen was out of the way.

Lee stood up and hitched at his gunbelt. "Let's ride, boys. We got us a legend to kill."

Chapter Eleven

But legends oftentimes grow out of fact. And Smoke Jensen was not an easy man to kill. There had been many over the long and bloody years who had thought that fact not to be true. Somebody had buried them all.

Smoke rode the big buckskin through the windy and lonely high country, once again a man with a price on his head. But this time, the price came from a corrupt judge. And Smoke would deal with him when this little matter in the mountains was settled. He didn't know just how he would deal with him, but deal with him he damn sure would.

Smoke sat the saddle like a man born to it. His back was straight and his eyes constantly moving, scanning the terrain ahead of him and on both sides.

He stopped to rest on a bluff high above the road that led to the little village, and he was not surprised to see wagon after wagon heading for the town. There were wagons and buggies of all descriptions and men on horseback, all heading for the town. It wasn't gold or silver that drew them there—although that was a part of it. It was the news that Smoke Jensen was a wanted man.

Smoke rested his horses and squatted down, his field glasses in his big hands, and studied the passing parade unfolding far below him.

He grunted as he picked out two of the West's most notorious bounty hunters: Ace Reilly and Big Bob Masters. They were riding together.

There was Lilly LaFevere in her fancy buggy, with several wagon loads of ladies of the evening right behind her. He saw several well known gamblers that he was on speaking terms with.

Then he laughed aloud. There was Louis Longmont, riding a beautiful high-stepping black, with a wagon pulled by four big mules right behind him, driven by his personal valet and cook . . . he wondered if it was still Andre? Louis Longmont, a millionaire professional gambler who owned a casino in Monte Carlo, who owned banks and railroads and entire blocks of cities, and who was one of the most feared gunfighters in all the world. In the wagon would be jars of caviar, cases of fine French wines, and plenty of Louis' favorite scotch whiskey, Glenlivet.

Smoke felt a lump knot up in his throat as he scanned the road below. There was Cotton Pickens from up in Puma County, Wyoming. Their paths had crossed a time or two, when Smoke had pulled Cotton out of a couple of bad spots. Now he'd come to help out Smoke.

"Well, I'll just be damned!" Smoke whispered, as he focused his glasses on Johnny North, who had a ranch about twenty miles from Smoke and Sally's Sugarloaf. Johnny had married the Widow Colby and hung up his six-shooters years back. Now he had cleaned them up, oiled the leather, and strapped them on and was coming to help his neighbor.

"My God!" Smoke said, as his eyes touched upon

137

a man with gray shoulder-length hair. "I was told you were dead!"

He was looking at the legendary Charlie Starr.

Smoke chuckled. "Going to get real interesting around the town very soon," he muttered. "Real interesting."

Smoke leaned back against a huge boulder and rolled a cigarette, lighting up. If he was right in his thinking, Lee Slater was probably right now splitting up his gang into small groups and starting a concentrated search for their prey . . . that being Smoke Jensen. Smoke smiled. He hoped Lee would do that. Small groups were easier to handle.

He smoked his cigarette and carefully extinguished it. He took his field glasses and once more studied the increasing traffic on the road below.

The town was going to boom for a time. The stage line would put on more stages and roll them in and out at least once a day from north and south, and maybe more than that.

"Well, now," Smoke said, as he picked out Dan Diamond, another bounty hunter. The man riding with him was familiar, but it took Smoke a minute or so to put a name on the face. Nap Jacobs. Nap was a thoroughly bad man. Fast with a gun and seemingly without a nerve or a scruple in his entire body. And he didn't like Smoke at all. And there was Morris Pattin, another bounty hunter who hated Smoke Jensen.

Smoke tightened the cinch on Buck and put the pack back on the pack animal. "Time to go, boys. I'm going to find you both a nice little box canyon, with good graze and water and let you both rest for a time. Then I'm going to lay out some ambushes."

* * *

"Good to see you again, Earl!" Louis said, stepping up on the boardwalk and shaking hands with the Englishman.

"By the Lord! It's grand to see you, Louis. It's going to get rather interesting around this little village before very long. Who are your friends?"

"Johnny North, a neighbor of Smoke Jensen's. Cotton Pickens, a rancher from up Wyoming way, and this, Earl, is Charlie Starr."

"I am awed and humbled, sir," Earl said, with genuine emotion in his voice. "You rank among the few men who have become a legend in your own time."

"Thank you, sir," Charlie replied, shaking hands with the gambler/gunfighter. "I may take it that you are a friend of Smoke Jensen?"

"You may. Let's go into my office, and I'll bring you up to date on Smoke's troubles."

Larry Tibbson had taken the first stage out of Big Rock, heading down to where Smoke was hiding out. He kept a very low profile and kept his big mouth shut concerning his opinions of Smoke Jensen. He decided that since the town was growing so quickly—he didn't have sense enough to know what was causing the rapid growth, nor that it would very likely bust as quickly as it boomed—he would hang out his shingle in the newly named town of Rio. Everybody needed the services of a good attorney from time to time, and this looked like the ideal spot to make some quick money.

But my word! Larry thought, stepping off the stage, it was so rowdy here. All these rough-looking fellows carrying guns and knives right out in the open. Shocking! He had never seen anything like it.

And their boorish behavior was offensive to someone of Larry's gentle sensibilities. All the more reason to stay, he thought. Bring some refinement to the savages.

He managed to get the last room available in the hotel — and he did that by paying five times the usual going rate.

"Them sheets ain't been slept on but three times," the man told him, in protest over Larry's demand for clean sheets. "The last feller used 'em didn't appear to have no fleas."

"Change the sheets!"

"All right, all right," the newly hired room clerk grumbled.

Larry turned to the stairs and was stopped in his tracks at the sight of Louis Longmont dismounting and shaking hands with what appeared to be a constable of some sort. It was hard to tell in this barbaric setting, since lawmen, for the most part, did not wear uniforms denoting their profession, as was the case in more civilized parts of the nation.

Louis Longmont . . . here? Larry walked to the window of the saloon and looked out, seeing the six-guns belted around the millionaire's waist. So the rumors were true after all, Larry mused. The man was an adventurer. But was he here to hunt down Smoke Jensen, or to aid the gunfighter?

And who was that long-haired, grizzled-looking older man shaking hands with the constable? Obviously some sort of gunfighter, but it was hard to tell, since all those gathered around the constable wore two guns, tied down. It was so confusing out here.

With a sigh, Larry turned to climb the stairs. He angled over and spoke to the room clerk, whose small station was at the end of the bar.

"Do you have inside facilities?" Larry inquired.

"Huh?"

"Water closets inside."

"Hell, no!"

Larry shook his head and headed for the room.

"You forgot your bags," the room clerk called.

"Carry them up for me."

"Tote your own damn bags, mister!"

Larry climbed the stairs, sweating under the load of his trunk. All in all, he thought, the West just had to be the most barbaric and inhospitable place he had ever traveled.

"How many men in Slater's bunch?" Johnny asked.

Earl spread his hands. "Fifty to seventy-five are the numbers I keep hearing."

"Smoke's a tough ol' boy," Charlie Starr said. "But he's not indestructible. He's gonna need some help with this one. Come the morning I'll provision up and head out for the lonesome. Louis, I think you and Johnny and Cotton ought to stay close to here. This town's a-fixin' to bust wide open and Earl, here, is gonna need some help keepin' order. 'Sides, Smoke needs all the friendly ears he can use right here."

"I agree," Louis said. "Sooner or later, Smoke is going to tire of the mountains and come into town, and to hell with the U.S. Marshals. We need to be here to back him up."

Johnny had left Big Rock before Larry Tibbson started with all his mouth, so all he knew about the Eastern lawyer was that he'd come trying to spark a

141

married woman, Sally, and that was a stupid thing to do. If Smoke had been home, the lawyer would be cold in the ground with the worms playing the dipsy-doodle around his sewed-together lips. Which was about the only way anybody could get a lawyer to shut up.

Someone had set up a portable saw mill and was already backed up with orders for lumber. The sounds of sawing and hammering and nailing and cussing overrode any other sound in the town. With Earl Sutcliffe as the marshal, few dared to fire a pistol, even for fun. And the whole town knew within minutes of their arrival that Cotton Pickens, Johnny North, Charlie Starr, and Louis Longmont were on the side of the law with Earl Sutcliffe. That knowledge smoothed out just a whole bunch of otherwise sharp and explosive tempers. It would take a puredee damn fool to go up against those five.

"Now," Earl said, "we have to see about rooms for you gentlemen."

Louis shook his head. "No need. Andre is hiring people now to erect my saloon and gambling hall. We'll have board floors and wooden sides, but a canvas top. I'll have the workmen build an addition to the saloon for us. Until then, we'll sleep out under God's blanket."

"I'm gonna start puttin' my provisions together," Charlie said. "I get it done soon enough, I just might take off while there's a few hours of daylight left."

"Get whatever you need and charge it, Charlie," Earl told him. "Your money is no good in this town."

Charlie looked at the man. "I ain't no broke saddle bum, Earl."

142

"Of course, you're not," Louis said with a smile. "If you wish, you can settle up when you return from the mountains."

"I just might do that. See you boys." The old gunfighter left the office.

"Whew!" Johnny said. "That, fellers, is one randy ol' puma."

"I concur," Louis said. "Have you ever seen him in action, Earl?"

"No, never."

"Awesome. He's a little slower than he used to be, I would imagine. But still one of the fastest guns around. And he never misses."

"I would like to get word to Smoke that you are here," Earl said. "But I haven't the foggiest where he might be."

Louis shrugged his shoulders. "Knowing Smoke as I do, he probably already knows. Although how he manages to learn those things mystifies me."

"Indians say that eagles come tell him," Cotton said.

"I've heard that, too," Johnny said.

"If he knows you gentlemen are here," Earl said drily, "it is probably because he squatted on a mountain and watched the road below through field glasses."

"I like the eagle story better," Louis said, and the men burst out laughing.

A bounty hunter they called Slim Williams wasn't laughing. He had left the road miles from the newly named town of Rio and headed into the high country. He'd come upon tracks: a man riding and a pack horse behind.

143

He found where the man had stopped and dismounted for a drink of water at a rushing mountain stream. A big man, judging by his boot tracks. And Smoke Jensen was a big man.

Then he lost the trail. Slim wandered around for a hour and never could pick it back up. He had sat his horse for a time, smoking a cigarette and thinking things through. His eyes caught movement in the timber, about a hundred yards away. Then the man—and he was sure it was a man—was gone.

"What the hell?" Slim said. He rode his tired horse over to the spot where he'd seen the movement and dismounted. There were tracks, and the print was about the same size as those he'd seen back at that little crick. But this man was wearing moccasins. And it hadn't been no Injun, neither. Slim was sure of that. This man seemed to have some sort of black bandanna tied around his head, and his hair had been cut short.

He walked back to where he'd left his horse reined. The damn horse was gone!

"Shotgun!" Slim called. "Come on, Shotgun. Come to Slim, boy."

Silence greeted him from the high country timber.

Slim began to worry. He could make it back to the road; he wasn't worried about that. But all his possessions were in the saddlebags or tied in his bedroll.

"Shotgun! Now come on, boy. Come to Ol' Slim, Shotgun."

Slim spun around, a Colt leaping into his hand as the voice came out of the timber. "Shotgun was tired. He needed a rest."

"Who the hell are you, mister? You gimmie back

my damn horse, you thief!"

"A back-shooting murderer calling me a thief." The voice laughed. "That's very funny."

Slim cussed him.

Smoke said, "You looking for Smoke Jensen?"

"That ain't none of your concern, mister."

"I can lead you to him."

"Oh, yeah?"

"Yeah. I get half the reward money, though."

"You go suck an egg, mister." Slim thought for a moment. "Tell you what I'll do, mister. You step out so's I can see you, and we'll talk."

"You put that gun up, and I'll do that." The voice was closer, and coming from a different location each time.

Damn, Slim thought. The man moves like a ghost. And I know that voice from somewheres. "Deal." Slim holstered his gun, thinking that if the man was planning to kill him, he'd have done so already.

"Turn around." The voice came from behind him.

Slim turned, and felt his stomach do a slow roll-over. He was facing Smoke Jensen. "Hello, Smoke. It's been a long time. Years."

"You should have stayed home, Slim," Smoke told him.

"Man's got to make a livin', Smoke."

"You know damn well those warrants out on me are bogus. You're a man-hunter, Slim. Out for the money. I got no use for scum like you."

"You ain't got no call to talk to me like that, Smoke. This ain't nothin' personal 'tween us. You've kilt more'un your share of men. You ain't no better than I am."

"We'll let God be the judge of that, Slim. You

came looking for me, now you've found me. Make your play."

Slim began to sweat. He hadn't planned on this. He'd planned on back-shootin' Smoke. His tongue snaked out to wet dry lips. "We can deal, Jensen. I can just ride on out of here and not look back."

"That's the same deal you made with the breed, Cloudwalker. Then you shot him in the back, all the time knowing he was an innocent man."

"Hell, Smoke, he was a damn Injun!"

"He was an innocent man. I've stayed with Crows and Utes and Sioux and Cheyenne. I have a lot of good Indian friends. It doesn't make any difference to me if a man is red, white, Negro, or Oriental."

"Don't preach to me, Jensen!" Slim got his dander up. "I don't need no goddamn gunslick sermonizin' to me."

"Draw, Slim!"

Slim grabbed for iron. Smoke's .44 slug caught him dead center in his chest and knocked him back against a tree. He finally managed to pull iron, and Smoke's second shot tore into his belly.

Slim screamed as the .44 slug ripped through his innards like a white-hot branding iron. His .44 dropped from dying fingers. He slumped to the cool ground.

"You gonna bury me proper, ain't you, Jensen?" he gasped the question.

"I'll toss some branches and rocks over you, Slim. I don't have a shovel."

"I hate you, Jensen!"

"I don't understand that, Slim. What did I ever do to you to cause you to hate me?"

"Jist . . . bein' . . . you!" Slim closed his eyes and died.

146

Smoke went through Slim's pockets before he piled branches and rocks over the body to discourage smaller animals, all the while knowing that a bear could, and probably would, rip it apart in seconds. He would give the money to some needy family. There was no indication that Slim had a family. Smoke shoved one of Slim's .44s behind his gunbelt and kept the other one in leather, hanging on his saddle horn. He inspected the late Slim's Winchester .44-.40. It was in excellent condition, and this one had an extra rear sight, located several inches behind the hammer, for greater accuracy. He found three boxes of .44-.40s in the saddlebags. Slim also had a nice poke of food: some bacon and bread and biscuits and three cans of beans that would come in handy on the trail.

Smoke hesitated, then carved Slim's name on the tree that towered over the man. He put the date below the name and mounted up and pulled out, knowing that shots carry far in the high thin air of the lonesome.

He stopped once, looking back at Slim Williams' final resting place. "You should have picked another line of work, Slim. That's about the best I can say for you. God's gonna have the final word anyway."

Chapter Twelve

"Them was shots," Crocker said. "Come from over yonder." He pointed. "Let's go!"

"That's Horton's assigned area," Graham said.

"Hell with Horton," Crocker blew away the myth about honor among thieves. "Don't you want that money? Man, that's five thousand apiece if we cut it up."

"What'd you mean: if we cut it up?" Causey asked.

"All right, when we cut it up. Does that make you feel better?"

"Let's ride!" Woody said. "Damn all this jibber-jabber. Smoke'll be in the next county 'fore we get done talkin'."

They found where Smoke had carved Slim's date of death in the tree.

"Knowed him," Dale said. "He was good with a gun."

"Not good enough," Haynes summed it up. "Let's drag him out and go through his pockets."

The men tore away the rocks and branches and searched the stiffening form of Slim. They found nothing of value. Woody did take the man's boots, putting them on and throwing his worn-out boots by the body. They left Slim sprawled on the ground, one big toe sticking out of the hole in his dirty sock.

A bear came lumbering out of the timber and sniffed the dead man. He dragged Slim off a few hundred yards and covered him up with branches. When Slim ripened some he would be back for a meal.

"Hey, old man!" the young man called out to Charlie Starr, as Charlie sipped his whiskey prior to hitting the saddle for the high lonesome.

Charlie ignored him.

"I'm talkin' to you, old shaggy-haired thing you!"

Most of the men in the crowded saloon were chance-takers and gamblers and gun-hands and bounty hunters. None of them knew the gray-haired man with the tied down guns, the wooden handles worn smooth, but they could sense danger all around him.

Charlie took a small sip of his whiskey—holding the glass in his left hand—and decided to wait it out. He'd been around for a long time, and knew there was a chance—albeit a small one—that he could avoid having to deal with this young smart-mouth. Maybe his friends would sit him down. Maybe.

"Damn!" the young gunslick yelled. "His hair's so shaggy it's blockin' his ears. Maybe we ought to give him a haircut."

We! Charlie thought. More than one. But maybe his friends will stay out of it. Maybe.

"Bobby . . ." a young man said, pulling at the young smart-mouth's arm.

"Shut up!" Bobby said. "You don't have the balls for this, stay out of it."

Charlie sipped his drink. The whiskey tasted good after the dust of the road. He'd been a hard-drinkin' man in his younger days. Now he enjoyed just an occasional drink, liked to linger over it. In peace. Young Bobby was pushing. Hard. Just a few more words and he would step over the line. Charlie hoped the young man would just sit down and shut up.

"Goddamn mangy old fart!" Bobby yelled. "You wear them two guns like you think you're hot stuff. Turn around and prove it!"

There it was, Charlie thought. He would have liked to just finish his drink and walk out the door. But the code demanded that he do otherwise.

No, Charlie corrected that. It wasn't just the code. It was much more than that. It came with manhood. It was part of maintaining one's self-respect. It . . .

Larry Tibbson walked down the rickety stairs and stepped into the barroom.

. . . was just something that a man had to do. Right or wrong, and Charlie had thoughts about that, it just had to be.

"I called for hot water!" Larry said.

"Shut up and git out of the way," the bartender told him.

"You goddamn old turd!" Bobby hollered. "Turn around and face me."

"What on earth is taking place here?" Larry asked, looking around him. "And where is my hot water. I want to take a bath."

The barkeep reached over the bar and pulled Larry to the far end of the long bar. "Shet your trap, boy," he told Larry. "Lead's a-fixin' to fly."

Charlie finished his drink and slowly set the glass

on the bar. He turned around, his hands by his side. "Go home, boy," he told Bobby. "I ain't lookin' for trouble."

"Well, you got it!" Bobby told him.

"Why?" Charlie asked. "I don't know you. I never seen you before in my life. Why me?"

" 'Cause I think you maybe believe you're a gunhawk, that's why."

"Son, I was handlin' guns years before you were born. Now why don't you just sit down and finish yur drink, and I'll just walk out the bats?"

"Yellow!" Bobby sneered at him. "The old man's yellow. He's afraid of Bobby Jones."

Charlie smiled. "I never heard of you, Bobby. Are you lookin' for a reputation? Is that it?"

"I got a rep!"

"I ain't never seen none of your graveyards, boy."

"You just ain't looked in the right place. As far as that goes, where's your graveyards?"

"All over the land, son. From Canada to Mexico. From Missouri to California."

"You say!"

"That's right, son. I say."

Earl Sutcliffe pushed open the batwings and stood there, sizing up the situation. "What's the trouble here?"

"Stay out of this, marshal," Bobby said. "This is between me and this old goat here."

"You know who that old goat is?" Earl asked.

"Don't make no difference to me. I don't like this old coot's looks, and I told him so. He's afraid of me."

Earl laughed. "Boy, that man is not afraid of anything. That's Charlie Starr."

Bobby looked like a horse just kicked him in the

151

belly. His face turned white and sweat popped out on his forehead. But he had made his bed—or in this case, dug his grave—and now he would be forced to lie in it. Unless he backed down.

"Give it up, son," Earl told him. "Sit down and live."

Bobby's hands hovered over the pearl handles of his brand new matching .45s. Those raggedly-looking guns of Charlie's looked to Bobby like they was so old they probably wouldn't even fire. Looked like they'd been converted from cap and ball to handle brass cartridges.

Bobby stepped down into the damp, chilly grave he'd just dug for himself. "You're yellow, old man!" he shouted. "Charlie Starr's done turned yellow. You're standin' on your reputation, and I'm gonna be the man who jerks it out from under you."

Charlie straightened up, his mouth tight and his face grim. Earl knew it was nearly over. A man can only take so much, and Charlie had given the young punk more than ample opportunity to back down. "Enough talk," Charlie said. "Make your play, you stupid little snot."

"Here now!" Larry said. "This has gone entirely too far. You there," he said to Charlie. "You stop picking on that boy."

"Shut up," Earl told him.

Louis Longmont, Johnny North, and Cotton Pickens had walked into the saloon, standing on either side of Earl. "Fifty dollars says the kid never clears leather," Louis offered up a wager.

"You're on," a young man at the table where Bobby should have stayed seated said. "That there's Bobby Jones. He's faster than Smoke Jensen."

"He couldn't lick Smoke's boots," Charlie said.

"What!" Bobby screamed. "Draw, you old fart!"

"After you, boy," Charlie told him. "I don't ever want it said that I took advantage of a young punk."

"I ain't no punk!"

"Then show that you're a man by sittin' down and lettin' me buy you a drink. That's my final offer, son."

"You mean, that's your final statement. 'Cause I'm gonna kill you, Starr."

"That's it," Louis muttered. He knew, as did everyone else in the bar, that those words, once spoken, were justification to kill.

Charlie shot him. His draw was so smooth, so practiced, so fast, so professional, that it was a blur to witness. Flame shot out the muzzle of his old long-barreled .44. Gray smoke belched forth, obscuring vision. Bobby was jarred back as the slug ripped his belly and wandered around his guts, leaving a path of pain wherever it traveled.

He imagined himself jacking the hammer back on his .45 and pulling the trigger. He actually did just that. But his guns were still in leather. He leaned against a support post and finally dragged iron.

Charlie let him cock his .45 before he put another slug in the punk's guts. Bobby yelled and slumped toward the floor, sliding down the post and sitting down heavily. He pulled the trigger and blew off several of his own toes. He screamed in pain and tried to lift the .45. It was just too heavy.

The .45 clattered to the littered floor.

"By God," one of Bobby's friends declared. "That'll not go unavenged." He stood up, a pistol in his hand.

Charlie drilled him in the brisket and doubled the young man over like the closing of a fan. The young man fell, landing on Bobby.

Bobby screamed in pain.

"You still owe me fifty dollars," Louis reminded the gut-shot punk who'd wanted revenge for Bobby.

"Help me!" the second punk bellered. "Oh, Lordy, Lordy, my belly's on fire."

"My God!" Larry yelled. "Somebody get a doctor and call the police."

He was ignored.

Bobby's other friends sat quite still at the table, their faces a sickly shade of green.

"Gimme a drink and one of them eggs over yonder," Charlie told the bartender. "Shootin' always makes me hungry."

"You barbarian!" Larry yelled at him.

Charlie noticed the man wasn't wearing a gun, so he did the next best thing. He walked over to him and slapped Larry across the mouth, knocking him down.

"I'll sue you!" Larry hollered.

Bobby broke wind and died.

His friend yelled, "Help me!"

Charlie punched out his empties, loaded up full, holstered his gun, and began peeling the egg.

"Somebody run fetch that new undertaker feller that just set up business down the street," the barkeep suggested. "I wanna see that shiny black hearse and them fancy-steppin' horses."

"You're all mad!" Larry said, getting to his shoes. "Somebody get a doctor for that poor boy."

"Ain't no doctor," a man told him. "Go get the barber."

"The barber!" Larry exclaimed in horror.

"There's a Ute medicine man down on the La Jara. But that young pup'll done be swelled up and

154

stinkin' something awful time he gets here. That old Ute's pretty good, but I ain't never heard of him raisin' the dead."

"Halp!" the second punk yelled.

His voice was getting weaker.

"Won't be long now," Earl said, bending over the gut-shot young man. "Where's your next of kin, lad?"

"I don't wanna die!"

"Then you should have chosen your companions with a bit more care. Next of kin?"

"I got a sister up in Denver. But she threw me out a couple of years ago."

The batwings flapped open, and a man dressed all in black stood in the space. "I heard shooting!"

"My, but your hearing is quite keen," Earl commented drily.

"I am the Reverend Silas Muckelmort. A minister of the gospel. I have come to this town to bring the word of God to the sinners who lust for blood money. Has that young man passed?" He pointed to Bobby.

"Cold as a hammer," Cotton told him.

"Then it is my duty to tend to his needs," the Rev. Muckelmort said.

"You keep your shit-snatchers off my body!" a small man dressed in a dark suit said, stepping into the barroom. "I'm the undertaker in town."

"His spiritual needs, you jackass!" Silas thundered.

"Pass the salt and pepper," Charlie told the barkeep. "I can't eat an egg without salt and pepper."

Smoke holed up in the most inhospitable place he

155

could find, very near the timber line, knowing the outlaws would, most likely, find the most comfortable spot they could to bed down for the night. He had already found a spot he would use to leave his horses, in an area so remote it would be pure chance if anyone stumbled upon them. Tomorrow he would ride there and leave them, packing on his back what he felt he would need in his fight against the bounty hunters and the Lee Slater gang.

Smoke rolled up in his blankets and went to sleep. The next several days were going to be busy ones.

He was up and riding before dawn, having committed to memory the trail to the cul-de-sac where he would leave the horses. He was there by midmorning. He transplanted several bushes over to the small opening and carefully watered them. To get to the opening, he had to ride behind a thick stand of timber, then angle around a huge boulder, and finally take a left into the lush little valley of about ten acres with a small pool next to a sheer rock wall. The grass was belly high in places; ample feed for the horses for some time. If he did not return, they could easily find their way out.

Smoke put together a pack whose weight would have staggered the average man. He picked it up with his left hand.

He sat for a time eating a cold . . . what was it Sally called a mid-morning meal? Brunch, yeah, that was it, and wishing he had a potful of hot, strong, black coffee. But he couldn't chance that. He would hike a few miles and then have a hot dinner—lunch, Sally called it—and drink a whole a pot of strong cowboy coffee. He wanted the scum and crud to see that smoke. He wanted them to come right to that spot. By the time they got there, he would have a few surprises laid out for them.

He walked over and spoke with Buck for a few moments. Rubbing his muzzle and talking gently to the big horse. Buck seemed to understand, but then, everybody thinks that of their pets and their riding horses. Shotgun, the pack animal, and Buck watched Smoke pick up his heavy pack and leave. When he was out of sight, they returned to their grazing.

Smoke hiked what he figured was about three miles through wild and rugged country, then stopped and built a small, nearly smokeless fire for his coffee and bacon and beans. While his meal was cooking and the coffee boiling, he whittled on some short stakes, sharpening one end to a needle point. After eating, he cleaned plate and skillet and spoon and packed them away. Then he went to work making the campsite look semi-permanent and laying out some rather nasty pitfalls for the bounty hunters and outlaws.

That done, he tossed some logs on the fire and slipped back into the timber where he'd hidden his pack. He waited.

Curly Rogers and his pack of hyenas were the first to arrive.

Smoke was back in the timber with the .44-.40, waiting and watching.

The outlaws didn't come busting in. They laid back and looked the situation over for a time. They saw the lean-to Smoke had built, and what appeared to be a man sleeping under a blanket, protected by the overlaid boughs.

"It might not be Jensen," Taylor said.

"So what?" Thumbs Morton said. "It wouldn't be

the first time someone got shot by accident."

"I don't like it," Curly said. "It just looks too damn pat to suit me."

"Maybe Slim got lead into him?" Bell suggested. "He may be hard hit and holed up."

Curly thought about that for a moment. "Maybe. Yeah. That must be it. Lake, you think you can Injun up yonder for a closer look?"

"Shore. But why don't we just shoot him from here?"

"A shot'd bring everybody foggin'. Then we'd probably have to fight some of the others over Jensen's carcass. A knife don't make no noise."

Lake grinned and pulled out a long-bladed knife. "I'll just slip this 'tween his ribs."

As Lake stepped out with the knife in his hand, Smoke tugged on the rope he'd attached to the sticks under the blankets. What the outlaws thought to be a sleeping or wounded Smoke Jensen moved and Lake froze, then jumped back into the timber.

"This ain't a gonna work," Curly said. "We got to shoot him, I reckon. One shot might not attract no attention. Bud, use your rifle and put one shot in him. This close, one round'll kill him sure."

Bud lined up the form in the sights and squeezed the trigger. Smoke tugged on the rope, and the stickman rose off the ground a few inches, then fell back.

"We got him!" Bell yelled, jumping up. "We kilt Smoke Jensen. The money's our'n!"

The men raced toward the small clearing, guns drawn and yelling.

Taylor yelled as the ground seemed to open up under his boots. He fell about eighteen inches into a pit, two sharpened stakes tearing into the calves of his legs. He screamed in pain, unable to free himself from the sharpened stakes.

Bell tripped a piece of rawhide two inches off the ground and a tied-back, fresh and springy limb sprang forward. The limb whacked the man on the side of his head, tearing off one ear and knocking the man unconscious.

"What the hell!" Curly yelled.

Smoke fired from concealment, the .44-.40 slug taking Lake in the right side and exiting out his left side. He was dying as he hit the ground.

"It's a trap!" Curly screamed, and ran for the timber. He ran right over Bell in his haste to get the hell into cover.

Smoke lined up Bud and fired just as the man turned, the slug hitting the man in the ass, the lead punching into his left buttock and blowing out his right, taking a sizeable chunk of meat with it.

Bud fell screaming and rolled on the ground, throwing himself into cover.

Thumbs Morton jerked up Bell just as the man was crawling to his knees, blood pouring from where his ear had once been, and dragged him into cover just as Smoke fired again, the slug hitting a tree and blowing splinters in Thumbs' face, stinging and bringing blood.

"Let's get gone from here!" Curly yelled.

"What about Taylor?" Thumbs asked, pulling splinters and wiping blood from his face.

"Hell with him."

With Curly supporting the ass-shot Bud, and Thumbs helping Bell, the outlaws made it back to their horses and took off at a gallop, Bud shrieking in pain as the saddle abused his shot-up butt.

Smoke lay in the timber and listened to the outlaws beat their retreat, then stepped out into his camp. He looked at Lake. The outlaw was dead. Smoke took his ammo belt and tossed his guns into the brush. He walked over to Taylor, who had passed out from the pain in his ruined legs. He took his ammunition, tossed his guns into the brush, and then jerked the stakes out of the man's legs. The man moaned in unconsciousness.

Smoke found the horses of the men, took the food from the saddlebags, and led one animal back to the campsite. He poured a canteen full of water on Taylor. The man moaned and opened his eyes.

"Ride," Smoke told him. "If I ever see you again, I'll kill you."

"I cain't get up on no horse," Taylor sobbed. "My legs is ruint."

Smoke jacked back the hammer on his .44. "Then I guess I'd better put you out of your misery."

Taylor screamed in fear and crawled to his horse, pulling himself up by clinging to the stirrup and the fender of the saddle. He managed to get in the saddle after several tries. His face was white with pain. He looked down at Smoke.

"You ain't no decent human bein'. What you're doin' to me ain't right. I need a doctor. You a devil, Jensen!"

"Then you pass that word, pusbag. You make damn sure all your scummy buddies know I don't play by the rules. Now, ride, you bastard, before I change my mind and kill you!"

Taylor was gone in a gallop.

Smoke shoved Lake's body over the side of the small plateau and began throwing dirt over the fire, making certain it was out. Then he sat down, rolled a cigarette, and had a cup of coffee.

All in all, he concluded, it had been a very pro
ductive morning.

Chapter Thirteen

The townspeople all turned out for the funeral parade that morning. Bobby had had enough money on him to have a fine funeral, complete with some wailers the Reverend Muckelmort had hired. He'd found someone with a bass drum and a fellow who played the trumpet. It was a sight to see, what with the thumping of the bass drum and the tootin' on the trumpet.

Muckelmort was something of a windbag. By the time he'd finished with his lengthy graveside harangue, nobody was left but the wailers—they were paid to stay—everybody else had retired to the saloon.

Nobody knew the second punk's name, and he'd only had ten dollars on him, so he was wrapped in a blanket and stuck in an un-marked hole. Two dollars went to the gravedigger, two dollars for the blanket, two dollars for the preacher, and the remaining four bucks went to buy drinks after the service. Somebody recalled that four of them had ridden into town together. But the other two had split just after the shooting. One of them was heard to say that milkin' cows wasn't all that bad after all. He was headin' back to the farm.

The RCMP had ridden in and collected the last prisoner, and the jail was empty.

When the morning stage rolled in, it was filled with reporters, all from back East. "Be another stage in this afternoon," the driver told Earl. "We're gonna be runnin' two a day while this lasts. We must have passed five hundred people on the road, all headin' this way."

Sheriff Silva rode in, looked around, cussed, and then commented to Earl that he reckoned he'd better hire some more deputies. Fifteen minutes later, he swore in Louis, Johnny, and Cotton. Louis asked him if he'd received warrants for Smoke's arrest.

"I tossed 'em in the trash can," the sheriff said. "There ain't no lawman out here gonna try to arrest Smoke Jensen. Not none that has a lick of sense. I know all about that shootin' in Idaho years ago. It was a fair fight, if you wanna call Smoke bein' outnumbered twenty to one fair. Those warrants are bogus."

A miner riding into town loping his mule as hard as he could cut off the conversation. He pulled up short at the sight of all the activity. When he'd been here last month there hadn't been more than seventy-five people in the whole damn town. Now it looked to him like there was more than a thousand.

With a confused look on his face, he tried to kick the mule into movement. But the mule was smarter than the rider. When a mule is tired or is loaded too heavily, it just won't move and no amount of cussing or kicking or threatening will make it move. The miner slid out of the saddle and ran up to Sheriff Silva and the other deputies.

The mule sat down in the street.

"Big shootin' about ten miles out of town, Sheriff," the miner said, pointing. "I don't know if they was outlaws or bounty hunters—one and the same if

163

you ask me. But anyway, the man who stopped by my tent for bandages and sich had one ear tore slap off. He said another man dropped into a pit of some sort that had sharpened stakes in it; run through both his legs. Terrible sight to see, he said. Another feller was shot dead and another was shot plumb through his ass—both sides!"

"Stay out of the mountains," the sheriff told the man. "And tell other miners to do the same. That's the Lee Slater gang—and some bounty hunters— chasing a man. It looks like some of them caught up with him."

"All them fellers chasin' after just one man? Good Lord, who are they after?"

"Smoke Jensen."

"Smoke Jensen!" the miner hollered. "Then they all must be nuts! I'd sooner run up on a pack of grizzly bears than tangle with him."

"I think they're beginning to discover that," Earl remarked. "But I'll wager they'll press on because they have no choice in the matter. They have to get Smoke out of the way."

The miner wandered off, muttering about crazy people. He tried to get his mule up off his butt, but the mule just brayed at him, telling him in no uncertain terms to get lost. He was tired, he was going to rest, so beat it.

"Has Luttie and his crew been back into town?" Sheriff Silva asked.

"No. Not in days."

The sheriff lit a cigar and said, "Main reason I rode down here was to tell you that Luttie's hirin' fightin' men. Payin' top wages. Whole passel of them rode through my town. Me and the boys sent them packin'. One-Eyed Jake and that Mexican gunslinger, Carbone, was among the bunch."

"I know them both," Johnny said. "They're top guns. Did you recognize any of the others?"

"Yeah. Nick Johnson, the twins, the Karl Brothers—Rod and Randy, and Rich Coleman."

"That's a whole army right there," Cotton said, hitching at his gunbelt. "Earl's told us something about this Luttie Charles. About his bein' the brother to Lee Slater. About how it's a good bet that he's tied up in all this. Ain't they enough evidence to move against him and shut him down?"

"Not . . . quite," Silva said with a sigh. "I received a wire from the governor this morning. Early this morning. He's not happy with all the press we're getting. He's afraid this town is going to blow wide open, and personally I think there is a good chance of that happening. There's a federal judge in Denver working very hard to overturn those warrants against Smoke, but that's going to take time. The governor said Smoke was on his own in this. I wired him back and told him that Jensen was one of my deputies, and he damn sure was not alone in this. Whatever he was doing up in the mountains comes under the business of keeping the law and order. I expect by the time I get back, I'll have several replies on my desk." Silva smiled. "They should make for interestin' readin'."

"Reading between the lines, Sheriff," Johnny said. "Smoke's on his own in the mountains, except for Charlie—and you want us to stay in Rio, right?"

"I'd appreciate it, boys. If the governor has to send the state militia in here, that's gonna make him very unhappy."

"Then here we'll stay, Sheriff," Louis assured the man. "Do you think Luttie has plans to attack the town, strip it bare, and leave this part of the country?"

"It's a possibility that I've considered. At first I think his plan was to hit the miners and the stages carrying gold and silver out. Maybe he might still do that. But I think now that Jensen has his brother's men out looking for him, he just might turn his back on Lee and use the men he has to wipe this town clean."

"Brotherly love doesn't run very deep in that family, does it?" Earl said softly.

Silva shrugged. "That's just a guess on my part. Who the hell really knows what Lee and Luttie will do?"

The men fell silent in the noisy, busy town, their eyes on the mountains that loomed around them. All of them had one overriding thought: Could Smoke pull this off?

Charlie Starr watched with some amusement in his hard eyes as Curly's group tried to treat the wounded. He had left his horse and walked to within fifty yards of the outlaw band's camp, casually leaning up against a tree at the edge of the clearing.

Bud was lying on his stomach, his britches down around his boots, his bare butt shinin' in the sunlight, while Thumbs Morton poured alcohol on the bullet holes. That set Bud off, jerking and squalling.

One side of Thumb's face was swollen and red-looking.

Bell Harrison had a bloody bandage wrapped around his head, and Taylor's legs, from the knees down, were wrapped in dirty, bloody bandages.

"I'm a-gonna kill that son of a bitch!" Bell said, considerable heat in his voice. "Torture him. Make it last. Burn him. I'll start with his feet in a fire and work up. I hate Smoke Jensen."

Charlie grinned. Smoke had really done a job on this bunch of no-goods.

"My legs is real hot, boys," Taylor said with a moan. "I'm burnin' up. I think Jensen put something on them stakepoints. Poison, maybe."

Probably so, Charlie thought. He probably found him some bear shit and smeared the points with it. Or he might have used some poisonous plant leaves. Ol' Preacher taught him every mean and dirty trick in the book when it came to survival. You boys done grabbed hold of a grizzly bear's tail when you decided to take on Smoke Jensen.

"I can't do no more for you, Bud," Thumbs said.

"I hate Smoke Jensen!" Bell said.

Charlie worked his way around the clearing until he had reached a spot about twenty yards from the bitching and moaning group of deadbeats. He pulled both .44s from leather and jacked the hammers back.

"What the hell was that?" Curly said, grabbing up a rifle and looking all around him.

"I didn't hear nothin'," Taylor said.

"I wonder if Jensen give Lake a decent buryin'?" Thumbs said.

"About the same as I'm gonna give you," Charlie said, and stepped out and started shooting.

Curly recognized the man at once. Charlie Starr! He jumped away from the group and headed for the horses, none of whom had been unsaddled. Curly wanted no part of Charlie Starr. Smoke Jensen was bad enough, but combine him with Charlie, and that was just too much.

Curly left his fearless little group to fight it out by themselves.

Charlie's first slug knocked Bell sprawling, his right arm hanging broken and useless by his side. Thumbs Morton was hit in the right side, the bullet shattering a rib and angling off to tear through a kidney. He lifted his six-gun, a curse forming on his lips, and got off one round, which missed.

Charlie didn't miss. He didn't even flinch as the slug from Thumbs' gun tore bark from a nearby tree. He leveled his long-barreled .44 and shot Thumbs in the belly, knocking the man down, hard-hit and dying.

Bell struggled to his boots and lifted his left-hand gun. Charlie perforated the man's belly, and Bell would never again have to worry about indigestion or how to keep his hat on his head with only one ear. Now all he had to worry about was facing God.

Charlie stepped back into the timber and was gone, leaving Bud and Taylor alive in the middle of carnage. He'd seen Curly Rogers hightail it out. Charlie knew Curly from way back. Knew him for the coward and the bully he was. Let him go; they would meet up again.

Charlie walked swiftly back to his horse, reloading as he went. He swung into the saddle, and was gone, a warrior's smile on his lips.

"Oh, my God!" Taylor yelled, the pain in his legs fierce. "What are we gonna do, Bud?"

Bud couldn't even stand up. His britches and his galluses were all tangled up around his boots. "Oh, Lord, I don't know!" Bud wailed. "I wish I'd never heard of Smoke Jensen. I wish I'd never left the farm."

"I think I'm gonna die, Bud. My legs is swellin' something awful."

"Hell with your legs. My ass hurts," Bud moaned.

Several of the groups had returned to base camp as night grew near. They all gathered around as Lee Slater listened to Curly's babblings, a disgusted look on his ugly face. He finally had enough and waved Curly silent. "Goddamnit, boys!" he yelled. "Smoke's jist one man. You're lettin' him buffalo you all."

"What about Bud and Taylor?" Horton asked.

"What about them?" Lee demanded. "Hell, they know the way back to base. We've all been shot before and managed to stay on a horse. If they got so much baby in them they can't ride through a little pain, we don't need them."

The young punks, Pecos, Miller, Hudson, Concho, Bull, and Jeff, all nodded their agreement and hitched at their gunbelts. None of them had ever been shot so they really didn't know what they were agreeing to. It just seemed like it was the manly thing to do.

"We put out guards this night," Lee said. "They'll be no more of Jensen slippin' up on us."

Miles away, Smoke had no intention of slipping up on anything that night, except sleep. Let the outlaws sweat it out and get tired and nervous. He would fix a good meal and rest.

Charlie had found him a nice comfortable little hidey-hole and was boiling his coffee and frying his bacon. He would get a good night's sleep and start out before dawn the next morning.

169

Back in Rio, a half dozen more rowdies had ridden in, on their way to the Seven Slash Ranch. They reined up in front of the saloon and swung down from the saddle, trail weary from a long day's ride. A whiskey would taste good.

"Keep movin', boys," the voice from behind them said.

They turned, and what they saw chilled them right down to their dirty socks. Louis Longmont, Cotton Pickens, Johnny North, and Earl Sutcliffe stood in the now quieted street, all of them with sawed-off shotguns in their hands. To a man they kept their hands very still.

"We just wanted to buy a drink of whiskey, Earl," John Seale said.

"You won't buy it here. None of you. Ride on to the Seven Slash if you want a drink."

"How'd you know? . . ." Mason Wright cut that off in mid-sentence. But it was too late; he'd tipped his hand and he knew it.

The others gave him dirty looks.

"Pack it in, Louis," Frankie Deevers said, looking at the millionaire gambler. "If you don't, you're gonna lose this pot. Believe me."

Louis smiled. "And who says life is not a game of chance, eh, Frankie?"

"Put them Greeners down, and we'll take you all right here and right now," a gunny snarled at Louis.

"Now, now, Willis," Louis said. "You know how talking strains your brain."

Larry chose that time to step out of the saloon/hotel for a breath of fresh air. The beery, sweaty odor from those unwashed cretins in the bar had drifted up to his room and was making him nauseous. But Larry was wising up to the West and

170

after giving the group in the street a quick look, he moved down the boardwalk, well out of the way.

"Longmont," Willis said. "I ain't never liked you. You got a smart damn mouth hooked to your face. I've always heard how bad you was, but I'm from Missouri, and I gotta be showed. So why don't you just show me?"

Louis lowered the shotgun and leaned it against a water rough. He swept back his coat and said, "Anytime you're ready, Willis."

Johnny, Earl, and Cotton backed off, still holding the express guns up and pointed at the gunnies.

"You can take him, Willis," Frankie said. "He's all showboat; that's all he is."

"A hundred dollars says he can't," Louis smiled the words.

"You got a bet, gambler!"

Willis made his play. Louis shot him just as the man cleared leather, the slug knocking him back on the steps leading up to the boardwalk. Willis lifted his gun and Louis plugged him again. Bright crimson dotted his dirty white shirt.

"You dirty son!" Willis gasped, still trying to jack back the hammer of his .45.

His friends desperately wanted to get into the fray, but the muzzles of those sawed-offs were just too formidable to breech.

"I can still do it!" Willis said, his blood staining his lips. He cocked his .45 and lifted it.

Louis shot him a third time, this time placing his shot with care. A blue/black hole appeared in the center of Willis' head. He died with his mouth and his eyes wide open.

"You owe me a hundred dollars," Louis said, looking at Frankie.

171

"I'll pay you," Frankie spoke through tight lips.

A young gunny who had ridden in with the hard-cases and had not been recognized by any of the lawmen asked, "Is Jensen faster than you?"

"Oh, yes," Louis told him. "Smoke Jensen is the fastest man alive."

The young gunny took off his gunbelt and looped it on the saddle horn. "If it's all right with you boys, I'll just have me one drink to cut the dust, a bite to eat at that cafe over yonder, and then I'll ride out of town. Not in the direction of the Seven Slash."

"You yellow pup!" Mason Wright told him. "I knowed you didn't have no good sand bottom to you."

"Shut up, Mason," Earl said. "The boy is showing uncommonly good sense." He looked at the young man. "Go have your drink and something to eat."

"Thank you kindly, sir." The rider walked up the steps and entered the barroom, the batwings slapping the air behind him.

Louis walked to Frankie. "A hundred dollars, Frankie. Greenbacks or gold."

Frankie paid him. "Your day's comin', Louis. You just remember that."

"If it comes from the likes of you, Frankie, it'll come from the back." Frankie flushed deeply. "Because you don't have the courage to face me eye to eye, with knife or gun or even fists, for that matter." Louis was a highly skilled boxer, and Frankie knew it.

"We'll see, Louis. We'll see."

"How about now, Frankie?" the gambler laid down the challenge. "You want to bet your life?"

"Let's go, Frankie," Mason urged him. "We can

deal with this bunch later."

Incredible! Larry thought. The man is a millionaire and is risking his life in a dirty street of a backwater town. I do not understand these men and their loyalty to someone of Smoke Jensen's dubious character.

The gunhands rode out of town, leaving Willis' body still sprawled on the steps of the saloon. Muckelmort and the undertaker came running over, squabbling at each other.

"Get a good night's rest, Smoke," Johnny North muttered, looking at the darkening shapes of the mountains all around the little town. "There's gonna be hell to pay in the morning, I'm thinkin'."

Chapter Fourteen

The body of Willis was toted off — Muckelmort and the undertaker would go through his pockets to determine the elaborateness of the funeral — and the town began once more coming back to life as darkness settled in. The saloon was doing more business than it could handle, and the owner actually wished the other saloons would hurry up and get their board floors down and the canvas sides and roof up to take some of the pressure off his place.

Louis volunteered to take the first shift, and the others went to bed early — they each would do a four hour shift.

In the mountains, the outlaws slept fitfully, not knowing when or even if Smoke Jensen or that old warhorse Charlie Starr would strike.

Charlie and Smoke, camped miles apart, slept well and awakened refreshed. They rolled their ground sheets and bedding, boiled their coffee and fried their bacon, then checked their guns, and made ready for another day.

The members of Lee Slater's gang, their size now cut by three more, were quiet as they fixed their breakfast and drank their coffee. Taylor and Bud had ridden in during the early evening, and Taylor's condition had both depressed and angered the outlaws. His legs were swollen badly, and the man had slipped into a coma as blood poisoning was rapidly taking his life.

"That there's the most horriblest-lookin' thing I ever did see," Woody commented, looking at Taylor. "Smoke Jensen don't fight fair a-tall."

"My ass hurts!" Bud squalled.

"Pour some more horse liniment on it," Lee told a man.

Bud really took to squalling when the horse medicine hit the raw wounds. Everyone was glad when he passed out from the pain and the hollering stopped.

The men mounted up and pulled out, a silent and sullen group of no-goods.

"How long do we intend to remain here?" Albert asked Mills, over breakfast.

"Until we come up with a plan to capture Smoke Jensen," the senior U.S. Marshal said. "Anybody got one?"

No one did.

"Pass the beans," Mills said.

Back in Washington, D.C., the chief of the U.S. Marshal's Service looked across his desk at a group of senators. The senators were very unhappy.

"Smoke Jensen is a national hero," one senator said. "He's had books and plays written about him. School children worship him, and women around the nation love him for the family man he is. The telegrams I'm receiving from people tell me they don't believe these murder warrants are valid. I want your opinion on this matter, and I want it right now."

Without hesitation, the man said, "I don't believe

the charges would stick for a minute in a court of law. But a federal judge signed them, and we have to serve them." He smiled. "But the information I'm receiving indicates that our people out West are not at all eager to arrest Smoke Jensen." He lifted a wire from Mills Walsdorf. "They have, shall we say, dropped out of sight for a time."

"Then the Marshal's Service is out of the picture?" another senator questioned.

"For all intents and purposes, yes."

The senator lifted a local newspaper. "What about these hundreds of bounty hunters chasing Jensen?"

The marshal shook his head. "You know how that rag tends to blow things all out of proportion. The reporter they sent out there to cover this story wouldn't know a bounty hunter from a cigar store Indian. He's never been west of the Mississippi River in his entire life . . . until now."

Another senator lifted a New York City newspaper and started to speak. The marshal waved him silent. "That paper is even worse. Smoke Jensen is probably up against a hundred people . . ."

"A hundred?" a Senator yelled. "But he's just one man."

The marshal smiled. "You ever seen Smoke Jensen, sir?"

"No, I have not."

"I have. One time about ten years ago when I was working out West. Three men jumped him in a bar in Colorado. When the dust settled, two of those men were dead and the third was dying. Smoke was leaning up against the bar, both hands filled with .44s. He holstered his guns, drank his beer, fixed him a sandwich, and went across the street to his hotel room for a night's sleep. I'm not saying he can pull this thing off and come out of it without taking some lead, but if anyone can do it, Smoke Jensen can. I can wish him well. But other than that, my hands are tied until some other federal judge overrides those warrants."

"Judge Richards has left town on a vacation," a senator said. "He'll be back in two weeks, so his office told me."

"He'd better stay gone," the marshal said. " 'Cause when Smoke comes down from those mountains, I got me a hunch he's Washington bound with a killin' on his mind."

"Well, now!" another senator puffed up. "We certainly can't allow that."

The marshal smiled. "You gonna be the one to tell Jensen that, sir?"

The senator looked as though he wished the chair would swallow him up.

Smoke released his hold, and the thick springy branch struck its target with several hundred pounds of impacting force. The outlaw was knocked from the saddle, his nose flattened and his jaw busted. He hit the ground and did not move. Smoke led the horse into the timber, took the food packets from the saddle bags, and then stripped saddle and bridle from the animal and turned it loose.

Smoke faded back into the heavy timber at the sounds of approaching horses.

"Good God!" a man's voice drifted through the brush and timber. "Look at Dewey, would you."

"What the hell hit him?" another asked. "His entar face is smashed in."

"Where's his horse?" another asked. "We got to get him to a doctor."

"Doctor?" yet another questioned. "Hell, there ain't a doctor within fifty miles of here. See if you can get him awake and find out what happened. Damn, his face is ruint!"

"I bet it was that damn Jensen," an unshaven and smelly outlaw said. "We get our hands on him, let's see how long we can keep him alive."

"Yeah," another agreed. "We'll skin him alive."

Smoke shot the one who favored skinning slap out of the saddle, putting a .44-.40 slug into his chest and twisting him around. The man fell and the frightened horse took off, dragging the dying outlaw along the rocks in the game trail.

"Get into cover!" Horton yelled, just as Smoke fired again.

Horton was turning in the saddle, and the bullet missed him, striking a horse in the head and killing it instantly. The animal dropped, pinning its rider.

"My leg!" the rider screamed. "It's busted. Oh, God, somebody help me."

Gooden ran to help his buddy, and Smoke drilled him, the slug smashing into the man's side and turning him around like a spinning top. Gooden fell on top of the dead horse, and Cates screamed as the added weight shot pain through his shattered leg.

Horton and Max put the spurs to their horses and got the hell out of there, leaving their dead and wounded behind. Smoke slipped back into the timber.

The screaming and calling out for help from Gooden and Cates were soon lost in the ravines and deep timber of the lonesome. Dewey lay on the trail, still unconscious.

Smoke seemed to vanish. But even as he made his way through the thick brush and timber, he knew he had been very lucky so far. He fully understood that there was no way he was going to fight a hundred of the enemy without taking lead at some point of the chase and hunt.

He just didn't know when.

Lee and his bunch muscled the dead horse off Cates and to a man grimaced at the sight of his broken and mangled leg.

"We got to set and splint it," Curly said. "Anybody got any whiskey?"

A bottle was handed to him. Curly gave the bottle to Cates. "Get drunk, Cates. 'Cause this is gonna hurt."

Cates screamed until he passed out from the pain.

Gooden was not hurt bad, just painfully, the slug passing through and exiting out the fleshy part of his side. Dewey's face was a torn, mangled mess. He was missing teeth, both eyes were swollen shut and blackened with bruises, and his nose and jaw were shattered.

"We got to get 'em, boss," Boots said. "Both Jensen and that old coot, Charlie Starr. This is gettin' personal with me, now. Me and Neal go way back together."

"What you got in mind? I'm damn shore open to suggestions."

"I go in after him on foot. Hell, he can hear horses comin' in from a long ways off. My daddy was a trapper and a hunter up in Northwest Territories. I can Injun with the best of them."

Lee shook his head. "I like the idea, but two would be better than one. You might get him in a crossfire."

"I'll go with him," Harry Jennings volunteered. "I'd like to skin that damn Jensen alive."

Both Jennings and Boots were old hands in the timber, and they carried moccasins in their saddlebags. They left behind boots and spurs, took two day's provisions and struck out, following the very faint trail that almost anyone leaves in the brush: bent-down blades of grass, a broken twig or lower limb from a scrub tree, a heel print in damp earth.

"He ain't that far ahead of us," Boots whispered, after having lost the trail at mid-morning and then picking it up a few minutes later. Boots was a thieving, murdering no-account through and through, but he was just about as good a trailsman as Smoke. "Grass hadn't started springin' back yet. No talkin' from now on—he's close. Real close. Come on."

Smoke had watched his backtrail. He had felt in the back of his mind that sooner or later somebody would try him on foot. Leaving his pack on the ground in some brush, he climbed a tall tree and began scanning his backtrail with his field glasses. On his second sweep he caught the two men as they skirted a small meadow, staying near the timber.

Smoke backtracked and left a trail, not a too obvious one, for that would be a dead giveaway, but a trail a skilled woodsman would pick up. He had a hunch those two men behind him were very good in the woods, for he hadn't been leaving much of a trail for anyone to follow.

Back at a narrow point in the game trail, he

quickly rigged a swing trap, using a young sapling about as big around as his wrist. The shadowy brush-covered bend in the trail should keep even the most skilled eyes from seeing the piece of dirt-rubbed rawhide he'd placed as the trip.

Smoke carefully backed off about twenty yards and bellied down against the cool earth under some foliage and took a sip of water from his canteen. Tell the truth, he was grateful for the time to rest.

"Pssttt!" he heard the call from one of the men.

He could not yet see them, but they were very near.

Stay on the trail, boys, he silently wished. Just stay on the trail. Do that, and I'll soon have just one to contend with.

Jennings eased forward, his smile savage as he saw the just crushed foliage on the trail. He touched it; it was very fresh. Smoke Jensen was only minutes ahead of them. Just minutes away from being dead meat, and Jennings and Boots would be thousands of dollars richer.

His left boot stepped over the trip; the right toe of his boot snagged it. Jennings experienced a savage blow in his belly, just below the V of the rib cage. Then the pain hit him. The most hideous pain he had ever experienced in his life. He forced his eyes to look down. He screamed at the sight.

A stake had been rawhided to the sapling. He had tripped a wire or something that had released the booby trap. The stake was now buried in his belly, his blood gushing out.

"Jesus God!" Boots whispered as he crept around the dark trail and saw what Smoke Jensen had done.

"Oh, my Lord!" Jennings wailed. "I cain't stand

the pain. Shoot me, Boots. Shoot me!"

"Yeah," Smoke's voice came out of the thick vegetation beside the trail. "Shoot him, Boots."

"You son of a bitch!" Boots yelled, dropping to his knees on the old trail. "You ain't no decent human bein'. This ain't fightin' fair a-tall."

Smoke laughed at the protestations of the outlaw/murderer/rapist. His laughter was taunting.

Jennings' screaming was a frightful thing to hear. He stood in the center of the game trail, afraid to move, both hands clutching the bloody end of the stake.

Smoke tossed a stick to his right. As soon as the stick hit the ground, Boots's rifle barked three times, as fast as he could work the lever.

Smoke laughed at his efforts.

Boots cussed Smoke. Called him every ugly and profane and insulting name he could think of, anything to draw the man out where he could get a clear shot at him.

Nothing worked.

"You ain't got no right to do this!" Boots yelled. "This ain't the way it's supposed to be."

"Jesus Christ, Boots," Jennings moaned. "You got to help me. I cain't stand no more of this."

Boots thought hard for a moment. He knew there was nothing he could do for Jennings. He was dying before his eyes. Not even a doctor right now could save him. Blood was dripping from Jennings' lips; that told Boots the stake had rammed right through the man's stomach. The point of the stake was sticking out the man's back.

Jennings died before Boots' eyes. The man's legs were spread wide, and both hands held onto the end of the stake. The thick sapling kept him in an upright position.

Boots didn't know what the hell to do. He knew that Smoke was over yonder, just ahead and to his right . . . at least the last time he'd laughed he was. But the way the man moved, hell, he might be anywhere by now.

Boots got down on his belly and started crawling away from the bloody scene. He was scared; he wasn't ashamed to admit it. A thrown stick landed just a few inches from his nose, and Boots almost crapped his longhandles.

"Wrong way, Bootsie," Smoke called.

"Stand up and fight me like a man, goddamn you!" Boots yelled. "Give me a chance."

"The same kind of chance you gave those little girls you raped and tortured and scalped and killed, Bootsie?"

"I didn't scalp nobody! That was Dolp what done that. And you done kilt him."

"I'm going to kill you, too, Bootsie."

"I surrender!" Boots shouted. "I give up. You got to take me in for a trial. That's the legal way."

"I'm a wanted man, Bootsie," Smoke said with a chuckle. "I've got murder warrants out on me. That's why you boys are chasing me. To collect those thousands of dollars. Now how in the hell can you surrender to me?"

Boots silently cursed. Didn't do no good to cuss out loud. Jensen wasn't gonna be rattled by that. Boots knew he was caught between a rock and a hard place. He could shuck his guns and stand up, his hands in the air. But as sure as he done that, Jensen would probably gut-shoot him. He knew how Jensen felt about criminals.

He was a thug and a punk and a lot of other

sorry-assed things—he knew that, wasn't no point in makin' excuses for what he'd done—but Boots was a realist, too. He knew damn well he was a dead man anyway it went. "I'm a gonna stand up, Jensen," he called. "My rifle's on the ground. My gun's in leather. We'll fight this out man to man. I'll . . ."

He screamed in fright as a hard hand closed around one ankle and jerked just as he was standing up. Boots hit the ground, belly-down, knocking the breath from him. Something with the strength of a bear flipped him over and tore the gunbelt from his waist. He watched belt and guns go sailing into the woods.

He looked up into the cold brown eyes of Smoke Jensen. God, the man was big.

"Get up," Smoke told him.

Boots crawled to his moccasins and watched as Smoke smiled at him and lifted his hands, clenching them into big leather-gloved fists. Boots grinned. Bare-knuckle, stomp and kick fighting was something he liked. He might have a chance after all.

"Okay, Jensen. Now you're playin' my game. I'm a-gonna stomp you into a greasy puddle."

Smoke hit him flush in the mouth and knocked him up against the bloody body of Jennings. Boots recoiled in horror and lunged at Smoke, both fists flailing the air.

Smoke hit him a combination left and right that staggered the outlaw and pulped his already split lips. Boots shook his head and tried to clear it. But Smoke pressed him hard, not giving him a chance to do anything except try his best to cover up.

Boots held his fists in front of his face. Smoke hammered at his belly with sledgehammer blows. Boots felt ribs crack and knew that Jensen was going to beat him to death. He tried to run. Smoke grabbed him by his dirty shirt collar and threw him back onto the trail.

"Get up and fight, you yellow bastard," Smoke told him.

Boots crawled to his feet, wondering if Smoke was going to kick him. That's what he would have done if it had been Jensen on the ground. He started to raise his fists, and Smoke drove a right through his guard and flattened his nose. Blood and snot flew from his busted snout, and Boots backed up against a tree as his eyes watered and his vision turned misty.

He heard Smoke say, "This is for those little girls back on the trail, Boots. For that poor woman and that man you sorry lumps of shit used for target practice."

Pain exploded in wild bursts in Boots' chest and belly and sides as Jensen pounded him unmercifully. Ribs popped and splintered like toothpicks. The last thing Boots would remember for awhile was those terrible cold eyes of Smoke Jensen.

He knew then why people called him the Last Mountain Man.

Chapter Fifteen

Al Martine and his bunch came upon Jennings and Boots in the midafternoon. Several of the outlaws lost their lunch when they found them.

Boots screamed hideously when the outlaws tried to move him.

"Jensen busted all his ribs," Al said, a coldness touching his guts. "Them ribs is probably splintered into his innards." He looked down at Boots. "There ain't nothin' we can do for you, Boots."

"Shoot me," Boots whispered.

Al just looked at him. "We'll get Jensen for you, Boots. That's a promise." Boots whispered something. "I can't hear you, Boots. What'd you say?"

"Give it up," Boots said through his pain. "Leave the gang. Leave the mountains. Go to farmin', or something. If you're gonna outlaw, git a thousand miles away from Jensen. He's a devil. Leave him alone."

"You don't mean that?" Zack said. "That's just your pain talkin'."

"Don't you want revenge?" Lopez asked.

Boots grinned a bloody curving of the lips. "Hell, boys. That ain't gonna do me no good. I'm dead." And he died.

Since none of them had shovels, they wrapped Boots Pierson and Harry Jennings in their blankets and covered them with branches. None of them had a Bible, either. The outlaws just stood around and looked at each other for a time. The gang of young punks rode up just as the last branch was put on the pile.

"Taylor's dead," Pecos announced. "Blood poisonin' kilt him, I reckon."

"This ain't workin' out like we planned, Al," Crown said. "This was supposed to be an easy hunt. Ever' day we're losin' two, three men to Jensen or Charlie Starr. Another week and there ain't gonna be none of us left."

"Yeah," Lopez said. "And Jensen could be Injunin' up on us right now."

All of them quickly found their mounts and hauled out of there. They rode until they came upon Ray's group and brought them up to date.

"A stake through his belly?" Keno said, his voice filled with horror. He shuddered. "Jesus, man, that ain't no fair way to fight no fight."

Concho said, "Jensen ain't playin' by no rule-book."

"Did we ever?" Pedro asked softly in an accented voice. "Unlike the rules set forth in lawbooks and courts of formal law, Jensen is giving us what we have given so many other people over the years. The way I see it, there is only two things we can do: continue the hunt until we kill Jensen or he kills us, or turn tail and run away."

"I ain't runnin' from Jensen," the young punk Concho said, swelling out his chest. "I think I can take him in a stand-up shoot-out."

"You are a fool," Lopez told him bluntly. "I have seen Jensen work. He is smooth, my young friend, and very, very quick. His draw is a blur that the

187

eyes cannot catch."

"I'm faster," Concho said.

Lopez shook his head and said no more. Let the young punk find out for himself, he thought. When he challenges Smoke Jensen, he will have a few seconds of life left him to ponder his mistakes as the gunsmoke clears, and he rides to Hell.

"It'll be dark in a few hours," Al said, looking up at the sky. "And it's gonna rain. Let's get back to the base camp and tell Lee what happened."

Smoke sat in his lean-to and drank his coffee and ate his early supper. He felt that outlaws being what they were, he would be reasonably safe from search in the cold, pouring rain. They would be too busy staying dry to look for him.

But he still carefully put out his fire before he rolled up in his blankets and closed his eyes.

Since Mills and his marshals were going to stay a spell where they were, they made their camp a secure and snug one, using canvas and limbs. The quarters were close together, with a cooking area just in front, easily accessible to all.

"This should bring the killing to a halt for a time," Mills said, looking out at the driving rain. "Maybe," he added. "I don't approve of what Smoke is doing, but I understand why he's doing it."

"There is a strange code out here," Albert said. "One that I'm sure our fathers swore to—at least to some degree."

"Or swore at," Sharp said.

"Probably a little of both." Harold poured a cup

188

of coffee and stared out at the silver-streaked gloom of late afternoon.

"Even after all this is said and done," Winston said. "We're still going to have to enforce the law once the warrants you requested on all those outlaws arrive."

"Yes," Mills said. "The San Francisco office is supposed to be getting them to Denver by train, then stagecoach to Rio. I requested them to be posted to the local marshal's office. I'll ride into town in a few days and check. By that time, I hope all this . . . nonsense concerning Smoke will be over."

The deputy U.S. Marshals looked at each other. They hoped the same thing. None of them wanted to confront Smoke Jensen with an arrest warrant. None of them knew if they would even try to do that. Aside from the fact that he was the most famous gunslinger in the West, they all genuinely liked the man.

Most of the miners within a forty-mile radius of the fight had left the mountains and descended on Rio. They didn't want to be caught up in the middle when the lead started flying. As it was, many of them had been close enough to hear the shots from Smoke and Charlie's guns. And from the guns of the outlaws.

Made a man plumb edgy.

Louis' saloon and gambling hall had been erected—due in no small part to the fact that Louis paid three times what others did for workmen. A smaller building had been built in the rear; this housed the kitchen, living quarters, and a privy attached to the building for maximum comfort and privacy. Cotton was on duty on the streets, and Louis and Johnny sat in the rear of the big wood and canvas saloon and talked in as low tones as the drumming of the rain overhead would permit. Earl was out of town.

"You heard that miner over yonder, Louis," Johnny said, cutting his eyes to a miner who had just come into town and was now sucking on a mug of beer. "What'd you think?"

"As near as I can figure—discounting the inevitable exaggeration—Smoke and Charlie have killed seven or eight of Slater's gang, and a couple of bounty hunters. This storm will probably blow out of here sometime tonight—it's raining too hard to keep this up long—so the hunt will resume tomorrow. Slater has to be getting frustrated, and frustration leads to desperate and careless acts. Smoke is fighting several fronts, and using varying tactics, including guerrilla warfare. Guerrilla warfare is a nasty business. It's demoralizing for those on the receiving end of it. Slater's people and the bounty hunters will be shooting at shadows from now on. And it's going to be just as dangerous in those mountains for Smoke and Charlie as it is for the outlaws and bounty hunters. Smoke will take some lead in this fight, my friend. I don't see how he can avoid it, and I would imagine he has already mentally prepared himself for it."

Johnny listened to the rain beat against the canvas for a moment. "Seems like trouble has been on Smoke's backtrail nearabouts all his life. Ever since I've known him—and years before that—all Smoke wanted was to be left alone to run his ranch, love his wife and kids, and live in peace. He changed his name and hung up his guns for several years, but no man should have to do that. That just isn't right. He never wanted the reputation of gunfighter. Never got a dime out of any of them Penny Dreadful books or plays about him. He didn't want the money. But he's a man that won't take no pushin'. Man pushes Smoke, Smoke'll push back twice as hard as he got. Them mountains best be cleaned good by this rain, 'cause come the mornin', they're gonna run red with outlaw blood."

The terrible storm raged over the mountains and then trekked east. Before dawn, Smoke was wide awake and looking at a star-filled sky. It was still dark when he broke camp, picked up his heavy pack, and headed down out of the high lonesome to face the ever-growing numbers of bounty hunters and the Lee Slater gang.

"Come on, boys," he muttered to the chattering squirrels and the singing birds. "Let's get this over with. I want to get back to Sally and the Sugarloaf."

A rifle cracked and bark stung the side of his face. Smoke hit the ground, struggled out of his pack, and wormed his way forward, the .44-.40 cradled in his arms.

"I seen him go down!" a man yelled.

"Down is one thing," another voice was added. "Out is another. Jensen's hard to kill."

"Move out," a third voice ordered. "But watch it. He's tricky as a snake."

Three men, Smoke thought. Bounty hunters or outlaws? He didn't know. He didn't really care. Man comes after another man for no valid reason, that first man better be ready to understand that

191

death is walking right along beside him.

"Where is the bastard?" the shout echoed through the lushness of timber.

Smoke saw a flash of color from a red and white checkered shirt, and put a .44-.40 slug in it. The man screamed and went down, kicking and clawing. Lead sang around Smoke's position, whining and howling as fast as the hunters could work the levers on their rifles. Smoke stayed low, and the lead sailed harmlessly over his head.

"Oh, God!" the wounded man moaned. "My shoulder's broke. I can't move my arm."

Smoke watched as a hand reached up and shook a bush, trying to draw his fire. He waited. The hand reached up again and exposed a forearm. Smoke shattered the arm. The man screamed in pain. Smoke fired again, and the man's screaming choked down to silence.

"Back off, John," a voice called. "He's got the upper hand now."

"What about Ned?" a pain-filled voice called.

"Ned's luck ran out."

Ned, Smoke thought. Ned Mallory, probably. A bounty hunter from down New Mexico way. He lay still and listened to the two men back off and move through the brush. After a few minutes, he heard their horses' hooves fade away. He made his way to Ned and stood over the dead man. His first slug had broken the man's forearm; the second slug had taken him in the throat. It had not been a very pleasant way to die. But what way is?

Smoke refilled his .44 loops with the dead man's cartridges and left him where he lay. He was not being unnecessarily callous; this was war, and war is not nice any way one chooses to cut it up.

He figured the shots would draw a crowd, and he headed away from that location, but every direction he walked, he saw riders coming before they saw him.

Smoke cussed under his breath. "All right," he muttered. "If this is the way it's going to be, all bets are off. I can't fight any other way."

He lifted his .44-.40 and blew a man out of the saddle, the slug taking him in the center of his chest.

"Over yonder!" another man yelled, pointing, and Smoke sighted him in. The man moved just as he squeezed the trigger, and that saved his life, the slug hitting his shoulder instead of his chest. The rider managed to stay in the saddle, but he was out of this hunt, his arms dangling uselessly by his side.

A round stung Smoke's shoulder, drawing blood, and another just missed his head. Smoke emptied another saddle, the rider pitched forward, his boot hanging in the stirrup. The horse ran off, dragging the manhunter.

Smoke slipped back into the timber and jogged for several hundred yards before he was forced to stop to catch his breath. He chose a spot where his back and his left flank would be protected and rested. He could hear the sounds of horses laboring up the grade.

"He's trapped!" a man shouted. "We got him now, boys. Let's go." He forced his tired horse up the slope, and Smoke sighted him in, squeezed the trigger, and relieved the nearly exhausted animal of its burden. The hunter bounced on the ground and then lay still.

Smoke drank some water and ate a piece of dry bread and waited. He was in a good spot and thought he saw a way out of it should it come to that. But he didn't think it would. The manhunters would soon realize that the advantage was all his—this time—and probably back off.

After a few minutes, a shout rang up the slope. "Give it up, Jensen! They's a hundred men ringin' this range. You can't get out. Come on down, and we'll take you in alive for trial."

"Sure you will," Smoke muttered.

A man deliberately ran from his cover for a short distance, exposing himself for no more than two or three seconds.

"Fool's play, boys," Smoke whispered. "You must have cut your teeth on amatuers."

He held his fire.

The manhunters began firing indiscriminately, the slugs howling around the rocks and trees. They were trying for a ricochet, not knowing that Smoke had taken that into consideration when he chose the spot to hole up. They wasted a lot of lead and hit nothing.

Another group rode in, and the men began arguing among themselves. Smoke shouted, "Why don't you boys try for the Slater gang? The mountains are full of them. There's about fifty of them, and they're all wanted by the law."

"Nickel and dime re-wards, Jensen," he was told. "You're worth a lot more."

"Look around you," Smoke verbally pointed out. "The ground is covered with the blood of those who thought the same thing. Think about it."

The bounty hunters fell silent as some of them did just that.

Rested, Smoke took that time to slip through the rocks and make his way around his left flank. But

194

he had to leave his heavy pack, taking with him only what he absolutely needed for survival. He packed that in his bedroll and groundsheet, tied it tight, secured it over one shoulder, and Injuned his way out of the rocks.

When he had worked his way several hundred yards above his last location, he paused and looked down. The sight did not fill him with joy. There were at least thirty men in position, grouped in a semicircle, around where the manhunters believed him to be.

A grim smile curved his lips. He took four sticks of dynamite from his roll and planted them under four huge boulders, making each fuse slightly longer than the other. Then he lit the fuses and got the hell gone from there.

The explosives moved three of the huge boulders, sending them cascading down the mountain, picking up small boulders as they tumbled. Even from his high-up location, he could hear the screaming of the men as the boulders, large and small, crushed legs and arms and sent the manhunters scrambling for cover.

"You opened this dance, boys," he said. "Now it's time to pay the band."

"Good God!" Cotton said, as the first of the shot up and avalanche victims came limping and staggering back into town.

Johnny stepped out into the muddy street and halted the parade of wounded. "Where'd you boys tangle with Smoke Jensen?"

A man with a bloody bandage tied around his head said, "Just south of Del Norte Peak. They's a half a dozen men buried under the rocks. Jensen is a devil! He caved them rocks in on us deliberate."

"And I suppose you boys were just ridin' around up there takin' in all the scenery, huh?" Johnny said sarcastically.

The man didn't answer. But his eyes drifted to the badge on Johnny's chest. "You the law. I want to swear out a warrant agin Smoke Jensen."

Johnny laughed at him. "Move on, mister. There's a new doctor just hung out his sign down the street."

"You ain't much of a lawman," another bounty hunter sneered at him. "What's your name?" He spoke around a very badly swollen jaw.

"Johnny North."

The manhunter settled back in his saddle with a sigh and kept his mouth shut.

"Move on," Johnny repeated. "And don't cause any trouble in this town or you'll answer to me."

Cotton and Louis had stepped out, Louis out of his gambling house and Cotton out of the marshal's office to stand on the boardwalk and watch the sorry-looking sight.

Cotton and Johnny joined Louis. "I count twelve in that bunch," Louis said. "Did he say there were half a dozen buried under rocks?"

"Yeah. Smoke musta started a rock slide. Earl said he took a case of dynamite with him. When's Earl gettin' back? I ain't seen him since he rode up to the county seat."

"Today, I would imagine. He said he'd be gone three days. He was going to send some wires. I don't know to whom, but I suspect they concern Smoke."

"You think he really knows the President of the

196

U-nited States?" Cotton asked.

"Oh, he probably does." Louis smiled. "I do."

Smoke reared up from behind the man, jerked the rider off his horse and slammed on to the ground. He hit him three times. Three short vicious right-hand blows that crossed the man's eyes, knocked out several teeth, and left the rider unconscious. Smoke knew the guy slightly. Name of Curt South. He was from Utah, Smoke remembered. A sometimes cowboy, sometimes bounty hunter, sometimes cattle thief, and all around jerk. He released Curt's shirt, and the man fell to the ground, on his back, unconscious. Smoke left him where he lay and swung into the saddle. The stirrups were set too short, but he didn't intend to keep the horse long.

Smoke headed across country, for the deep timber between Bennett Mountain and Silver Mountain. After a hard fifteen minute ride, Smoke reined up and allowed the horse to blow while he inspected the bedroll and saddle bags. The blankets smelled really bad and had fleas hopping around them. He threw them away and kept the ground sheet and canvas shelterhalf. He found a side of bacon wrapped in heavy paper and some potatoes and half a loaf of bread that wasn't too stale. He smashed Curt's rifle against a rock and swung back into the saddle.

Minutes later, he came around a clump of trees and ran right into the outlaw Blackjack Simpson — literally running into him. The two horses collided on the narrow game trail and threw both Lee and Smoke to the ground, knocking the wind out of

197

both of them. Blackjack came up to his knees first and tried to smash Smoke's head in with a rock. Smoke kicked him in the gut and sent the man sprawling.

Guns were forgotten as the two men stood in the narrow trail and slugged it out. Blackjack was unlike most gunmen in that he knew how to use his fists and enjoyed a good fight. He slammed a right against Smoke's head and tried to follow through with a left. Smoke grabbed the man's arm, turned, and threw him to the trail. Blackjack got to his feet, and Smoke busted his beak with a straight right that jarred the man right down to his muddy boots. The blow knocked him backward against a tree.

With the blood flowing from his broken nose, Blackjack came in, both fists swinging. Smoke hit him a left and right combination that glazed the man's eyes and buckled his knees. Smoke followed through, seizing the advantage. He hammered at the man's belly with his big, work-hardened fists, the blows bringing grunts of pain from Blackjack and backing him up.

Smoke's boot struck a rock and threw him off balance. Blackjack grabbed a club from off the ground and tried to smash in Smoke's head. Smoke kicked him in the parts, and Blackjack doubled over, gagging and puking from the boot to his groin.

Smoke grabbed up the broken limb and smacked Blackjack a good one on the side of his head. Blackjack hit the ground and didn't move.

Smoke took the man's guns and smashed them useless, then caught up with the spooked horse. He took Blackjack's .44-.40 from his saddle boot and shucked out the ammo, adding that to his own supply. Then he smashed the rifle against a tree.

He knew he should kill Blackjack; the man was a murderer, rapist, bank robber, and anything else a body could name that was low-down and no-good.

But he just couldn't bring himself to shoot the man.

Trouble was, he didn't know what the hell to do with him.

"Can't do it, can you, Jensen?" Blackjack gasped out the words.

"Do what, Blackjack?" Smoke backed up and sat down on a fallen log.

"You can't shoot me, can you?"

"I'm not a murderer."

"That'll get you killed someday, Jensen." The man tried to get to his feet, and Smoke left the log and kicked him in the head.

Smoke took Blackjack's small poke of food from his saddlebags, cut Blackjack's cinch strap and slapped the horse on the rump. He swung into his saddle and looked at the unconscious outlaw.

"I should kill you, Blackjack. But I just can't do it. If I did that, I'd be across the line and joined up with the likes of you. God forbid I should ever enjoy killing."

He rode into the timber, straight for trouble.

Chapter Sixteen

Those men who came into Rio thinking the hunt for Smoke Jensen would be no more than a lark took one last look at those manhunters who staggered out of the mountains and hauled their ashes out of the country.

With their departing, they left behind them only the hardcases of the bounty hunting profession. Men who gave no thought to a person's innocence or guilt. Men who were there only for the money.

"Amazing," Earl said, gazing at the ever-growing number of manhunters converging on the town. "The mountains are full of members of the Lee Slater gang—all with a price on their heads—and these dredges of society would willingly consort with them to get to Smoke."

"There isn't much to them," Louis agreed. "I've seen their kind all over the West. Most lawmen don't like them, and few decent members of society have anything more than contempt for them. But I suppose in some instances, they do provide a service for the common good."

"Name one," Johnny said sourly.

"I would be hard-pressed to do so," Louis admitted. He cut his eyes. "Well, now. Would you just look at this."

The men looked up the street. Luttie Charles and

his crew were riding in, and his crew had swelled considerably. The men of the Seven Slash turned in toward the marshal's office, where Earl and the other 'deputies' were standing on the boardwalk. The men sat their saddles and stared at the quartet.

"Loaded for bear," Cotton whispered, taking in the bulging saddlebags and bedrolls.

"Yeah," Johnny said. "I got a hunch this ain't no good news for Smoke."

"I am here to announce our intentions, gentlemen," Luttie said.

Earl stared at the man, saying nothing.

"Smoke Jensen is a wanted man, correct?" Luttie asked, his smile more a nasty smirk.

"That is, unfortunately, correct," the Englishman acknowledged.

"That being the case," Luttie said, "we have come to offer our services toward the cause of law and order."

"Like I said," Johnny whispered. "No good news for Smoke."

"We want this to be legal and above board," Luttie said. "So we came to the appointed law first."

"Get to the point," Cotton said bluntly.

"We are going into the mountains to bring back the murderer Smoke Jensen," Luttie spoke around his smirky smile.

"Dead or alive," Jake said.

The Karl Brothers, Rod and Randy, giggled. Both of them were about four bricks shy of a load, and were men who enjoyed killing.

Johnny spat on the ground to show his contempt for the goofy pair.

Rod grinned at him. "If you wasn't wearin' that tin star, I'd call you out for that, North."

Johnny reached up, unpinned the badge, and put it in his pocket. "Then make your play, you stupid-lookin' punk."

"No!" Luttie's command was sharply given. "We have no quarrel with the law, and that's an order."

Rod relaxed and grinned at Johnny. "Some other time, North."

"I'm easy to find, goofy."

"Anything else you gentlemen need to know before we pull out?" Luttie asked.

"That about does it, I suppose," Earl told him.

"Ain't you lawmen gonna wish us luck?" One-Eyed Jake asked.

"Personally, I hope you fall off your horse and break your damn neck," Cotton told him.

"You ain't got no call to talk to me like that!" Jake protested.

"You wanna do something about it?" Cotton challenged.

"Let's ride, boys," Luttie said. "We got a killer to bring to justice."

"Maybe later," One-Eyed Jake said.

"Anytime," Cotton told him.

The Seven Slash crew and the hired guns who rode among them slopped out up the muddy street.

"Sixteen more after Smoke's hide," Johnny spoke the words bitterly. "Smoke's gonna need all the luck and skill he can muster to come out of this alive."

"How about them wires you sent, Earl?" Cotton asked.

Earl shook his head. "The marshal's service is out of it. But until a panel of federal judges can gather and review all the evidence against Smoke, the warrants stand."

"Damn!" Louis said.

"Quite," the Englishman said. "And Sheriff Silva said if we went into the mountains to help Smoke, there would be warrants issued for us. He said he was sorry about that, but that was the way it had to be."

"I can understand that," Johnny said. "He's stickin' his neck out pretty far for Smoke now."

Louis looked toward the mountains. "We've all been concentrating on how Smoke is doing. I wonder how Sally is coping with all this?"

"Sally's gone!" Bountiful yelled, bringing her buggy to a dusty, sliding halt.

"What?" Sheriff Monte Carson jumped out of his chair. "What do the hands say?"

"I finally got one of them to talk. He said he took her down to the road day before yesterday, and she hailed the stage there. He said she had packed some riding britches in her trunk, along with a rifle and a pistol. She was riding the stage down to the railroad and taking a train from there. Train runs all the way through to the county seat. Lord, Lord, Monte, she's just about there by now. What are we going to do?"

Monte led her into his office and sat her down. Bountiful fanned herself vigorously. He got her a drink of water and sat down at his desk. "Nothin' we can do, Miss Bountiful. Sally's gone to stand by her man. And them damn outlaws and manhunters down yonder think they got trouble with Smoke. I feel sorry for them if they tangle with Miss Sally. You know she can shoot just like a man and has done so plenty of times. She's a crack shot with rifle and pistol. Smoke seen to that."

"I just feel terrible about this. I should have guessed something was up when I saw her oiling up that .44 the other day. But out here . . . well, we all keep guns at the ready."

"T'wasn't your fault, Miss Bountiful. She's doin' what she feels she has to do, is all." He took off his hat and wiped his forehead with a bandana. "This situation is gettin' out of hand."

Lee Slater and his bunch came upon Blackjack just as he was getting back on his feet. The man's face was swollen from the kick he'd received from Smoke. That kick had put him out for nearly half an hour.

"Cut my cinch and smashed my guns," Blackjack mumbled. "I'm gonna kill that dirty bastard!"

"There's a lot of people been sayin' that," Ed told him. "So far the score is Jensen about fifteen and the other side zero. And we're the other side."

Someone rounded up a horse for Blackjack and loaned him a spare gun. Blackjack swung the horse's head.

"Where are you goin'!" Lee shouted.

"To kill Smoke Jensen," Blackjack snarled. "And this time I'm gonna do it."

Lee started to protest. Curt waved him silent. "Let him go. You know how he is. When he gets mad, he's crazy. Hell, we're better off without him until he cools down."

" 'Spose he gets to Jensen afore we do?" Ed asked.

"They'll be one less to share the re-ward money with," Curly said. "Blackjack ain't gonna take Jensen; 'lessen he shoots him in the back."

"Let's make some coffee," Ed suggested. "I could do me with some rest."

None among them had considered how, as wanted outlaws, they would collect any reward money should they manage to capture Smoke.

Nearly everyone on Main Street had seen the elegantly dressed lady step off the train and stroll to the hotel, a porter carrying her trunk. As soon as she signed her name, the desk clerk dispatched a boy to run fetch the sheriff.

Sally had signed the register as "Mrs. Smoke Jensen."

Sheriff Silva was standing in the lobby, talking to several men, and he nearly swallowed his chewing tobacco when Sally walked down the stairs.

She was wearing cowboy boots and jeans—which she filled out to the point of causing the men's eyeballs to bug out—a denim shirt which fitted her quite nicely too, and was carrying a leather jacket. She had a bandana tied around her throat, and a low crowned, flat-brimmed hat on her head. She also wore a .44 belted around her waist and carried a short-barreled .44 carbine, a bandoleer of ammo slung around one shoulder.

"Jesus Christ, Missus Jensen!" Sheriff Silva hollered. "I mean, holy cow. What do you think you're gonna do?"

"Take a ride," Sally told him, and walked out the door.

Silva ran to catch up with her. "Now you just wait a minute, here, Missus Jensen. This ain't no fittin' country for a female to be a-traipsin' around in. Will you please slow down?"

Sally ignored that and kept right on walking at a rather brisk pace.

She turned into the general store and was uncommonly blunt with the man who owned the store. "I want provisions for five days, including food, coffee, pots and pans and eating utensils, blankets, ground sheets, and tent. And five boxes of .44s, too. Have them ready on a pack-frame in fifteen minutes. Have them loaded out back, please."

"Now you just hold up on that order, Henry," Sheriff Silva said.

"You'd better not cross me, Henry," Sally warned him, a wicked glint in her eyes. "My name is Mrs. Smoke Jensen, and I can shoot damn near as well as my husband."

"Yes'um," Henry said. "I believe you, ma'am."

"And you," Sally spun around to face the sheriff, "would be advised to keep your nose out of my business."

"Yes'um," Silva said glumly, and followed her to the livery.

Sally picked out a mean-eyed blue steele that bared its teeth when the man tried to put a rope around it. Sally walked out into the corral, talked to the big horse for a moment, and then led it back to the barn. She fed him a carrot and an apple she'd picked up at the store, and the horse was hers.

"That there's a stallion, ma'am!" Silva bellered. "He ain't been cut. You can't ride no stallion!"

"Get out of my way," she told him.

"It ain't decent, ma'am!"

"Shut up and take that pack animal around to the back of the store."

"Yes'um," Silva said. "Whatever you say, ma'am." While Sally was saddling up, he turned to the hostler. "Send a boy with a fast horse to Rio. Tell them deputies of mine down there that Sally Jensen is pullin' out within the hour and looks like she's plannin' on joinin' up with her husband. Tell them to do something. Anything!"

"Sheriff," the hostler said, horror in his voice. "Don't look. She's a-fixin' to ride that hoss astride!"

"Lord, have mercy! What's this world comin' to?"

"Looking for me, boys?" Smoke called.

Crocker and Graham spun around, dropping their coffee cups, and grabbing for iron.

But Smoke was not playing the gentleman's game. His hands were already filled with .44s. He began firing, firing and cocking with such speed the sounds seemed to be a continuous roll of deadly thunder. Crocker literally died on his feet, two slugs in his heart. Graham was turned completely around twice before he tumbled to the earth. He died with his eyes open, flat on his back and staring upward.

Smoke reloaded, listened for a moment, and then walked to the fire, eating the lunch and drinking the coffee the outlaws had fixed and no longer needed.

He drank the pot of coffee, kicked out the fire and left his tired horse to roll and water and graze, throwing a saddle on a fresh horse that was tied to a picket pin. He took what was left of a chunk of stale bread, sopped out the grease in the frying pan to soften it up, and finished off his lunch.

He looked at Crocker and Graham. "Nothing personal, boys. You just took the wrong trail, that's all." He swung into the saddle and put the camp of the dead behind him. Ray's group came upon the

207

bodies of Crocker and Graham and sat their horses for a time, looking around the silent camp.

"I'd like to think they et a good meal 'fore Jensen or that damned ol' Charlie Starr come up on them," Keno said. "But if I was to bet on it, I'd wager that Jensen kilt 'em and then sat down an' et their food." He shook his head. "We're gonna lose this fight, boys. Somebody is shore to get lead in Jensen, least the odds lean thataway, but in the end, we'll lose."

Sonny shook his head. "It just ain't possible what he's a-doin'. By rights, we should have kilt him the first day or two. This makes nearabouts ten of us he's kilt—and half a dozen or more bounty hunters—and we ain't got no clear shot at him yet. I just ain't likin' this, boys."

Jerry nodded his head in agreement. "I got me a bad feelin' in my guts about this fight. But, hell, way I see it, we ain't got no choice 'cept to go on with it."

Ray swung down from the saddle. "Let's give the boys a buryin'. Stoke up that far, McKay, make some coffee."

"We got no quarrel with you, Charlie," Luttie told the old gunfighter. "It's Jensen we're after."

Charlie had stepped out of the timber, blocking the trail. His hands were by his side, by the butts of his guns, and his eyes were hard and unblinking. "You got a quarrel with Smoke, you got a quarrel with me. That's the way it is. So I hope you made your peace with God." He jerked iron and opened the dance.

Two of Luttie's hands went down before anyone could react to the sudden gunfire. Horses were rear-ing and screaming in fright; several of the riders were dumped from the saddle. Charlie shot Nick Johnson between the eyes, and he fell over against Luttie, knocking the man from the saddle and falling on top of him in the brush.

Charlie took a round in his side, flinched from the painful impact, jerked out two spare six-guns from behind his gunbelt and kept on throwing lead.

A young hand who fancied himself a gunslick pulled iron and jacked the hammer back. One of Charlie's slugs caught him in the chest and knocked him to the ground. He died calling for his mother.

Charlie's left leg folded under him as a .45 hit him in the thigh. He went down rolling into the brush. Just as he got to his boots and staggered off into the timber, toward his horse, he turned and blew another of Luttie's hired guns out of the saddle. Ted Danforth took the slug in the belly and hit the ground. He died on his knees.

Charlie managed to get into the saddle and point his horse's head south, toward Rio.

"No need to chase after him, Luttie," Jake said, after the spooked and screaming horses had been settled down. "He's had it. I seen him take at least three slugs. He's dead in the saddle by now."

Luttie looked around him at the carnage. "That old bastard just jumped out and killed five of my men. I ain't believin' this!" He was rubbing the bump on his head where his noggin hit a rock. "I started out with sixteen top guns, and my people has been cut damn near a third in less than a minute and a half. Jesus Christ!"

"But now Smoke is alone up here," One-Eyed Jake pointed out.

"Wonderful," Luttie said sourly.

* * *

Blackjack reined up when he spotted the ground-reined horse. That wasn't the horse Smoke had been riding, but he could have changed horses somewhere along the way. Blackjack stepped down from the saddle and took cover behind a tree, his eyes sweeping the area in front of him. He should have been looking behind him.

Blackjack was so mad he wasn't thinking straight. His head ached where Smoke had kicked him, and his nose and mouth hurt, too. All he could think about was killing Smoke Jensen. And he didn't want to do it quick, neither. He wanted Jensen to suffer. He had plans for Smoke Jensen. Painful plans.

But a higher power had already checked off Blackjack's name in the book of life.

"You should have stayed where I left you, Blackjack," Smoke said from behind the outlaw.

Blackjack whirled around, a curse on his lips and his right hand filled with a .45. Smoke shot him twice, in the belly and the chest as the .44 rose in recoil.

Blackjack sighed once and fell back against the tree he'd thought was giving him cover. The .45 fell from his numbed hand. "Damn you, Jensen!" he gasped.

"Sometimes the cards just don't fall right," Smoke told him.

The light was fading around Blackjack.

"Any family?" Smoke asked.

"None that would give a damn about me dyin'."

"Too bad."

"You're a . . . devil, Jensen! You musta . . . come here from somewhere's outta hell." His legs

210

would no longer support him. He slumped to the ground.

Smoke kicked the .45 far from Blackjack's reach and walked toward his horse, reloading as he walked. Blackjack's voice stopped him.

"Yes?" he asked.

"Stay with me 'til I'm gone, Jensen—please?"

"All right," Smoke said.

Smoke walked to him, reached down, and took the .41 derringer Blackjack had slipped from behind his big silver beltbuckle. Blackjack let his hand fall to his side.

"Damn you!" the outlaw moaned. "How'd you know?"

"I didn't. But people like you never change." He broke open the derringer and checked the loads. Full. He slipped the tiny gambler's back-up behind his belt.

"I'll see you in hell, Jensen!"

"Maybe. I've done some things that probably qualify me for that place."

Blackjack fell over on his side. "We was all so shore about this. Fifty, sixty . . . of us. One of you. I just cain't understand it." He shuddered and grabbed the ground in his pain. "What is it that . . . makes you so damn hard to kill?"

"Maybe it's because I'm right, and you boys are wrong."

Blackjack laughed bitterly.

"You got any money you want me to give to a church or an orphanage, Blackjack?"

Blackjack sneered past bloody lips and said some pretty terrible things about churches, orphans, the public in general and Smoke in particular.

He died with a curse on his lips.

"I don't understand it either, Blackjack," Smoke said to the dead outlaw.

Smoke stripped the saddle and bridle from Blackjack's horse and turned the gelding loose. "Run free for a time, boy. You earned it."

The last mountain man walked to his horse and swung into the saddle. "Let's go meet what I was born to meet, boy," he said. "No point in prolonging this."

Chapter Seventeen

"What?" Earl almost lost his English cool.

"That's what the sheriff said," the young man told him. "Missus Sally Jensen is headin' into the mountains."

Louis took off his badge and handed it to Earl. "I hereby resign my commission," he told him. "The rest of you stay here. I've got to get into the mountains and head her off."

"Look!" a citizen said, pointing up the muddy street.

"That's Charlie!" Johnny shouted, running toward the man who appeared to be unconscious in the saddle.

"Get the doctor!" Cotton yelled, running after Johnny.

They gently took Charlie from the blood-soaked saddle and laid him down on the boardwalk. Charlie's eyes fluttered open. "I'm hard hit, boys."

"You'll make it, you old war-hoss," Johnny told him.

"I put about five or six of 'em down 'fore they plugged me," the old gunfighter said. "Seven Slash bunch."

"Don't talk, Charlie," Lilly LaFevere said, kneeling down beside him.

213

"Hello, baby," Charlie grinned up at her. "I ain't seen you in ten years."

"Nine," she corrected him. "We was down on the border. Now hush your mouth."

"Tired," Charlie whispered. "Awful tired."

"Take him to my quarters and put him in my bed," Lilly told the men. "Move him gentle like. I count three bullet holes in his ornery old hide." She looked around her. "Where's that goddamn sawbones?"

"He's on the way," a citizen said. "Is that really Charlie Starr?"

"Yeah," Lilly said. "Now get the hell outta the way and give the man room to breathe."

"I'm gone," Louis said. "See you boys later."

"You got enough grub?" Cotton asked.

"They'll be food in the saddlebags of the outlaws," Louis told him. "I'll have a week's supply fifteen minutes after I hit the mountains."

He lifted the reins and was gone.

With his knife and strips of rawhide, Smoke made a pack out of two saddlebags, then carefully repacked all the supplies he'd taken from several dead men. He had a good five days' food and plenty of ammo.

He tried not to think about when his luck was going to run out.

But he knew it would, sooner or later. The odds were just too great against him.

He was only a few miles away from where he'd left his horses—as the crow flies—but he didn't want to head there, just yet. He stripped saddle and bridle from his borrowed horse and turned it loose to roll and water and graze. Then he picked up his pack and rifle and headed into the deep timber, to a place he remembered when roaming the country with old Preacher.

"You may get me, boys," he said to the sighing winds and the soaring eagles high above him. "But you'll pay a fearful price before you do."

"Scum," Louis said to the two riders.

"Huh?" one asked.

"I said you're scum," Louis repeated.

Stan and Glover had gotten separated from Noah's group. They'd been wandering around in circles when they came upon the tall, well-built man dressed all in black. Kind of a dudey lookin' fellow — except for those guns of his. They looked well-used. And his coat was brushed back to give him free access to the Colts. He was just standing in the middle of the trail, smiling sort of strange-like. Now he was insulting them.

"Git out of the way, fancy-pants!" Glover told him.

"I like it here."

"Well, you about a stupid feller, then. I might decide to just run you down with this here horse. What do you think about that?"

Louis smiled. "I think your blow-hole is over-loading your mouth, punk."

Glover and Stan exchanged glances. It just seemed like nothin' had worked out right since they'd left the West coast and come to Colorado. All them hayseeds and hicks out in the rural areas of the coast states knowed who the Lee Slater gang was, and they kowtowed and done what they was told. But it seemed like that ever since they'd come to Colorado, all that was happenin' was they

215

was gettin' the crap shot out of them. And nobody seemed to be afraid of them.

"You a bounty hunter, mister?" Stan asked.

"You might say that. I hunt punks. And it looks like I found me a couple."

"I'm gettin' tarred of you in-sultin' me!" Glover popped off.

"Yeah," Stan flapped his mouth. "We're lookin' for Smoke Jensen so's we can collect the re-ward money."

"You dumb clucks," Louis said with a chuckle. "You're part of the Lee Slater gang. You're all wanted men, with bounties on your own heads. How in the devil do you think you're going to collect any reward money?"

Stan and Glover exchanged another look. That hadn't occurred to either of them.

"Uhhh . . ." Glover said.

"Well . . ." Stan said.

"Get off your horses, throw your guns in the bushes, and start walking," Louis told them.

Stan told him what he could do with his orders. Sideways.

Louis shot him. His draw was like a blur and totally unexpected. Stan pitched from the saddle, and Louis turned his gun toward Glover just as the outlaw was jerking iron. Louis waited; a slight smile on his lips as the man cursed and jacked back the hammer.

That was as far as he got before Louis drilled him dead center in the chest, the slug knocking the outlaw out of the saddle, dead before he hit the ground. Quite unlike him, Louis twirled his six-shooter twice before dropping it back in leather.

"Punks," he said scornfully.

He went through their saddlebags and took out bacon, potatoes, bread, onions, and coffee. Fortunately, he did have with him his own coffee pot and small frying pan. The one he took from Stan's saddlebag was so coated with old grease and other odious and unidentifiable specks it was probably contagious just by touch. With a grimace of disgust, Louis tossed it into the bushes.

He stripped both horses of saddle and bridle and turned them loose, then swung back into the saddle and headed out. He did not look back at the dead outlaws lying sprawled on the trail.

It was nearing dusk when Al Martine and his bunch spotted Smoke high up near the timber line in the big lonesome.

"We got him, boys!" Al yelled, and put the spurs to his tired horse.

A rifle bullet took Al's hat off and sent it spinning away. The mountain winds caught it, and it was gone forever.

"Goddamn!" Al yelled, just as another round kicked up dirt at his horse's hooves, and the animal started bucking. It was all Al could do to stay in the saddle.

A slug smacked Zack in the shoulder and nearly knocked him from the saddle. The second shot tore off the saddle horn and smashed into Zack's upper thigh, bringing a scream of pain from the outlaw.

"He's got help!" Pedro yelled. "Let's get gone from here."

The outlaws raced for cover, with Zack flopping

around in the saddle.

Smoke looked down the mountain. "Now who in the devil is that?" he muttered.

Sally punched .44 rounds into her carbine and settled back into her well-hidden little camp in a narrow depression with the back and one side a solid rock wall.

"Who you reckon that was a-shootin' at us?" Tom Post yelled over the sounds of galloping horses.

"I don't know," Crown returned the yell. "But he's hell with a rifle, whoever he is."

Using field glasses, Sally watched them beat a hasty retreat, and then laid out cloth and cup, plate and tableware, and napkin for her early supper. Just because one was in the wilderness, surrounded by Godless heathens, was no reason to forego small amenities.

She opened a can of beans, set aside a can of peaches for dessert, and spread butter on a thick slice of bread. Before eating, she said a prayer for the continuing safety of her man.

"Hello the far!" the voice came out of the timber.

Louis edged back into the shadows and lifted his Colt. "If you're friendly, come on in."

"I reckon we're friendly," came the call. Two men stepped into the small clearing. "We're all in this together, a-huntin' that damn Smoke Jensen. Share your coffee, friend?"

"Why, certainly!" Louis called out cheerfully. "Step right on in, boys."

"Kind of you." The men stepped closer. "I'm

Nick Reeves, and this is my partner, Mike Beecham."

Louis knew them both. No-goods from down near the Four Corners.

"What might your name be, mister?" Mike asked, squatting down by the small fire. "I think I know the voice, but I cain't hardly see you in them shadows."

"Louis Longmont, you cretin!"

Both men yelled, cussed, and grabbed for iron. Louis had both hands filled with .44s, and the campsite thundered with shots, the moist evening air filling with gray smoke.

Louis reloaded then dragged the bodies away, heaving them over a small cliff. He went through their saddlebags and found more food, a goodly amount of .44 ammo, and some stinking socks and dirty longhandles. He kept the food and the ammo and turned their horses loose after relieving them of saddle and bridle. He returned to his fire and slowly ate his supper, scoured out his pan and plate, then broke camp and moved on about a mile, before bedding down for the night.

"Got more bounty hunters in the mountains than boys left in the gang," Lee Slater said glumly. He sat staring into the flames of the campfire and sucking on a bottle of rye whiskey.

His brother, Luttie, sat across the fire from him, equally morose. He took a drink from his bottle and wondered how all this was going to turn out. The shock of losing five of his men in a matter of seconds earlier that day still had not entirely left him. He wondered if his boys had man-

219

aged to get enough lead in that damned ol' Charlie Starr to kill him. He doubted it.

"Twelve dead, last count," Lee said. "Six wounded. And you lost five of your boys to Starr."

"You don't have to keep reminding me," Luttie said sourly. "This wouldn't have happened if you had kept a tight rein on your boys. The dumbest damn thing you did was attackin' Big Rock and shootin' up the place. The second dumbest thing you done was shootin' Smoke Jensen's wife. And the third dumbest thing you done is torturin' and rapin' and killin' that family up north of here."

"Aw, shut up!" Lee told him.

"Don't tell me to shut up! I told you to come straight here and stay out of trouble on the way. We could have had it all, Lee. We could have taken a million dollars worth of gold and silver from the miners and stages and banks and done been gone from this damn place. But, oh, hell, no. You had to surround yourself with idiots and screw it all up."

"If he's talkin' about idiots, he must be talkin' about you boys," Lopez said to the Karl Brothers.

Rod gave him a dirty look, and Randy gave him an obscene gesture.

"We got Smoke to the north of us," Curt said. "A damn good rifleman to the East of us, and it looks like Louis Longmont is to the south of us."

"And a bunch of U.S. Marshals camped at the edge of the mountains," Dale pointed out.

"Maybe it's time to haul out of here," Max suggested.

"I'll be damned!" Lee snarled at him. "Good God, people! Countin' Luttie's bunch, they's nearly fifty of us left, all told, and we're lettin'

220

two or three people whup us. What the hell's the matter with you? No one or two people ain't never whupped fifty people. We're doin' somethin' wrong, is all. We got to study this out and find out what it is."

"Smoke Jensen and Louis Longmont ain't no average two people," Al Martine pointed out. "And that rifleman that hit us this afternoon wasn't no pilgrim, neither. Now you think about this—all of you: hittin' Rio is out the winder. They'd shoot us to pieces in ten seconds. The miners has all shut down and gone into town; they ain't diggin' no gold, and they shore ain't shippin' none. The county seat is out of the pitcher; Sheriff Silva ain't no man to fool with. So where the hell does that leave us?"

"My ass hurts!" Bud complained.

"He's up there," Ace Reilly said, his eyes looking at the timber line. Good light of morning, the air almost cold this high up.

Big Bob Masters shifted his chew from one side of his mouth to the other and spat. "Solid rock to his back," he observed. "And two hundreds yards of open country ever'where else. It'd be suicide gettin' up there."

Ace lifted his canteen to take a drink, and the canteen exploded in his hand, showering him with water, bits of metal, and numbing his hand. The second shot nicked Big Bob's horse on the rump, and the animal went pitching and snorting and screaming down the slope, Big Bob yelling and hanging on and flopping in the saddle. The third shot took off part of Causey's ear, and he left the

221

saddle, crawling behind some rocks.

"Jesus Christ!" Ace hollered, leaving the saddle and finding cover. "Where the hell is that comin' from?"

Big Bob's horse had come to a very sudden and unexpected halt, and Big Bob went flying ass over elbows out of the saddle to land against a tree. He staggered to his feet, looking wildly around him, and took a .44 slug in the belly. He sank to his knees, both hands holding his punctured belly, bellering in pain.

"He's right on top of us," Ace called to Nap. "Over there at the base of that rock face."

Smoke was hundreds of yards up the mountain, just at the timber line, looking and wondering who his new ally might be. He got his field glasses and began sweeping the area. A slow smile curved his lips.

"I married a Valkyrie, for sure," he muttered, as the long lenses made out Sally's face.

He saw riders coming hard, a lot of riders. Smoke grabbed up his .44-.40 and began running down the mountain, keeping to the timber. The firing had increased as the riders dismounted and sought cover. Smoke stayed a good hundred yards above them, and so far he had not been spotted.

"Causey!" Woody yelled. "Over yonder!" he pointed. "Get on his right flank — that's exposed."

Causey jumped up, and Smoke drilled him through and through. Causey died sprawled on the still damp rocks from the misty morning in the high lonesome.

"He's up above us!" Ray yelled.

"Who the hell is that over yonder?" Noah hollered, just as Sally fired. The slug sent bits of rock into Noah's face, and he screamed as he was momentarily blinded. He stood up, and Smoke nailed him through the neck. Smoke had been aiming for his chest, but shooting downhill is tricky, even for a marksman.

Big Bob Masters was hollering and screaming, afraid to move, afraid his guts would fall out.

Smoke began dusting the area where the outlaws and bounty hunters had left their horses. The whining slugs spooked them and off they ran, reins trailing, taking food, water, and extra ammo with them.

"Goddamnit!" Woody yelled, running after them. He suddenly stopped, right out in the open, realizing what a stupid move that had been.

Smoke and Sally fired at the same time. One slug struck Woody in the side, the .44-.40 hit him in the chest. Woody had no further use for a horse.

Smoke plugged Yancey in the shoulder, knocking the man down and putting him out of the fight. Yancey began crawling downhill toward the horses, staying to cover. He had but two thoughts in mind: getting in the saddle and getting the hell gone from this place.

"It's no good!" Ace yelled. "They'll pick us all off if we stay here. We got to get out of range. Start makin' your way down the slope."

The outlaws and bounty hunters began crawling back, staying to cover. Smoke and Sally held their fire, neither of them having a clear target and not wanting to waste ammo. They took that time to take a drink of water, eat a biscuit, and wait.

Haynes, Dale, and Yancey were the first to reach the horses, well out of range of the guns of

Smoke and Sally.

Haynes looked up, horror in his eyes. A man dressed all in black was standing by a tree, his hands filled with Colts.

"Hello, punk!" Louis Longmont said, and opened fire.

Chapter Eighteen

The last memory Haynes had, and it would have to last him an eternity, was the guns of Louis Longmont belching fire and smoke. He died sitting on his butt, his back to a boulder. Yancey tried to lift his rifle, and Louis shot him twice in the belly. Dale turned to run, and Louis offered him no quarter. The first slug cut his spine, the second slug caught him falling and took off part of his head.

Louis reloaded his Colts, then picked up his rifle and took cover.

"We yield!" Nap Jacobs yelled.

"Not in this game," Louis called.

"Somebody come hep me!" Big Bob Masters squalled. "I cain't stand the pain!"

The pinned-down gunmen looked at each other. There were four of them left. Nap Jacobs, Ace Reilly, and two of Slater's boys, Kenny and Summers.

All knew Big Bob Masters was not long for this world. His yelling was growing weaker.

"I ain't done you no hurt, Longmont!" Ace yelled. "You got no call to horn in on this play."

"But here I am," Louis said. "Make your peace with God."

The silent dead littered the mountain battlefield. Below them, an outlaw's horse pawed the ground, the steel hoof striking rock.

"And I don't know who you is over yonder in the rocks," Nap yelled. "But I wish you'd bow out."

"I'm Mrs. Smoke Jensen!" Sally called.

"Dear God in Heaven," Ace said. "We been took down by a damn skirt!"

"Disgustin'!" Nap said.

Kenny looked wild-eyed all around him. He was mumbling under his breath. His eyes held a touch of madness, and he was breathing hard, his chest heaving. Drool leaked from his mouth. "I'm gone," he said, and jumped up.

Three rifles barked at once, all the slugs striking true. Kenny was slammed backward, two holes in his chest and one hole in the center of his forehead.

Nap looked over at Ace. "This ain't no cakewalk, Ace. We forgot about Smoke's reputation once the battle starts."

"Yeah," Ace said, his voice low. "Once folks come after him, he don't leave nobody standin'."

"I got an idea. Listen." Nap tied a dirty bandana around the barrel of his rifle and waved it. "I'm standin' up, people!" he shouted, taking his guns from leather and dropping them on the ground. "I walk out of here, and I'm gone from this country, and I don't come back." He looked at Ace. "You with me?"

"All the way—if they'll let us leave."

"I ain't playin', Ace. If they let us go, I'm gone far and long."

"My word on it."

"How about it, Jensen?" Nap shouted.

"It's all right with me," Smoke returned the shout. "But if I see you again, anyplace, anytime, and you're wearing a gun, I'll kill the both of you.

226

That's a promise."

"Let's go," Nap said. "I always did want to see what's east of the Mississippi."

The three of them shifted locations, leaving the dead bodies behind them. They knew all those shots would soon bring other troublehunters on the run.

Louis reached out to stroke the blue steele's head, and the stallion almost took some fingers off. Louis got his hand out of the way just in time.

"Vicious brute!" he said.

The stallion walled his eyes and showed Louis his big teeth.

"Gentle as a baby," Sally said, giving him a carrot.

The stallion took the carrot as gently as a house pet.

"We've got to get Sally out of here," Smoke said.

"I concur," Louis said. "However . . ."

"You can both go straight to hell!" she cut off Louis' words. "I didn't travel two hundred and fifty miles from the Sugarloaf to sit in some hotel room. I came to stand by my man, and that's exactly what I intend to do."

Smoke shrugged. "You were about to say, Louis? . . ."

"That it might not be possible to get Sally out of the mountains. Bounty hunters and assorted other crud and punks were still pouring into town when I left. We cut the odds down some today, but I'll wager that double that number came into the mountains."

Smoke had taken a big, tough-looking horse from the mounts that the dead would no longer need.

They had all carried food in their saddlebags, so that problem, at least, was solved. They had plenty of coffee and ammo as well.

"If we could just find a place to hole up until those warrants are lifted," Smoke said wistfully. He was weary of the killing. Weary of the blood and pain and sweat and tension.

Louis shook his head. "No, my friend. That wouldn't stop most of them. The blood lust is high and hot now. They're like hungry predators on a blood scent."

Smoke drained his coffee cup and tossed the dredges. "Let's get moving. We've got to find a place that we can defend."

"He'll make it," the young doctor said, stepping out of the room and gently closing the door behind him. "That is one tough man in there."

Charlie Starr was sleeping with the aid of some laudanum.

The doctor dropped three chunks of lead on the table. "I dug one out of his leg, one out of his side, and another was lodged in his arm. Another bullet grazed his head. He'll have a frightful headache for a time, and a hat would be uncomfortable, but he'll be flat on his back a long time before he needs a hat."

"Don't you bet on that," Lilly told him. "That's a warhoss in there in my bed." She grinned wickedly. "And it ain't the first time he's been in my bed." The doctor blushed. "I've wore him down to a frazzle a time or two myself. You got any pills you want me give him?"

"You're staying with him?"

"Night and day until I'm sure he's all right."

Earl stepped into the room. "You've got to see this, Johnny," he said. "You might never see another sight like it."

Johnny walked outside and stood with Earl and Cotton, staring at the lawyer Larry Tibbson. Larry had bought himself some cowboy clothes, from hat to boots, and was wearing two pearl-handled .45s and carrying a Winchester rifle. There was a bandoleer of ammo looped across his chest.

"He wants to be a deputy," Earl said.

"Boy," Johnny said, after he recovered from his shock at the sight. "Are you tryin' to get yourself killed?"

"I am going into the mountain to aid Miss Sally," Larry said stiffly.

"Miss Sally don't need no aid from you," Johnny bluntly told him. "Boy, if you go blundering around up in them mountains, you probably gonna get lost and eat up by a bear. That's the best way you might leave this world. The worst is gettin' taken alive by them outlaws and havin' them stick your bare feet in a fire for the fun of it."

"I am perfectly capable of taking care of myself," Larry informed him. "I'll have you know that I belong to the New York City Pistol Club, am a very good shot, and have been duck-hunting many, many times."

"That's good, Lawyer. Dandy," Cotton said. "I'm proud of your accomplishments. But have you ever faced a man who was shootin' at you? And plugged him?"

"Heavens, no!"

The men stood for fifteen minutes, begging and pleading with Larry to give up his plan. He stood

229

firm. Finally Earl sighed. "Go get me a badge, Cotton. We'll swear him in. That might give him some edge."

"Get him killed," Cotton said. He stepped off the boardwalk and paused, looking back. "I seen Mills in town just before the stage run. Did he say anything to any of you? He looked sort of jumpy to me. Excited, I guess it was."

"No," Earl said. "I saw him. He met the stage and was gone before I could talk to him. And I wanted to tell him about Charlie."

"I wonder what he's got up his sleeve?"

"I shall endeavor to join with that stalwart group," Larry said.

"Whatever that means," Cotton said, walking off.

"Here they are," Mills said excitedly, jumping from his horse. "The warrants on the Lee Slater gang. Saddle up, men! We're riding for the deep timber."

The men broke camp quickly and were in the saddle within fifteen minutes.

"We've got a few hours of daylight left," Mills said. "We'll get in close and camp, hit the outlaws at first light."

"Ah . . . Mills, we don't know where they are," Albert pointed out.

"We'll follow the sounds of shooting," Mills spoke the words in a grim tone. "And we'll put a stop to it before it can escalate further."

The marshals exchanged glances.

"Pin your badges to your jackets," Mills ordered. "These men have got to learn to respect the law."

"And you think these badges are going to do

that?" Moss asked.

"Certainly!"

"Right," Winston said, with about as much enthusiasm as a man going to his own hanging.

Larry was dismayed when he could not find a proper English riding saddle anywhere in town. But he was not discouraged. He left town armed to the teeth, sitting in a Western rig, bobbing up and down in the saddle as he had been taught. The horse wore a very curious expression on its face.

"He's gonna get killed," Cotton predicted.

"Maybe not," Earl said. "Men like that seem to lead a charmed life. But there is one thing for certain: he won't be the same man coming out as he is going in."

Not a single shot was fired in anger the rest of that day. When the news of the shoot-up on the slopes reached Lee and Luttie, they signaled their men back to camp for a pow-wow.

Even some of the bounty hunters had lost their enthusiasm for the chase.

"Has to be bad when Nap and Ace give it up," Dan Diamond opined.

"Big Bob gone," Morris Pattin said. "He was one tough son of a bitch."

Several bounty hunters—older, tougher, and wiser hands—quietly packed their gear and pulled out. In the Lee Slater group, Bud, Sack, Cates, Dewey, and Gooden rode into Rio under a white flag and turned themselves in to the sheriff's deputies. Bud had passed out in the saddle a half a dozen times from the pain in his buttocks.

"We might have to amputate," the doctor said, after winking at Johnny.

"Cut off my ass!" Bud yelled, then he really started bellering.

Smoke, Louis, and Sally worked until dark rigging their new defensive position above the timberline in the big lonesome. Smoke planted almost all of his dynamite under heavy boulders in carefully selected spots while Louis rigged deadfalls far below their position; they might not fall for them, but it would make them cautious. Then they all set about gathering up wood for a fire.

"We'll take a lot of them out," Smoke said. "But they'll eventually breech our position. Just before they do, we'll slip out through that narrow pass behind us and blow it closed. It'll take them half a day to work around this range. By that time we'll be long gone . . . hopefully," he added. "We'll have us a good hot meal this evening. They know where we are; our trail is too easy to follow. Anyway, we've got to have a fire this high up; we'd freeze to death without it. Let's settle in and rest and eat. It's going to get busy come first light."

Larry built a fire large enough to endanger the forest. And it wasn't just for heat. Spooky out here. All sorts of strange sounds were coming out of the darkness surrounding him. Larry imagined huge bears staring at him, vicious packs of wolves, and slobbering panthers waiting to pounce and eat him if he let the flames die down.

He needn't have worried about four-legged animals. No woods' creature would come within a mile of that mini-inferno he kept feeding during the night. All in all, Larry cleared about an acre of land getting fuel for the fire. It looked like Paul Bunyan had been on a rampage.

"Who in the hell is that down yonder?" Curley asked, looking at the glowing bright spot surrounded by a sea of darkness.

"That goofy lawyer we was told about," Carbone said, returning from his stint on guard. "The one with a crush on Sally Jensen."

"Oh," the others said, and dismissed Larry without another thought.

Mills and his marshals came upon Larry just after first light. He was trying—unsuccessfully—to fry a potato in bacon grease.

"You got to peel it and cut it up first," Moss told him.

"Oh," Larry said. "I employ a cook back home. I'm not much of a hand in the kitchen."

"I never would have guessed," Mills said. "Who are you?" He asked. He'd never seen anyone try to fry a whole potato.

"I am an attorney from back East. I have come into these battle-torn mountains to offer my assistance in bringing to justice the hooligans and ruffians who are endangering Miss Sally Jensen's life."

"Sally Jensen!" the marshals all hollered. Mills said, "Are you saying that Smoke's wife has joined him?"

"Most assuredly. I am not a man of violence, but with this new development, I felt compelled to pick up arms and race to the rescue."

"Let me fix breakfast," Hugh said. "After I build

another fire," he added. "I can't get within five feet of the one you got."

"Are you lost?" Winston asked.

"Oh, no." Larry smiled. "I may not be much of a cowboy — as a matter of fact, I'm not a cowboy at all — but I spent some time at sea. It would be difficult to get me lost anywhere. I take my bearings often."

"Can you use those guns?" Sharp asked.

"I've never shot a man before. But I'm quite good at target shooting. Have you ever shot a man?"

"Ah . . . no," Sharp admitted.

"Any of you?" Larry questioned.

The marshals all looked embarrassed.

"This is going to be quite an expedition we're mounting," Larry mused.

Far in the distance, the faint sounds of gunshots drifted to them.

"I think we'd better forego breakfast," Larry said.

"Let them bang away," Smoke said. "They're far out of range and shooting uphill. All they're doing is wasting ammunition."

Louis lay behind cover and counted puffs of smoke until he grew tired of counting. He looked at Smoke. "Over thirty down there."

"And more coming," Smoke replied, cutting his eyes to the East.

Sally was looking through field glasses. "Eleven of them. And another bunch right behind them."

"How many in the second bunch, honey?"

"They're too far off to make out yet. Now they've disappeared into the timber."

"Gathering like blowflies on a carcass," Louis said,

his words filled with contempt. "Blowflies one day and maggots the next."

The three of them were in a natural rock depression with a clear field of fire in all directions except the rear. They had hauled in branches and dead logs the previous afternoon and stacked them to their rear, against the stone face. The wood would soak up slugs and would prevent any ricochets. They had lain in a goodly supply of dry dead wood and had eaten a hardy breakfast and had a fresh pot of hot coffee ready to drink.

Sally suddenly giggled. Smoke looked at her. "You want to tell me what's so funny about this situation?"

"You remember me telling you about a man named Larry Tibbson?"

"The lawyer fellow from New York who tried to spark you when you both were in college?"

"That's him."

"What about him?"

She brought him up to date.

Smoke chuckled, the humor touching his eyes. "He's got nerve, I'll give him that. Does he have any idea what might have happened to him had I been home?"

"I think he does now."

Louis poured them all coffee in tin cups and passed them around. The air was cold early in the morning; the hot coffee and the small fire felt good to them as they waited.

The firing stopped.

"They'll be moving soon," Louis said. His eyes touched the eyes of Smoke. The gambler minutely nodded his head. While Sally had slept, Smoke and Louis had talked. Smoke and Sally's children could get along without a father, but they needed a mother. If bad turned to worse, Louis was to take Sally and make a run for it, even if he had to punch her unconscious to do it. The dynamite was in place, and if Smoke was trapped on this side of the narrow pass, so be it.

"They're moving," Sally said. "They'll be able to get within range of us."

"Yes. Then we'll start picking them off," Louis said. "We have all the advantage. Our position is like a fort. We're shooting downhill, and that is easier to compensate for than shooting uphill. We have food and water and warmth. Know this now, Sally: come the night, they'd overrun us. At dusk, we're going to start the avalance and make a run for it. I . . ."

"I heard you both talking last night," she said softly. "You won't have to knock me out to make me go." She opened her pack and took out a smaller package wrapped in canvas. "These are medicines and bandages, Smoke. Potions to help relieve pain and to fight infection. I did not include any laudanum. I knew even if you were badly hurt, you wouldn't take it."

He kissed her gently while Louis discreetly looked away, a smile on his lips. She clung to him for a moment, then pulled back and squared her shoulders and took several deep breaths, getting her emotions under control and blinking away the tears that had gathered. "You come back to me now, you hear me, Smoke Jensen?"

"Yes, ma'am," Smoke smiled at her. "I'm going to take some lead, honey," Smoke told her. "I'd have to be the luckiest man alive not to. But I'll make it out of this. And that's a promise."

236

A slug thudded into the logs they had placed against the rock wall behind them.

"They're in range," Louis said.

Smoke and Sally moved into position. Sally had lain aside her short-barreled carbine and had taken a longer-barreled, more accurate lever action from the saddle boot of a dead outlaw. She lined up the sights on part of a leg that was sticking out from behind a large rock and squeezed off a round.

The man started screaming hideously.

"You busted his knee, baby," Smoke told her.

"That's too bad," she said with a wicked grin. "I was aiming a little higher than that."

Chapter Nineteen

"Cease and desist," Mills shouted to a group of riders. "I'm a United States Marshal."

The riders all jerked iron and began pouring lead at the marshals and Larry. They dove for cover, leading their horses into timber.

"I'm a deputy sheriff of this county!" Larry shouted. "I order you in the name of the law to stop this immediately."

A slug howled past his nose and slammed into a tree, spraying him with bits of bark and bloodying his chin.

"Cretinous son of a bitch!" Larry mumbled, from his suddenly attained position flat on his belly on the ground. "No respect for law and order."

"You're learning," Mills said. "I had to."

The riders dismounted and took cover, continuing their firing at the marshals and Larry.

"Did you recognize any of them?" Winston asked.

"No. I think they're bounty hunters. But that doesn't make any difference now." Mills eared back the hammer on his Winchester.

"What do you mean?" Larry asked.

"They were warned as to who we are; they ignored that and fired at lawmen. That makes them criminals." Mills sighted in one of the manhunters who had taken cover behind a tree that was just a tiny bit too small. He shot the man and knocked him sprawling. "Fire, damnit!" he ordered his men.

Two of the outlaws, or bounty hunters—the trio on the mountain didn't know and didn't care which—tried to carry the man with the busted knee down the slope. Smoke and Louis dropped them. The wounded man began his long rolling slide down the slope, screaming in pain as he hit rocks and scrub bushes. When he reached a flat, he lay still, either dead or unconscious.

"Riders coming," Sally announced, handing Smoke the field glasses.

Smoke studied the men. "Luttie Charles and his bunch. I count . . . ten, no, eleven of them."

"Getting crowded down there," Louis remarked, biting the end off of an expensive imported cigar he'd taken from a silver holder and lighting up. When the ash was to his liking he laid the stogie aside and punched two more rounds into his rifle and jacked back the hammer, sighting in on an exposed forearm.

"That's a good hundred and fifty yards," Smoke said. "Five dollars says you can't make the shot."

"You just lost five dollars," the millionaire industralist/adventurer/gambler said, and squeezed the trigger.

The man yelled as the slug rendered his arm useless. He rolled to one side and exposed a boot. Smoke shot him in the foot, and the outlaw began the slow slide down the slope, hollering and screaming as he rolled and slid downward.

One man jumped out from cover to stop his buddy and Smoke, Sally, and Louis dusted the ground all around him. It was too far for accurate shooting, but after doing a little dancing, the outlaw jumped back into cover, unhit but with a new respect for those three on the mountain.

The arm and foot-shot outlaw rolled off a plateau and fell screaming for several hundred feet. His screaming stopped when he impacted with solid rock. It sounded like a big watermelon dropped from a rooftop to a brick street.

"Fall back! Fall back!" the shout drifted to the trio. "This ain't no good. We'll take them come the night."

"Nap time," Louis said, and promptly stretched out, his hat over his face, and went to sleep.

The bounty hunters—those left alive—called out their surrender to Mills. They had suffered two dead and four wounded. Mills ordered the dead buried. When that was done, he lined up the living.

"I just don't have the time to arrest you properly and transport you into Rio for trial and incarceration," he told them. "But I have your names—whether they are your real names is a mystery that might never be solved—and your weapons. Ride out of here and don't come back. If I ever see any of you again, I shall place you under arrest and guarantee you all long prison terms. Now, move!"

The manhunters gone, the marshals and Larry exchanged glances. They were all a little shaky from the fire-fight, but all knew they had grown a bit in the experience field.

"I would say we conducted ourselves rather well," Larry said, trying to stuff and light his pipe with trembling fingers. He finally gave it up and put the pipe into a pocket.

"You did well," Mills said, putting a hand on Larry's shoulder. "I believe we all proved our mettle. I'm proud to ride with you, Larry."

"The shooting appears to have stopped," Moss said, looking toward the high peaks where they believed Smoke to be holed up.

"That's still a good day's ride from here," Mills said. "Let's get cracking."

The day dragged slowly on without another shot being exchanged. The outlaws and bounty hunters built fires for cooking and for warmth and waited for the night.

Smoke was silent for a time, deep in thought. Finally he made up his mind. He looked at his wife. "I want you gone from here, Sally, while there is good light to travel. I don't see the point in waiting for the night. It's a pretty good bet that nearly all of the manhunters and outlaws are right down there below us. You should have an easy ride back to Rio. Louis, take her out of here."

"All right," the gambler said. "I agree with you. But first let's load you up full and get you all the advantage we can give you."

They had taken all the rifles from the saddle boots of the dead outlaws and bounty hunters, as well as a dozen pistols. They were all loaded up full and placed within Smoke's reach. It would give him a tremendous amount of firepower before having to stop and reload.

Louis slipped out behind the rock wall to saddle up the horses and give Smoke and Sally a few moments alone.

"I'll make one last plea and then say no more about it," Sally said. "Come with us."

Smoke shook his head. "They'd just follow us, and we'd have to deal with it some other place. They'd probably even follow us back to the Sugarloaf or into town and that would get innocent people hurt or killed. So I might as well get it over with here and now."

He leaned over and kissed her. "See you in Rio, honey."

"You better get there," she told him with a forced grin. " 'Cause if you don't, I'm going to be awfully angry."

"Let's go," Louis called from behind the rock wall. "We've got some clouds moving in."

Smoke shook hands with the gambler, and then they were gone, the rock wall concealing their departure from the many blood-hungry eyes below them.

Smoke put a fresh pot of coffee on to boil and gave the long fuses leading from his position to the dynamite a visual once-over. Everything seemed in order. He ate slowly, savoring each bite, and then rolled a cigarette and drank several cups of coffee. He knew it was going to be a very long and boring afternoon. But he was going to have to stay alert for any kind of sneak attack the outlaws might decide to launch at him.

Twice he went back to check on his horse. The animal seemed well rested and ready to go. The last time, with about an hour of daylight left, Smoke saddled him up and secured his gear.

As the shadows began to lengthen over the land, Smoke checked all his weapons. He could see the men moving toward him. A lot of men. He checked both flanks; men were moving in and out of the sparse timber and coming toward him. Still out of range, but not for long.

Smoke emptied the coffee pot and kicked out the fire, leaving only a few smoldering sticks. He drank his coffee and pulled his .44-.40 to his shoulder, sighting a man in and gently squeezing the trigger. The rifle fired, and the man fell to his knees, tried to get up, and then pitched forward on his face. Smoke shifted positions and emptied one rifle into the thin timber on his left flank. A scream came from the shadowy scrub. He emptied another rifle into that area and several men ran out, one limping badly, all of them heading down as fast as they dared, getting out of range.

Lead began howling off the rocks in front of him while others slammed into the logs behind him. Men began rushing from cover to cover, panting heavily in the thin mountain air. This high up, the heart must work harder. Smoke fired and one man did not have to worry about breathing any longer. The .44-.40 slug hit him in the face and tore off most of his jaw. He rolled and bounced his way down the mountain, leaving smears of blood along the way.

Rock splinters bloodied Smoke's face. He wiped the blood away and shifted to the other side, firing as he went, so the others would not know he was alone on the mountain.

On the right side of his little fort, Smoke noted with some alarm how close the manhunters were getting. He looked straight down the mountain. Men were moving in on him, working their way from sparse cover to sparse cover . . . but still coming. He ended the journey for two of them, head and neck shots. Smoke grabbed up a .44 carbine and began spraying the lead below him as fast as he could work the lever. That one empty, he grabbed up another and ran to the other side. The manhunters were getting closer. Too damn close. A slug ripped through the outside upper part of his left arm, bringing a grunt of pain.

Time to go!

He ignored the pain and ripped his shirt to see how bad it was. Not too bad. He tied a bandana around the wound, then picked up a smoldering stick and lit the fuses. Smoke ran behind the rock wall and grabbed the horse's reins, running and leading the horse toward the narrow pass. He did not want to be in the saddle when the explosives went off. It was going to make a hell of a lot of noise, and the horse would be spooked.

"I think we got him, boys!" a man yelled. "Let's go, let's go."

The outlaws and manhunters came screaming and yelling triumphantly up the mountain. When no shots greeted them, they began cheering and slapping each other on the back.

The explosives blew, each charge five to ten seconds behind the other. One of Lee's co-leaders, Horton, about seventy-five yards from the small fort, looked up in horror at the tons of rock cascading toward them. He put a hand in front of his face as if that alone would stop the deadly thunder. A watermelon-sized rock, hurtling through the air, took his hand and drove it into his head.

His buddy, Max, seemed to be rooted to the mountain side, numbed with fear. He would forever be a part of the mountain as tons of rock buried him.

Pecos and his gang of young punks had not advanced nearly so far as the others. Screaming in terror, they ran into the timber and were safe from the deadly cascade.

McKay's legs were crushed, and Ray was pinned under a boulder. Both lay screaming, watching their blood stain the ground and life slowly ebb from them.

Lee Slater and his group, Al Martine and his pack of no-goods, and part of another team watched from below as the carnage continued high above them.

Al lifted field glasses and grimaced as he watched through the thick dust as Sonny tried to outrun the rampaging tons of rock. He could see the man's face was tight and white from mind-numbing fear. Sonny was swallowed by the rocks. All but one arm. It stuck out of the huge pile, the fingers working, opening and closing for a moment, a silent scream for help. The fingers suddenly stiffened into a human claw and stayed that way. As soon as the buzzards spotted it they would rip, tear, and eat it to the bone.

Jere and Summers almost made it. They had lost their weapons and were running and falling and stumbling down the mountain. Their mouths were working in soundless screams, the pale lips vivid in their frightened faces. Several huge boulders hit a stalled rockpile and came over, seeming to gain speed as they traveled through the air.

"Split up!" Al yelled. But his warning came too late and could not be heard over the now-gradually dying roar of the avalanche.

The boulders landed square on the running men, squashing them against the rock surface of the

245

mountain.

Al Martine crossed himself and cursed the day he ever agreed to leave California.

A bounty hunter known only as Chris turned to look behind him and tripped, falling hard, knocking the wind from him. "No!" he screamed, just seconds before the tons of rock landed on him. One boot stuck out of the now-motionless pile of stone. The boot trembled for a moment, then was still.

Huge clouds of dust began drifting upward to join the night skies.

"I'd a not believed no one man could have done all this," Whit said, his voice husky from near exhaustion. He sank to his knees and put his hands to his face, trying to block from his mind all that he'd just witnessed.

Mac came limping out of the dust, dragging one foot. Reed was behind him. He did not appear to be hurt.

Luttie Charles, accompanied by his men, walked slowly up the slope to stand by his brother.

"Incredible," Luttie said, his voice small.

They all cringed and jumped, some yelling and running away, as another dull thud cut the darkening day.

"Musta been a pass back yonder," Milt said. "And Jensen just blowed it."

Rod and Randy giggled.

"Loco!" Lopez muttered.

Luttie started counting. Thirty men left standing here out of nearly seventy. Maybe eight or ten bounty hunters still working the wilderness alone. He coughed as the dust from the avalanche drifted down the mountain. Luttie waved his people farther back.

"We'll make camp at the base down yonder," he said, pointing. "Eat and rest and tomorrow we can take him."

"How you figure that?" his brother asked.

"You're forgetting, I know this country." He turned to his foreman, and the man grinned.

"I'll take two of the boys and plug up the only hole out of that area," the man said. "The gambler and the woman probably done made it out, but Smoke won't try it at night—too dangerous. We got him now, boss. Pinned in like a hog for slaughter."

The lonely cry of a lobo wolf drifted to them, abruptly changing into the blood-chilling scream of a big puma.

"Look!" the punk Peco yelled, pointing.

At the crest of the mountain, the men could just make out the figure of a man, sitting his saddle. The scream of the puma came again.

"It brings chills to my arms," Pedro said. "He is calling like el gato. Daring us to come and get him."

Smoke screamed his panther scream again, the sound drifting and echoing around the mountains, touching all those who hunted him. A big puma answered the call, the scream fading off into the puma's peculiar coughing sound.

Martine and Pedro looked at each other, neither of them liking this at all.

Smoke threw back his head and howled like a big wolf. It was so real that somewhere in the timber a big wolf replied, others joining in, lifting their voices in respect to a brother wolf.

"I've had it," Reed said. "The rest of you do what you want to, but as for me, I'm gone."

"You're yeller! Jeff," one of Peco's punks sneered

247

at Reed.

Wrong thing to do.

Reed palmed his .45 and put a hole in Jeff's chest. The punk hit the rocky ground and died.

"Anybody else want to call me yeller?" Reed said, jacking back the hammer of his pistol.

No one did.

"I'll watch your back for you, Reed," Dumas said. "You got a right to leave if'n' you want to."

"Let me tell you all something, boys," Reed said. "That man up yonder was born with the bark on. We've all hunted him, trapped him, cornered him, and he's tooken some lead. Bet on that . . ." He shivered as Smoke's wolf howl drifted to them; it was soon joined by others. "Jesus God, I can't stand no more of that. Makes my blood run cold. I think the man's got some animal in him. Injuns think so." He shook his head as if to clear it. "And he'll probably take some more lead afore this is all over. You might get a bunch of lead in him. But you'll all be dead, and he'll be standin' when it's all over. Bet on it. And I will be too. 'Cause I'm leavin'. Goodbye."

Smoke howled again.

The men looked toward the crest of the mountain.

Smoke was gone, but his call still wavered in the air.

"Where'd he go?" Crown asked, the question almost a cry of fear.

No one replied. No one knew.

Carbone lifted his hands and looked at them. They were trembling.

Lopez noticed the trembling hands. "Si," he spoke softly, in a voice that only Carbone could hear. "I understand. He is of the mountains, one with the

248

animals, brother of the wolf."

"And us?" Carbone asked in a soft tone.

"I think, amigo, that if we pursue the last moun tain man, we are dead."

Chapter Twenty

Smoke had approached the pass leading out of the valley very cautiously. He took his field glasses and squinted at the pass in the dim light the moon provided. The pass looked innocent enough, but warning bells were ringing in his head. He picketed his horse and approached the narrow pass on foot. The closer he got the more certain he became that the pass was guarded. He heard the faint whinny of a horse and stopped cold, listening. Another horse answered. Smoke began backtracking.

He returned to his horse and removed the saddle. He took his small pack, two rifles, and his saddlebags, then turned the animal loose. There was plenty of water and good graze in the valley. If the horse never found its way out, it would live a good and uneventful life.

Smoke returned to a spot near the mouth of the pass and rolled up in his blankets after eating a can of beans and the last of his now very stale bread. He slept soundly, awakening while the stars were still diamond-sparkling high above the mountains. He lay for half an hour, mentally preparing for the battle ahead.

They had him trapped, but he had been

trapped before. Smoke was outnumbered and outgunned. He'd been there before, too. He lay in his blankets and purged his mind of all things that did not pertain to survival. He'd had lots of practice at that. He became a huge, dangerous, predatory animal. He became one with the mountains, the trees, the animals, the rocks, and the eagles and hawks that would soon be soaring above him, looking for food.

He came out of his blankets silently. He rolled his blankets in the ground sheet and left them. If the fight lasted more than one day, and he was forced to spend another night in the mountains, well, he'd been cold before. More than once in his life he had lain down on a blanket of leaves with only fresh-cut boughs covering him. He slung one rifle and picked up the other.

He did not think of Sally or his children. He had no thoughts of friends or family. He forced everything except survival from his mind. He had told Louis where he had cached supplies and his horses. If he died in this valley, Louis would see to his stock.

Just as dawn was streaking the sky with lances of silver and gold, Smoke Jensen, the last mountain man, threw back his head and screamed like an enraged panther.

The chirping of awakening birds and chattering of playing squirrels ceased as the terrible scream cut through the forest and echoed around the mountains.

Smoke was telling his enemies to come on; he was ready to meet them.

* * *

"My God!" Mills said, standing at the base of the mountain where so many men had died of gunshots and the avalanche. The sunlight was bright on the side of the slope, the rays reflecting off of dark splotches of dried blood.

"The rumbling we heard yesterday," Larry said.

"Yes," Moss replied, looking at the hands and arms and legs sticking out from under tons of rock. His eyes touched upon what was left of two men who'd been crushed under huge boulders, the boulders rolling on after doing their damage.

"I can say in all honesty, I have never seen anything like this," Winston said.

"Do you suppose the fight is over?" Sharp asked.

"No," Albert called, squatting down off the rock face. "A group of men rode out of here. Heading that way." He pointed.

Mills consulted a map he'd purchased at the assayer's office. "If Smoke is still behind this death mountain, he's probably trapped. According to this, there is only one way in and one way out of that little valley. And you can bet the outlaws and bounty hunters know it and have sealed off the entrance."

"How far are we from the mouth of that pass?" Larry asked.

"I'm not sure, but—"

The sounds of a shot echoed to them.

"It's started," Hugh said.

Smoke opened the dance. His .44-.40 barked, the slug taking Dumas in the throat. The outlaw gasped and gurgled horribly and died as he

252

watched his life's blood gush from the gaping wound.

Smoke lay about seventy-five yards from the mouth of the pass and watched and waited with all the patience of a great puma sunning itself.

"We got ourselves an em-pass-see goin' here," Tom Post said.

"A what?" Lee asked.

"We can't go in, and he can't come out."

Rod and Randy giggled.

One-Eye looked at Morris Pattin and shook his head in disgust. Morris nodded his head in complete agreement.

"We got to go in," Luttie said. "We got to get him. It's a matter of honor, now. We're finished in this country. No matter what, we're done here."

Ed and Curt exchanged glances and began crawling toward the mouth of the pass. They passed the bloody body of Dumas and tried not to look at it. Slowly, one by one, the others followed them, staying low on their bellies, offering Smoke no target. They knew that some of them were going to die breeching the mouth of that narrow pass. They also knew that once inside, they could track Smoke Jensen down and kill him. The money was unimportant now. Not even a secondary thought. Their honor was at stake. One man, Smoke Jensen, with a little help, had nearly destroyed a huge gang. He had to pay. That was their code.

They understood it, and Smoke Jensen understood it.

Bobby Jackson jumped up and ran toward the rocky mouth of the pass, firing as fast as he could work the lever of his rifle. Smoke put a slug into

253

his belly, and the man folded up on the ground, his rifle clattering on the rocks.

But four outlaws had worked a dozen yards closer to the entrance.

A bounty hunter called Booker ran into the clearing and jumped for cover. He almost made it through unscathed. Smoke's .44-.40 barked, and the slug hit Booker in the hip, turning him in the air. He hit the ground hollering in pain. But he was inside the valley and still holding onto his rifle.

"Come on!" Booker shouted, and began laying down a withering fire, forcing Smoke to keep his head down.

Tom Post, Martine, and Mac made it inside the valley and fanned out. Smoke saw them and backed up, crawling on his belly into a thick stand of timber. The other manhunters poured into the valley, sensing victory. That was very premature thinking on their part.

A rifle slug grazed the side of Smoke's head, knocking him to one side and addling him for several moments. He felt the warm stickiness of blood oozing down his cheek. He forced himself to ignore it as he shifted positions.

Smoke found better cover and sighted in on a man. Mac took the slug just below his belt buckle and hit the ground howling, unable to move his legs. The bullet had angled up and exited out his back, tearing his spinal cord. Keno dragged the screaming man back toward the entrance to the valley.

"I cain't move my legs!" Mac hollered. "I'm crippled. Finish me, Keno."

"All right," the outlaw said, and shot the man

between the eyes.

Outside the valley, reporters and the curious had gathered nearby, but not so close as to risk getting shot. After Louis and Sally had told their stories, the town of Rio emptied in a rush. Saloonkeepers had set up shop and were doing a brisk business in the wilderness. They kept people busy racing back and forth to town for more whiskey.

Sally was bathing in Louis' quarters. She had no intention of returning to the wilderness. She would be waiting here for her man—when he returned. Not if. When.

Louis had posted one of his men at the front and at the back of his quarters, with orders to shoot to kill any man who tried to breech Sally's privacy.

Louis was sitting by Charlie Starr's side, in a chair by the bed. Charlie was pale and hurting, but getting stronger.

"I know that valley," Charlie said. "Found it with Kit back in '48. Peaceful, pretty little place."

"It isn't peaceful now," Louis told him.

"How many you guess are in there after him?"

"Twenty to thirty."

"He'll take lead."

"He knows it. And so does Sally. But this last round is his. He told me so."

"It's got to be that way, Louis. It's the code of the mountain man. Preacher taught him that. You and me, we just shortened the odds some." He sighed. "I've known that boy for a long time. Me and Preacher went way back together. Them gunnies in that valley now, they don't really know what they're up agin. It's been play time so far.

255

Now Smoke's gonna get nasty. He laid in his blankets this mornin' and put ever'thing out of his mind except stayin' alive. He Injuned and made his peace with the gods. Asked the wind and the rain and the lightning and the animals and the trees and the mountains to help him. He's not quite human now, Louis. And as bad hurt as he might get, when this is over, he might stay up there for several hours or several days, fixin' his mind so's he can once more be fit to associate with normal human bein's. Depends on how bad it gets in his head."

Louis stirred in his chair. "I never saw him the way you just described him."

"Be thankful. It's a fearsome sight."

Lilly came in and shooed Louis out. She took a bottle of sleeping medicine from the bureau and poured a tablespoon full. Charlie took it without grumbling. He smiled at the madam.

"When I get my strength back, I'm gonna repay you, Lilly." He winked.

She returned the wink. "The saddle'll be ready for you to ride, Charlie. Now go to sleep." She drew the curtains to the small quarters in the big wagon. As she stepped down to the ground, her eyes flicked to the mountains. She'd been knowing Smoke Jensen ever since he was just a little tadpole roaming the country with that old reprobate Preacher. She'd heard Charlie telling Louis about how Smoke turned into some sort of unstoppable inhuman creature when he got all worked up. She knew it to be fact. She'd seen it one time. She hoped to God she never had to see it again. But she would, at least one more time. And soon.

It was a terrible, fearsome thing to witness.

* * *

Steve Bolt was crawling through the lushness of the little valley. He had dreams of being the man who killed Smoke Jensen. The money wasn't important—it was the reputation he sought.

"Lars?" he whispered. His partner was supposed to be a few yards away, to his right.

Lars didn't reply.

"Lars! Come on, man, where are you?"

Steve raised up on his elbows, and his face froze with fear. Lars was standing up, sorta like a scarecrow, both arms wedged over low branches. His throat had been cut. Steve stood up to his knees, opening his mouth to scream.

A spear, about six feet long and sharpened on one end, caught him in the chest and drove all the way through him. Steve uttered a long, low moan as the pain registered in his brain. Both hands gripped the spear, and he tried to pull it out. He screamed in pain and gave that up.

"What's the matter, Steve?" another manhunter called in a low whisper.

Steve could only grunt in pain. His eyes were fixed on a tall, very muscular man who suddenly appeared about ten yards in front of him. He was hatless, his face bloody. His shirtfront was bloody. But it was his eyes that froze Steve's tongue. The brown eyes had a gold tint about them—they seemed to glow with rage. The man—it had to be Jensen—held several long spears in his left hand.

"Steve!" the call came again.

Steve found his voice and screamed like he had never done before in his life. He cut his eyes. The tall bloody man had disappeared.

257

"Good God!" the third bounty hunter said, running over to Steve. His eyes touched the lifeless body of Lars, hanging from the branches. "No," he whispered.

That was the last thing he whispered. A long spear, hurled with strength that the average man only dreams about, struck the manhunter in the chest with such force it knocked him back against a tree. He died on his boots.

Keno was the first to find the three bounty hunters. He immediately dropped to his knees for cover and looked wildly around him. His mouth and throat and lips were suddenly very dry. And he realized that he was scared. Very badly scared. He'd been an outlaw since no more than a boy; he'd done some terrible, awful things and seen even worse. But he had never before faced such a man as Smoke Jensen. There were no rules. Jensen was a savage, through and through. Worser than any damn Injun that ever lived.

"Martine?" Keno called as softly as he could and still have a chance to be heard.

" 'Bout twenty yards behind you, Keno. What you got?"

"Steve, Lars, and that other fellow. All dead. Lars' throat is cut ear to ear. Steve and his buddy was kilt with spears."

Martine cursed softly in Spanish.

"Que haces?" Lopez questioned.

Mason Wright came running up, both hands filled with Colts. His eyes became wild with rage when he saw the three dead bounty hunters. "Jensen!" he screamed. "Goddamn you, Jensen. Me and Lars was compadres. You'll pay for this, you cowardly bastard. Step out here, face me."

A rifle cracked and a blue-black hole appeared in Mason's forehead. The gunfighter slumped to the ground, stayed on his knees for a moment, then fell over on his face. Both Colts went off when he hit the ground, and Keno screamed in pain as a slug tore through his shin and exited out the back of his calf. He rolled on the ground, yelling.

"Oh, Jesus!" Keno squalled. "You shot me, you stupid idiot! Oh, God, it hurts."

Luttie ran up, looked around, and hit the ground. "Fill the woods with lead," he yelled. "Everybody start shooting."

Lead started flying from all directions in all directions. "Don't shoot at me, you fools!" Luttie screamed. "Form a skirmish line, left and right of me. Jesus Christ, men, think!"

The outlaws and bounty hunters formed up and began filling the timber ahead of them with lead. But Smoke was gone. He knew if he was to survive, he had to think twice as fast as the outlaws and be two steps ahead of them at all times.

He chanced a return to the pass entrance, hoping against hope. But after scanning the entrance, he knew it had been posted with men. Safely behind and to the north of the outlaws, Smoke paused for a short rest while he looked around him at the high peaks surrounding the valley. Was this valley really a box? He knew a lot of cowboys called any canyon or valley they could not ride a horse out of a box. Maybe it was—maybe it wasn't. He was going to find out. Only problem was, he had no blankets to combat the intense cold of the high lonesome should he be trapped up there and have to spend the night.

A bullet slammed into a tree, just missing his head. Smoke jumped for cover.

"Here he is!" came the shout. "Come on, boys. Now we got him."

"Where, Malone?"

"Work your way north towards me. I'll keep him pinned down. That'll put him 'twixt you and me."

Smoke put a .44-.40 'twixt Malone's ribs, right in the center of the V of the ribcage.

"Oh, God!" Malone yelled. "He plugged me."

Smoke ran to Malone and kicked the man's rifle away from him, smiling as he saw the rolled up ground sheet and blanket tied across the man's back. He tore it from him and took his pistols.

"Help me," Malone moaned.

Smoke pointed his rifle at Malone and jacked back the hammer.

"Oh, Jesus!" the outlaw squalled. "Not thataway!"

"Then shut up and die quietly." Smoke was gone, running into the timber north of the gutshot outlaw and at the base of a formidable-looking peak.

"He's run towards the mountains, boys!" Smoke heard Malone's yell, and knew he had to stand and fight for a time.

He bellied down behind a rotting log and punched rounds into his Winchester. One outlaw ran across the small clearing, running to help Malone. Smoke dropped him. The man threw his rifle high into the air and hit the ground. He did not move.

"You a devil, Jensen!" Malone yelled. "He was a-comin' to help me."

"Stay along the timberline," Luttie told his men.

260

"Don't expose yourselves."

"What about Malone?" Jake asked.

"You want to go help him?"

Jake did not reply. The men stayed in cover until Malone's screaming ceased. They did not know if he had passed out or if he was dead. Most didn't care one way or the other.

"He's tooken Malone's bedroll," Whit said. "See yonder. It's gone."

"He's going to try for the peaks," Lee said. "But you said this was a box."

"It is." But that nagged at Luttie. He knew there were only two ways that a man could ride a horse in or out. Jensen had blown one of them closed. But was it possible for a man to climb out? He didn't know. He'd never tried it, and didn't know of anyone who ever had.

Luttie silently cursed. But if any man could climb out, it would be that damn Smoke Jensen.

"Fan out," Luttie ordered. "We can't let him get into the highup. Remember what he done last time."

The outlaws and manhunters started cautiously fanning out. Some of them were rapidly losing their taste for the hunt and would leave if they got a chance. Honor be damned.

Smoke silently melted into the timber and the brush, climbing higher. He would pause now and then to scan the peaks with field glasses. A cup of coffee would taste good right now, but he didn't have any and could not dare risk a fire even if he did.

He found a small pool of clear, cold water and bathed his wounds carefully, treating them with the medicines Sally had packed for him. The wounds were not serious, and he knew that high altitudes slowed infections.

Smoke took the time to rig some deadfalls and other more lethal traps. That done, he hiked up another hundred yards and found a good location. To hell with it! He was tired and was going to rest.

"Come on, boys," he muttered. "You want me, here I am!"

Chapter Twenty-one

They almost got him.

It was one of those freak shots that had nothing at all to do with skill. The slug howled off a rock, hit a tree a glancing blow, and struck Smoke in the side. Had it not lost much of its force, it probably would have killed him.

Smoke looked at the hole in his side. The bullet had hit the fleshy part of his back and exited out the front. It looked awful, hurt like hell, but was not a serious wound. It was, however, going to impede any attempts at climbing.

Smoke shifted positions, working his way out of the rocks and getting into a natural depression that offered less chance of a ricochet. He checked the sun. About ten o'clock, he figured. It was going to be a very long day.

Smoke sighted in what appeared to be a man's arm and fired. He missed his shot, but the outlaw yelled and scrambled back down the hill, finding a more protected spot.

Smoke kept his head down while the lead hammered and howled all around him. He knew they were advancing toward him during the fusillade, but it couldn't be helped. While the outlaws frantically punched fresh rounds into their rifles, Smoke sighted in a man running hard for cover . . . and alarmingly near Smoke's position. The .44-.40 slug busted him, turning him around like a top. Smoke's second shot ended the spin.

"He got Tap!" a man yelled, jumping up in anger and excitement.

Smoke got him, too. He couldn't tell if it was a killing shot, but the man went down limp and didn't move.

"Damn!" he heard a man say. "Whit's had it."

"I've had it too," another man said. "I'm gone. Done. Finished."

Two more agreed with him, and Smoke let them leave, even though he had a clear shot at one of them and a maybe shot at another.

Smoke pulled back. He was so muddy and bloody he blended in with the earth and the foliage. He ached all over and longed for a hot tub of water with a big bar of soap. What he got was dirt and rocks and twigs kicked into his face by a bullet. He wiped his vision clear and slipped into cover, his face bleeding.

He watched through a sturdy mountain bush as a man limped from one tree to another. Smoke ended his limping with a single shot.

"Damnit!" a man said. "I told Keno to head back out of the valley."

"He shore ain't goin' nowheres now," another man said. 'Ceptin' the grave, if he's lucky."

"I want his boots," a man yelled. "I was with him when he stole 'em. Them's brand new. Mine's wore slap out."

Keep talking, Smoke thought, shifting around to

face the direction of the closest voice and earing back the hammer on his Winchester.

He waited and saw what he felt was the tip of a boot. The boot moved just a bit, exposing several more inches of leather. He laid a bead and squeezed the trigger. A howl of pain erupted from behind the cluster of low rocks.

"My foot's ruint!" a man yelled. "Oh, God, it hurts! He blowed my toes off."

"Now you shore need some boots," a man told him, ending it with a dirty laugh.

Smoke put three fast rounds into the bushes where he felt the smart-mouth was hiding. He watched as a man rose slowly to his feet. He looked down at his bullet-perforated and bloody shirt front. "You bastard," the outlaw said, then toppled over on his face.

"It ain't workin', Luttie," the sound came to Smoke. "He's pickin' us off one by one."

"Then leave, you yeller-belly!" Luttie said. "You're paid up. Haul your ashes."

"I believe I'll just do that little thing. I'm pullin' out, Jensen. You hear me?"

"I hear you."

"Don't shoot. I'm gone."

Smoke let him go while the remaining outlaws poured lead into Smoke's position. Smoke stayed low, hating it, knowing they were inching closer, but unable to prevent it.

He heard panting coming from only a few feet away and knew if he didn't move, they would have him cold.

"Goddamnit, he must have moved!" the voice was only inches away.

"He's got to be in there. Are you stone blind,

Crown?" Lee yelled.

No. Crown was just stone dead. Smoke shot him in the belly at point-blank range, pulled out the man's twin Remingtons and emptied them downhill. He lunged out of the hole and ran into the bushes, lead whining and howling and clipping branches and thudding into trees all around him.

"Somebody kill him, damnit!" Luttie screamed. "Cain't nobody shoot straight no more?"

Smoke climbed higher, pausing often to rest. His wounds were taking a toll on him, gradually sapping his strength. Although still bull-strong, he couldn't last another day; he knew that. He had to bring this fight to an end.

Something slammed into his head and knocked him spinning. The last thing he remembered was falling into darkness.

"They claim they killed him," Mills said, after speaking to several people in the huge crowd around the mouth of the valley entrance.

"I don't believe it," Winston said.

Mills shrugged his shoulders. "Smoke is a mortal man, Winston. A big tough bear of a man, but still mortal. Look, I don't want to believe it either, but face facts. He's been fighting terrible odds for days."

"Where's the body?" Larry asked, a sick feeling in the pit of his stomach.

"They said he fell down into a ravine. No way to retrieve the body. But they have his rifle."

"Oh, my God!" Hugh shook his head. "It must be true."

"We'll arrest the outlaws as they come out," Mills ordered. "If they offer just the slightest hint of resistance, kill them on the spot."

"You don't mean that, Mills!" Sharp said.

"The hell I don't!"

Sally looked up into the face of Lilly LaFevere. Johnny North, Cotton, Earl, and Louis were with her. All their faces were grim.

"Give it to me straight," Sally said.

"Word is they killed your man, honey."

"Where's the body?"

"A bounty hunter told a reporter that it can't be recovered. Smoke supposedly fell off into a ravine after being shot in the head," Louis said grimly. "We're riding to the valley. Sheriff Silva and a posse are here now, to keep order. Stay with her, Lilly."

"I'll do that."

Cold.

Smoke opened his eyes and for one panicky moment felt he was blind. But it was dried blood that had caked his eyes shut. He dug the blood away with as little movement as possible, not wanting to draw attention. His entire left side hurt, and the right side of his head throbbed with pain. But not his left side. Curious. He wondered how that could be?

When his vision cleared, he realized just how bad his position was.

He was lying on a ledge that jutted out a few yards from the face of the ravine. It was about a five hundred foot drop to the bottom. Smoke looked up and guessed that he'd fallen no more than fifteen or twenty feet. When he hit, the bedroll had protected his head. That was why only the bullet-creased side ached. When he hit, he had rolled against the face of the cliff, protected from eyes above by a little outcropping of rock. He was stiff and sore and bruised all over . . . but he was alive.

He lay still for a moment, going over his problems, and they were many. He rolled over on his stomach and had to stifle a groan of pain as his torn and bruised body protested.

The ledge snaked around a bend. He had no idea what lay around that bend. He had no rope to aid in his climbing out. He had no idea how badly hurt he might be. He had no idea how far the ledge ran. If he stayed where he was, he would die. It was that simple. If he tried to climb out, the odds of his making it were slim to none.

But he damn sure was going to try.

Food. He had to eat. He fumbled around in his saddle bag and found some hard crackers. He ate them, drank a swallow of water left in his busted canteen, and felt better. If I felt any worse, he thought with dark humor, I'd be dead.

Smoke wriggled around on the ledge, being very careful not to get too close to the edge, for the rock looked very flaky and unstable there. On his belly, he checked his guns which had stayed in leather thanks to the hammer thongs. The guns were dirty, and he carefully cleaned them, working the action and reloading. He checked the knife on his belt and the shorter-bladed knife in his leggings. Both were still in place and both still sharp enough to shave with.

Smoke was tired, so very, very tired. He would have liked to just lay his head on his arm and go to sleep. Maybe just rest for a few moments. He shook himself like a big shaggy dog. No time for rest. He felt for his pocket watch and was not surprised to see it busted, the hands stopping at eleven-thirty-five. He judged the time to be close to four, maybe four-thirty. He didn't have all that much daylight left him.

Taking a deep breath, he crawled forward. Wouldn't it be interesting, he thought, to come face to face with a mountain lion on this narrow trail with a five hundred foot drop below?

He decided it would not be interesting. Just deadly for one of them.

He crawled on, smiling at what faced him a few yards around the curve in the trail. The mountain pass ended, but it did not end sheer; it ended in an upside down V. Now, if there were just sufficient handholds or jutting rocks that were stable, he could climb out. It was only about twenty feet to the top, and he could hear no sounds above him except the sighing of the mountain winds. He reached the end of the narrow ledge and rested for a time. God, he was worn out.

Smoke crawled to his knees and put one foot on the other side of the narrow gorge. He willed himself not to look down. The slight protruding of rock felt secure under his foot, and he leaned forward, gripping two outcroppings, one in each hand. He lifted his left foot to a toehold about two feet off the trail, and now he was committed to the mountain.

It took him twenty minutes to climb about twenty feet, and using brute strength while dangling over a five hundred foot drop was not something he wished to repeat. Ever.

When he crawled over the top he was exhausted. If he had not been wearing leather gloves, he probably would not have made it; the rocks would have cut his hands to bloody ribbons. He belly-crawled into a copse of timber and rolled up in his blankets. He had to rest.

"Can you believe this?" Mills almost shouted the words, as he waved a court order that was hand-delivered to him that afternoon.

"Yeah, I can believe it," Johnny said. The marshals and the deputies had returned to town after the court order had been delivered.

Judge Richards had obviously pre-signed pardons for all the outlaws in the Lee Slater gang. The order had just been found and delivered.

"I turned all the jailed outlaws loose," Earl said. "I thought Sheriff Silva was going to have a heart attack."

It was midnight in Rio, and the town was sleeping. The outlaws were due to ride in the next day, as soon as the reward money was stagecoached in on the afternoon stage, to collect their blood money. And outlaws being what they are, they were also going to collect the reward money that had been on the heads of their now departed friends.

"The end of an era," Larry said, soaking his feet in a bucket of lukewarm water. "I would have liked to have met Mr. Smoke Jensen, to shake his hand and tell him how wrong I was about him."

"Don't sell Smoke short," Louis said. "I'll not believe he's dead until I see the body."

"But he fell off a mountain!" Mills said. "Or rather down into a deep chasm."

"Yes," the gambler said. "And chasms and ravines have outcroppings that are not always visible from above. I don't believe he's dead."

"Neither do I," Johnny said. "Hurt, yes. Dead?" He shook his head. "No." ·

"Sally?" Earl asked.

"I don't think she believes it either."

"I aim to be in the street when them outlaws ride in tomorrow," Johnny said.

"Me, too," Cotton said.

"I'll be with you boys," Earl made three.

"I shall certainly be there," Louis said, standing up.

"Count me in," Larry surprised them all. "I owe this much to his memory. I certainly maligned the man while he was alive."

Six U.S. Marshals' badges hit the desk. "And we shall be standing with you," Mills said.

"Gonna be a hell of a party," Cotton summed it up with a wicked grin.

Smoke awakened at midnight. He was aching and sore, but feeling a lot better. His clothes were stiff with dried blood and mud and sweat, but his hands opened and closed easily. He rolled his blankets and started walking. Less than an hour later, he found a riderless horse, still saddled and bridled. Probably had belonged to one of the dead outlaws or bounty hunters. He stripped saddle and bridle from the animal and let it graze and roll while he went through the saddlebags and poke-sack and found food, coffee, frying pan, and coffee pot.

He checked out the rifle in the boot; it was loaded full with .44s. He led the horse back behind some boulders and picketed the animal. Then he built a fire and fried bacon and potatoes and made a pot of coffee. Being a coffee-loving man, he drank the coffee right out of the pot while his food was cooking, then he settled down and ate leisurely and drank more coffee out of a cup.

An hour later, he had carefully put out the fire and was in the saddle, riding for the pass. The pass was deserted when he rode through it. On the other side of the pass, however, he could see where it looked like hundreds of people had held a wild party. Empty beer kegs and empty whiskey bottles lay all over the place.

"I wonder if they were celebrating the news of my death?" he muttered, then rode on.

He came upon what appeared to be a dead man lying by the side of the road that led to Rio. He dismounted and knelt down beside him, rolling him over. Not dead, just dead drunk. Smoke slapped him awake.

The man opened his eyes and started to scream when he recognized the man standing over him. Smoke put a hand on the man's mouth, shushing him.

"Don't yell," he told him. "You understand?"

"But you're dead!" the man said, after Smoke removed his hand.

"I'm a long way from being dead," Smoke corrected him. "Do I look dead to you?"

"No. But you shore look some terrible tore up."

"Tell me what went on back by the pass."

The man brought Smoke up to date, still convinced he was conversing with a ghost.

"I see," Smoke said, when the man had finished. "You're going to freeze to death if you lay out here the rest of the night."

"It don't seem to have bothered you none! 'Sides,

I got me a claim about a mile from here. I can make it, providin' I don't run into no more ghosts."

Chuckling, Smoke left the man and rode on. Just about ten miles outside of town, Smoke found a good place to camp and bedded down for the rest of the night. He slept deeply and awakened well after dawn, feeling at least part of his enormous strength once more returning to him. He did a few exercises, copied after a great cat's stretchings, to get the kinks out of his muscles, then cooked the last of the dead outlaw's food and boiled the last of the coffee.

He pulled out his makin's sack and rolled a cigarette, enjoying that with the last cup of coffee. He found a spare sixgun in the saddle bags and dug out the two extra he had in his pack. He checked them all out and loaded them up full, then checked the rifle again.

He talked to the horse for a moment before saddling up, and the horse seemed eager to ride. He wondered if Louis had gone back and gotten his horses. He would soon know.

He had traveled about three miles, he reckoned, when the sounds of galloping horses reached him, coming up fast behind him. He pulled off into timber and waited.

The Lee Slater gang, Luttie with them, along with One-Eyed Jake and his bounty hunters. Smoke wanted them to get into town and have one good drink of whiskey before he threw down the challenge.

He stopped to water his horse, and as he knelt down to drink, he was shocked at the reflection staring back at him. His face was bloody and cut and swollen. His hair was matted with dried blood from where the slug had grazed him—on both sides. He looked like something out of Hell.

Which was fine with him. The gunhands better get used to Hell, 'cause that's where Smoke intended to send them.

Chapter Twenty-two

Smoke reined up and dismounted at the edge of town. He looked up at the sun. Directly overhead. High noon. He pulled saddle and bridle off the horse and turned it loose to water and roll and graze.

Smoke loosened his guns in leather, then stuck the extra .44s behind his gun belt, the fifth .44 jammed down into his legging, right side. He waved a burly, bearded man over to him.

"Yeah?" the man asked, walking over to him. He took a long second look, his mouth dropping open. "Holy Christ!" the man whispered.

"Clear the streets," Smoke told him.

"Yes, sir, Mr. Smoke. Ever'body said you was dead!"

"Well, I'm not. I just look it. Move."

The miner ran toward the marshal's office and threw open the door, and almost got himself shot for that rash act. "Whoa!" he cried, as Johnny, Louis, Earl, and Cotton jerked iron. "I ain't even carryin' no sidearm. Smoke Jensen just rode into town. He's up yonder." He pointed. "He looks like death warmed over. But he said to clear the streets. He's all muddy and bloody and mean clear through. Got guns a-hangin' all over him."

"Hot damn!" Earl said.

"I'll run tell Charlie!" Mills said. "Sharp, take the men and clear the streets of people and horses."

Louis pointed a finger at Cotton. "Go to Sally. Tell her the news."

"I'm gone!" Cotton ran from the office.

"This is Smoke's fight," Louis said. "But we can keep a eye out for ambushers and back-shooters."

The men took down sawed-off shotguns, stuffed their pockets with shells and stepped out of the office. The main street was already deserted.

Luttie was lifting his second glass of rye to his lips when the wild scream of an enraged panther cut the still, hot air. He spilled half his drink down his shirt-front.

"Jesus Christ!" Tom said.

"It can't be!" Pecos shouted, frantically brushing at his crotch where he'd dropped his cigarette. "He fell off a damn mountain."

Rod and Randy giggled.

Dan Diamond looked at One-Eyed Jake, disbelief in his eyes.

Frankie Deevers loaded up his guns full.

Martine's fingers were trembling as the cry of a panther changed to the howling of a lobo wolf. He crossed himself and stood up.

Charlie Starr chuckled in his bed and propped a couple of pillows behind him, then lifted the canvas and tied it back. He pulled out his long-barreled six-guns and checked them.

Sally smiled and put on a pot of coffee. Smoke would want a good strong cup of coffee when this was over. She knew her man well.

Larry Tibbson loaded up a sawed-off express gun and took a position near the center of the boom town.

The stage rolled in, the driver and guard taking a quick look at the deserted street. "Oh, my God!" the driver said, his eyes touching on the tall bloody man standing at the end of the long street. He threw the strongbox and mail pouch to the ground and yelled at his horses to get gone.

Mills tore open the mail pouch and jerked out a letter, quickly scanning it. With a yell of excitement, he jumped up and said, "Here it is! The warrants against Smoke Jensen have been dropped. It's signed by the President of the United States!"

"Damn that President Arthur!" Luttie said.

Morris Pattin stepped out of the barber shop where he'd just had a haircut and a bath. He brushed back his new coat, freeing his guns, and walked up the street toward Smoke Jensen. He was shocked at the man's appearance. Jensen looked like something out of hell.

"I'll take you now, Jensen," he called.

"You'll kiss the devil's behind before you do," Smoke told him, then lifted his rifle in his left hand and drilled the bounty hunter from a hundred yards out.

The slug hit the manhunter in the center of his chest, and Morris was down and dying without ever having a chance to pull iron—not that it would have done him a bit of good at that distance.

Sally moved the coffee pot off the griddle and decided she would wait a few minutes before dumping in the coffee. She wanted Smoke to have a good hot fresh cup of coffee.

Charlie caught movement by the edge of a building and jacked back the hammer on his old six-gun. It would be a good shot for him, but he figured he could do it. He smiled as he recognized the gunfighter from down Yuma way. Couldn't think of his name. Didn't make no difference; the gravedigger could just carve "Yuma" on the marker.

Yuma lifted his rifle and sighted Smoke in. Charlie took him out with a neck shot at seventy-five yards.

"Damn good shootin'," Charlie complimented himself, as Yuma slumped to the dirt. "I'd a not done 'er with one of them new short-barreled things."

Photographers had quickly set up their boxy equipment, filled the flash-trays, and were ready to record it all for posterity.

Smoke stepped out of the street and ducked into an alley.

Tom Post looked up and down and all around. "Where'd he go?" He asked Lopez. The men were in the general store, pricing new suits of clothes they planned to buy with the reward money. Or steal them, now that the shopkeeper and his woman had locked themselves in the storeroom.

"Right behind you," Smoke said calmly.

Tom and Lopez turned, jerking iron.

They were far too slow.

Smoke had leaned the rifle up against a counter and stood with both hands filled with Colts, the Colts spitting lead and belching fire and gunsmoke.

Lopez took two rounds in the chest, dropped his guns, staggered backward, and fell out one of the big storefront windows. He crashed to the boardwalk and lay amid the broken glass, kicking and cursing his life away.

Tom was doubled over with two slugs in his belly. He fell to the floor and lay moaning. Smoke kicked the man's gun away and reloaded his own. He took a sawed-off shotgun from the rack and broke it

278

open, shoving in shells and filling his pockets from the open box.

"You a no good sorry son!" Post groaned.

"Don't lose any sleep over it," Smoke told him, then stepped out to the back of the store.

The young punk Bull, from Pecos' gang, was running up the alley, wild-eyed, cussing, and both hands full of guns. Smoke let him have both barrels of the sawed-off twelve gauge. The buckshot lifted the punk off his boots and sent him crashing into an open-doored outhouse. The punk died sitting on the hole, crapping into his pants.

Smoke punched fresh rounds into the Greener and walked on, pausing when he heard the sounds of someone running.

Curt Holt rounded a corner, running as hard as he could, his hands full of six-guns. He slid to a halt and lifted them. Smoke blew what was left of him—after the man took two rounds of buckshot at pointblank range in the guts—through a window of someone's living quarters behind a saddleshop.

"Good Jesus Christ!" he heard someone shout from inside. "What a mess."

"I believe Mr. Jensen is very upset," Larry muttered to Sharp, who had joined him.

"I wholeheartedly agree," the U.S. Marshal said.

In the saloon, Rod and Randy giggled insanely, Rod saying, "Come, brother. We'll put an end to this nonsense."

Johnny North was waiting on the boardwalk. As soon as the brothers stepped through the batwings, Johnny started shooting, cocking and firing in one long continuous roar of thunder and smoke. The Karl Brothers did a macabre dance of the dying on the boardwalk as they soaked up lead. Randy fell into a horsetrough and died with both arms hanging over the sides. Rod lay draped over a hitchrail. He giggled as he died.

Dewey and Gooden, freshly released from jail, stepped out into the street and yelled at Johnny, knowing his guns were probably empty.

Louis stepped out of his gambling hall, his eyes hard. He emptied his guns into the pair. They lay in the dust, their outlawing days over.

Reporters were scribbling and photographers' flashpans were puffing as they recorded it all for their readers back East.

The foreman of the Seven Slash stepped into the alley and faced Smoke, both hands hovering over the butts of his guns. "You ain't got the balls to drop that Greener and drag iron with me, Jensen."

"Courage has nothing to do with it," Smoke told him. "But time is of the essence."

He pulled the triggers on the express gun, and the foreman's earthly cares and woes were a thing of the past.

Smoke walked up the alley to stand in the cool shadows, looking out into the street.

In the saloon, Luttie looked at Lee. "It's been a good, long run, Lee. Now it's over."

Lee swore. "It may be over for you, but it ain't over for me. I'm gonna kill that damn Jensen oncest and forever."

"I wish you luck," his brother said, lifting a shot glass in salute.

Lee walked out the back of the saloon.

"You're a fool, brother. But then, I've always known that." Luttie drank his whiskey and turned around, his back to the bar, facing the batwings.

Smoke heard the hammer cocking behind him

280

and dropped to his knees in the alley just as the slug hammered the pine boards above his head. Smoke leveled the shotgun, and gave Curly a gut-full of buckshot. Curly's boots flew out from under him, and he smashed down to earth, lying on his back; the charge had nearly cut him in two.

Smoke was out of shotgun shells. He laid the Greener down and pulled his Colts, jacking the hammers back. He scanned the street for trouble. He couldn't see it, but knew it was there, waiting for him.

Smoke eased back down the alley, a .44 in both hands. He was facing south, the sun just beginning its dip toward the west. A thin shadow fell across the end of the alleyway. Smoke paused, pressing against the outside wall of the building.

"You see him, Milt?" someone called in a hoarse, softly accented whisper.

"Naw," the voice came from just around the corner, back of the building, belonging to the shadow that was still evident on the weedy ground.

Milt stepped out and Smoke drilled him, the slug snapping his head back as it hit him in the forehead.

Smoke hit the ground and rolled under the building.

Pedro jumped out, a puzzled look on his face. Smoke shot him twice in the belly, and the puzzled look was replaced by one of intense pain. The outlaw fell to his knees, both .45s going off, blowing up dirt and dust and rocks. He cursed for a moment, then fell over, still alive, but for how long was something that only God could answer.

Dan Diamond and One-Eye were walking boldly down the boardwalk, toward the sounds of shooting when Cotton stepped out of a doorway and faced them.

"I told you it'd be someday, One-Eye," Cotton said. "Why not now?" He jerked iron and shot the manhunter in the belly.

Dan fired just as Cotton stepped to one side, the slug knocking a chunk out of the building. He missed but Cotton didn't. Dan folded and sat down heavily on the boardwalk for a moment. He looked up at Cotton.

"Is Pickens really your last name?"

"That it is."

"Cotton Pickens," Dan said, then died with a smile on his lips.

Smoke was standing in the alley when the manhunters Davy and Val rode out. He nodded at them and they nodded at him and then were gone. Smoke let them go. They just came after the wrong man, that's all.

Smoke stepped out and walked up the steps to the boardwalk. The town was eerily quiet. Most of the citizens were either inside looking out of windows, or had locked themselves behind doors. The reporters and photographers were the only ones other than the combatants on the street, crouching behind horsetroughs and peeking out of open alleyways. Smoke had always figured that reporters didn't have a lick of sense.

A man stepped out of the shadows. Lee Slater. His hands were wrapped around the butts of Colts, as were Smoke's hands. "I'm gonna kill you, Jensen!" he screamed.

A rifle barked, the slug striking Lee in the middle of his back and exiting out the front. The outlaw gang leader lay dead on the hot dusty street.

Sally Jensen stepped back into Louis' gambling hall and jacked another round into her carbine.

Smoke smiled at her and walked on down the boardwalk.

"Looking for me, amigo?" Al Martine spoke from the shadows of a doorway. His guns were in leather.

"Not really. Ride on, Al."

"Why would you make such an offer to me? I am an outlaw, a killer. I hunted you in the mountains."

"You have a family, Al?"

"Si. A father and mother, brothers and sister, all down in Mexico."

"Why don't you go pay them a visit? Hang up your guns for a time."

The Mexican smiled and finished rolling a cigarette. He lit it and held it to Smoke's lips.

"Thanks, Al."

"Thank you, Smoke. I shall be in Chihuahua. If you ever need me, send word, everybody knows where to find me. I will come very quickly."

"I might do that."

"Adios, compadre." Al stepped off the boardwalk and was gone.

Smoke finished the cigarette, grateful for the lift the tobacco gave him. His eyes never stopped moving, scanning the buildings, the alleyways, the street.

He caught movement on the second floor of the saloon, the hotel part. Sunlight off a rifle barrel. He lifted a .44 and triggered off two fast rounds. The rifle dropped to the awning, a man following it out. Zack fell through the awning and crashed to the boardwalk. He did not move.

Rich Coleman and Frankie stepped out of the saloon, throwing lead, and Smoke dived for the protection of a water trough.

"I got him!" Frankie yelled.

Smoke rose to one knee and changed Frankie's whole outlook on life—what remained of it.

Rich turned to run back into the saloon, and Smoke fired, the slug hitting him in the shoulder and knocking him through the batwings. He got to his boots and staggered back out, lifting a .45 and drilling a hole in the water trough as he screamed curses at Smoke.

Smoke finished it with one shot. Rich staggered forward, grabbing anything he could for support. He died with his arms around an awning post.

The thunder of hooves cut the afternoon air. Sheriff Silva and a huge posse rode up in a cloud of dust.

"That's it, Smoke," the sheriff announced. "It's over. You're a free man, and all these other yahoos are gonna be behind bars."

"Suits me," Smoke said, and holstered his guns.

Luttie Charles stepped out of the saloon, a gun in each hand, and shot the sheriff out of the saddle. The possemen filled Luttie so full of lead the undertaker had to hire another man to help tote the casket.

"Damnit!" Sheriff Silva said, getting to his boots. "I been shot twice in my life and both times in the same damn arm!"

"No, it ain't over!" the scream came from up the street.

Everybody looked. Pecos stood there, his hands over the butts of his fancy engraved .45s.

"Oh, crap!" Smoke said.

"Don't do it, kid!" Carbone called from the boardwalk. "It's over. He'll kill you, boy."

"Hell with you, you greasy son of a bitch!" Pecos yelled.

Carbone stiffened. Cut his eyes to Smoke.

"Man sure shouldn't have to take a cut like that, Carbone," Smoke told him.

Carbone stepped out into the street, his big silver spurs jingling. "Kid, you can insult me all day. But you cannot insult my mother."

Pecos laughed and told him what he thought about Carbone's sister, too.

Carbone shot him before the kid could even clear leather. The Pecos Kid died in the dusty street of a town that would be gone in ten years. He was buried in an unmarked grave.

"If you hurry, Carbone," Smoke called, "I think you could catch up with Martine. Me and him smoked a cigarette together a few minutes ago, and he told me he was going back to Chihuahua to visit his folks."

Carbone grinned and saluted Smoke. A minute later he was riding out of town, heading south.

Chapter Twenty-three

Smoke soaked in a hot tub of water for a hour before he would let the doctor tend to his wounds.

"You're a lucky man," the doctor told him, after shaking his head in amazement at the old bullet scars that dotted Smoke's body. "That side wound could have killed you."

"What happened to John Seale and the others?" Smoke asked the sheriff, who was lying on the other table in the makeshift operating room.

"I gave them an option: a ride or a rope. They chose to take a ride. What are you going to do about all those reporters gathered outside like a gaggle of geese?"

"What I've always done. Ignore them."

"You plan on staying around here for any length of time?"

"Two days and I'm gone."

"Good. Maybe then this county will settle down."

"You can't ride in two days!" the doctor protested.

"Watch me," Smoke told him.

Two days later, Smoke and Sally rode out with Johnny North. Smoke on Buck, Sally on the blue steele stallion.

Charlie Starr stood with Lilly and Earl and Louis

on the boardwalk and watched them leave. Cotton and Mills and Larry stood with them.

"That's a hell of a man there," Larry said, looking at Smoke Jensen.

Louis smiled. "The last mountain man."

THE MOUNTAIN MAN SERIES BY
WILLIAM W. JOHNSTONE